THE CARTAGENA AFFAIR

A CAT SLOANE THRILLER

KIRA LENNOX

THE CARTAGENA AFFAIR
A Cat Sloane Thriller

This is a work of fiction. Names, characters, businesses, places, events, and incidents are either the products of the author's imagination or used in a fictitious manner. Any resemblance to actual persons, living or dead, or actual events is purely coincidental. While real locations are referenced, all events depicted in these settings are entirely fictional.

Published by Carentan Press
ISBN: [Your ISBN here]
First edition: 2026
www.kiralennox.com

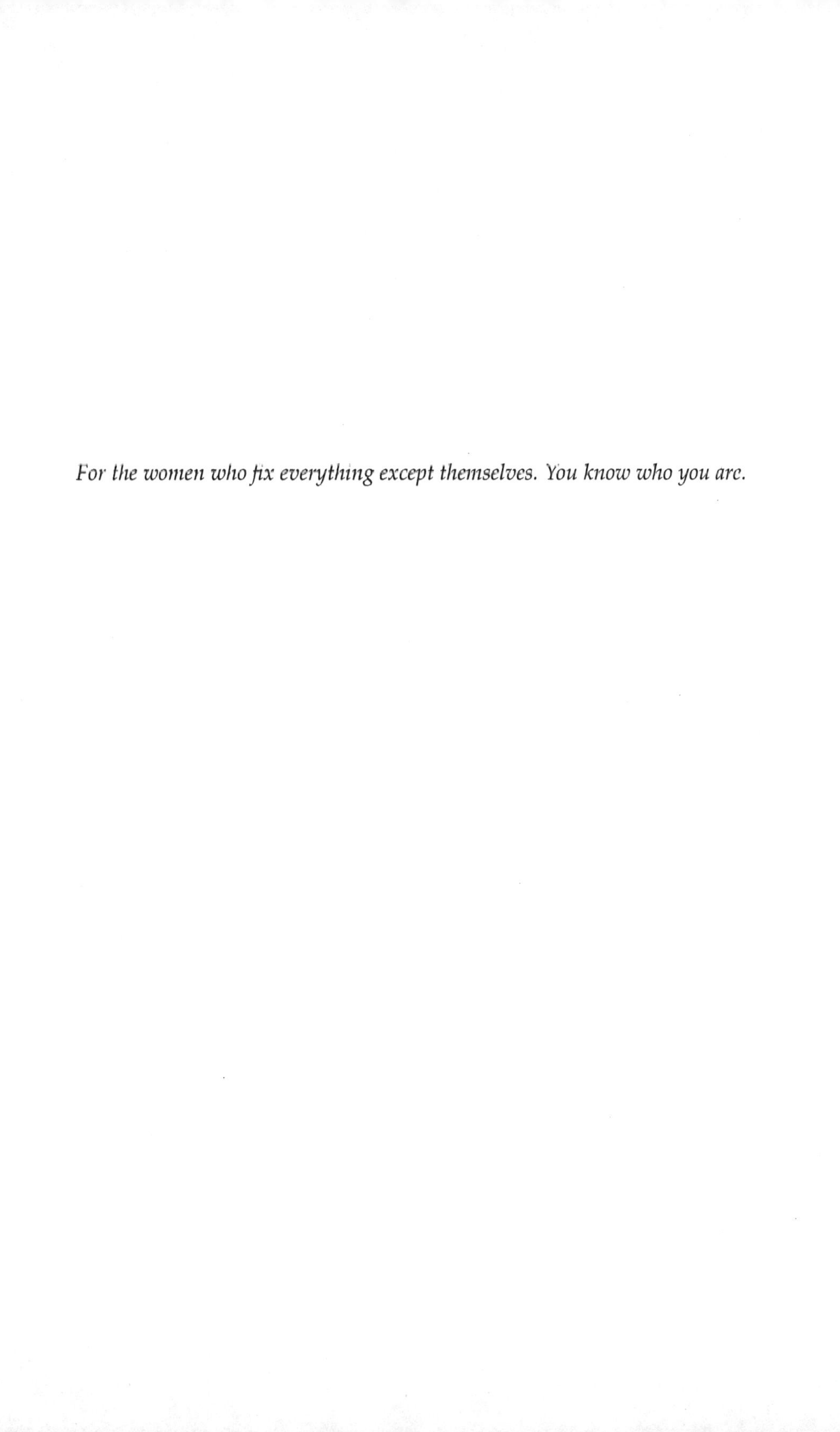

For the women who fix everything except themselves. You know who you are.

PROLOGUE

ST. *Barts — Four Days Ago*

The woman on the terrace was someone else's wife, and Cole Hartwell knew this the way he knew most inconvenient things—clearly, completely, and not nearly soon enough to matter.

She stood at the railing with her back to him, looking out over Flamands Bay, and the wind pressed her dress against her body in a way that made thinking difficult. Below them the Caribbean was doing that thing it does at dusk, going from turquoise to ink in slow, impossible gradients, the kind of color that doesn't exist anywhere else on earth and that rich people pay obscene amounts of money to watch from exactly this angle.

He'd rented the villa for the week. Five bedrooms, a staff of four, an infinity pool that seemed to pour directly into the ocean. The kind of place his father's press secretary would have called "optically unfortunate." Cole didn't care. He was thirty-two years old and he ran a venture capital fund that had returned forty-one percent last year, and if he wanted to spend a week on an island where a bottle of rosé cost more than a car payment, that was his money and his business.

Gabriela was not his business. She was someone else's entirely. And yet.

They'd met three days ago at the bar at Eden Rock. She'd been sitting alone with a glass of champagne and a paperback novel in Spanish, and he'd asked what she was reading, which was the kind of line that never works except when it does. She'd looked up at him with dark eyes that held a quality he couldn't name, amusement, maybe, or the particular fatigue of a woman who'd been beautiful long enough to be bored by men who noticed. She'd told him the title. He'd admitted he didn't speak Spanish. She'd smiled and said, "It's about a woman who burns down her husband's house."

"Is it good?"

"It's satisfying."

Three days. That's all it had been. Three days of dinners that started in restaurants and ended on this terrace, of conversations that felt like discovering a door in a room you thought you'd already mapped, of the slow, excruciating awareness of wanting someone you have no right to want. He hadn't touched her until the second night. She'd touched him first, her hand on his wrist as he reached for a wine glass, so brief it could have been accidental if not for the way her eyes held his when she did it.

Now it was the last night. She was flying back to Colombia in the morning, back to the life she'd described only in the spaces between words—a home she didn't choose, a marriage she couldn't leave, a world whose walls she'd stopped trying to see beyond.

She turned from the railing and looked at him.

"Stop thinking," she said.

"I'm not thinking."

"You're calculating. I can see it. You're trying to figure out how this ends." She walked toward him, barefoot on the warm stone. "It ends tomorrow morning. We already know that. So stop."

She kissed him and he tasted salt and wine and something that felt reckless in the way only borrowed time can feel. Below the terrace, the Caribbean went black. Above them, stars appeared with the vulgar abundance they reserve for places where the light pollution is zero and the real estate is infinite. Somewhere in the garden, an unseen bird made a sound like a question being asked and not answered.

They did not sleep that night. They talked. They made love. They lay in tangled sheets while the ceiling fan turned and the tropical dark pressed against the windows, and she told him about growing up in Bogotá and he told her about growing up in the particular prison of being a president's son, and for a few hours they were just two people who'd found each other in the wrong life at the wrong time, which is the oldest story there is and the one that never stops hurting.

At dawn, she dressed in the bathroom and came out looking like a different woman—composed, remote, the recklessness of the night folded away so completely it might never have existed. She kissed him once, on the forehead, which was worse than any other kind of goodbye. Then she left.

Cole stood on the terrace and watched the sun come up over the bay and felt the specific emptiness that follows the departure of someone who was never yours to keep.

His phone buzzed at 7:14 AM.

Unknown number. A photograph. Him and Gabriela on this terrace, last night, her face tilted up to his, his hand in her hair. The image was sharp. Professional. Taken from below, from the hillside, with a long lens by someone who'd been watching.

Below the photograph, three words:

I'll be in touch.

Cole Hartwell set the phone down on the railing and looked out at the Caribbean, which was turquoise again, and beautiful, and completely indifferent to the fact that his life had just ended.

CHAPTER
ONE

THE PATTERN

His name was either Brian or Ryan, and I should have cared enough to remember which, but I didn't, and if I'm being honest. And I'm always honest with you, if not with anyone else. That was the point.

He was on top of me and he was doing fine. Better than fine, technically. He had good hands and a nice mouth and the kind of body that suggested a gym membership he actually used, and he was attentive in the way that men are when they're trying to impress a woman they've just met, which is to say he was paying careful attention to all the wrong things. Checking my face for feedback like a student watching for the teacher's nod. Adjusting his rhythm when I shifted underneath him, which showed effort but not instinct.

I closed my eyes and let the sensation build. Not because of him. Despite him, maybe. My body knew what to do with this—the weight of another person, the friction, the specific heat of skin against skin in a dark room. My body had always been good at this part. It was the rest of me that had trouble.

I rolled us. Put myself on top. He made a sound that was gratifying in a simple, animal way, and I planted my hands on his chest and found my own rhythm, and for a few minutes I wasn't thinking about anything at all, which is the only state of grace I reliably achieve and the reason I keep doing this.

When I came it was sharp and brief and mine. I'd taken it for myself the way I take most things, efficiently, on my own terms, without asking permission. He finished shortly after, and I rolled off and lay beside him in the dark and felt the familiar tide—the sixty seconds of chemical peace, the warmth, the slowing pulse, and then, right on schedule, the quiet arrival of the thing that always follows. Not sadness, exactly. More like clarity. The room reassembling itself. The man beside me becoming a stranger again, which he'd been all along, which was the point, which was always the point.

"That was amazing," he said to the ceiling.

"Mm."

"Can I get you anything? Water?"

I almost smiled. The post-sex water offer. It's the modern gentleman's equivalent of a curtain call, polite, performative, and entirely beside the point. "I'm good. Thank you."

He turned on his side and looked at me, and I could feel him trying to decide whether to touch my hair. I gave it a beat. He reached.

"So," he said. "Should we—"

"I have an early morning."

The gentlest possible no. I'd perfected it over the years. Warm enough to preserve his dignity, clear enough to preclude ambiguity. He took it well. They usually did. He got dressed in the half-dark with the slightly hurried movements of a man recalibrating his expectations, and I watched him from the bed and felt—nothing. Which was not the same as feeling nothing. It was a specific feeling, the feeling of nothing, and I'd learned to recognize it the way I'd learned to recognize the sound of a lie or the weight of a loaded room. It had a texture. Cool. Smooth. Like river stones.

"Call me?" he said at the door.

"Absolutely."

I wouldn't. He knew I wouldn't. We both performed the fiction anyway, because that's what adults do when the truth is too small to bother telling.

The door closed. I lay still for a moment, listening to his footsteps recede down the hall, and then I got up and walked naked to the bathroom and turned the shower as hot as I could stand it.

My apartment is on the fourteenth floor of a building on the Upper West Side that a real estate agent once described as "prewar with character," which is Manhattan code for "the elevators are slow and the doorman has opinions." I'd bought it in 2017 with the fee from a case I can't discuss, and I'd furnished it with the same philosophy I apply to most things in my life: nothing extra, nothing sentimental, everything in its place.

The living room had a gray linen sofa, a walnut coffee table, a single floor lamp, and a view of the Hudson that did more decorative work than any painting could. The bookshelves were full but organized. The kitchen was clean because I'd cleaned it, not because I didn't cook. There was one photograph on the mantel: my parents on their wedding day, my mother in a dress that was too much lace and not enough hem for 1976, my father grinning like a man who'd won something he hadn't deserved. They'd been married forty-nine years. I didn't know how they did it. I didn't know how anyone did it.

I made coffee—a pour-over, because ritual matters when everything else is chaos—and stood at the window in a robe and bare feet and watched a barge move down the Hudson with the unhurried patience of something that knows exactly where it's going. I envied the barge. I'd been envying simple, purposeful things a lot lately—boats, dogs, Sophie's conviction that the world made sense. Maybe it did. Maybe I'd just been in the wrong rooms.

The intercom buzzed.

"Ms. Sloane, Sophie's here," said George, the doorman, who had in fact been working in this building since before I was born and who I suspected would outlast the building itself. He adored Sophie. Everyone adored Sophie. It was one of the more annoying things about her.

"Send her up."

Sophie Navarro arrived the way she always arrived, like a small, organized hurricane. She came through the door with two coffees (she never trusted that I'd made my own, which was insulting and also correct about forty percent of the time), a leather portfolio under one arm, and the particular energy of a twenty-four-year-old who believed that mornings were for accomplishing things rather than for staring at rivers and contemplating one's failures.

"You're up," she said, handing me a coffee and scanning the apartment in a single, efficient sweep that I recognized because I'd taught it to her. She was checking for two things: anything out of place, and evidence that I hadn't slept. She found neither, because I'd slept fine and because Brian-or-Ryan had been neat about his exit.

"I'm always up."

"You're not always showered and dressed before eight. Big night?"

"Small night. Very small. Tell me about my week."

She sat on the sofa and opened the portfolio and became, in the space of a breath, the most competent person in any room she occupied. This was the thing about Sophie that made my chest do something I didn't have a name for, the transformation from a young woman who texted in abbreviations and had strong opinions about reality television to a professional who could brief a security operation with the precision of someone twice her age. She'd gotten that from Jimmy. The switch. The ability to be casual and then, instantly, not.

I didn't think about Jimmy. I didn't think about the way Sophie pushed her hair behind her ear with her left hand, which was exactly the gesture her father had used, a muscle memory passed down like eye color or the shape of a jaw. I didn't think about the forty-seven minutes.

I took a sip of coffee and sat down across from her and listened.

"Two inquiries came in yesterday. Both referrals. One's a hedge fund manager in Greenwich with a custody situation that's gotten complicated. His ex-wife is alleging he's hiding assets offshore and she's hired investigators. He wants us to get ahead of it."

"Is he hiding assets offshore?"

"Almost certainly."

"Pass. I'm not cleaning up a rich man's divorce. What's the other one?"

"A tech founder in Austin. Deepfake situation. Someone's created a synthetic video of him that's convincing enough to move markets if it leaks. He wants it traced and killed."

"That's more interesting. How'd he find us?"

"Through the Kessler chain. His general counsel used to work for the Hartwell campaign."

The Kessler chain. Every case I'd taken in the last three years traced back, eventually, to Martin Kessler—the White House Chief of Staff, the man who'd seen what I could do and had decided I was worth knowing. Not worth trusting, necessarily. Kessler didn't trust anyone, which was one of the reasons he'd survived four years in the most paranoid building on earth. But worth knowing. Worth calling when the problem was too strange, too sensitive, or too dangerous for anyone with a government email address.

"Set up a call for Thursday," I said. "Get his file to Ezra first. I want to know everything about the deepfake before I talk to the client."

Sophie typed a note. Her phone was military in its organization, color-coded calendars, encrypted messaging apps, a filing system that made my own look primitive. She'd built it herself. No one had taught her. She'd simply looked at the chaos of my operation and imposed order on it, the way her father had once imposed order on a forward operating base in Al Anbar Province with nothing but a whiteboard and a box of markers.

I didn't think about that either.

"Anything else?" I asked.

"Your sister called. Twice. Something about Easter."

"It's February."

"Angela plans ahead."

"Angela plans like she's coordinating a military operation, which is ironic given that she teaches second grade."

Sophie almost smiled. She knew about my family the way I knew about hers, in careful, partial pieces, the way people who work closely together learn the shape of each other's lives without ever looking directly at them. She knew I had a sister who called too much and a brother who called too little and parents who were still alive and still married and still living in the same house in Alexandria where I'd learned to ride a bike and argue about politics and believe that institutions worked.

I didn't believe that anymore. But I still called my mother every Sunday, because some habits are older than disillusionment and stronger than grief.

My phone rang.

Not my regular phone. The other one. The one that lived in the top drawer of my bedside table and that only five people in the world had the number for. I looked at Sophie. She looked at me. Neither of us said anything, because we both knew that when that phone rang, everything else on the schedule stopped.

I walked to the bedroom and picked it up.

"Catherine." Martin Kessler's voice was the same as always: measured, deliberate, the voice of a man who had learned to control every frequency of human communication the way a conductor controls an orchestra. But there was something beneath it. A hairline fracture in the composure.

"Martin."

"I need to see you. Today. In person. Can you come to Washington?"

I looked at the clock. 8:22 AM. If I left within the hour, I could be at Union Station by noon.

"How serious?"

A pause. Martin Kessler did not pause. Martin Kessler spoke in complete, considered sentences that arrived fully formed, like legislation. A pause from Kessler was the equivalent of anyone else screaming.

"The most serious call I've ever made to you."

I looked at myself in the bedroom mirror, still in my robe, hair wet, the face of a woman who'd had mediocre sex and good coffee and was about to have a very interesting day.

"I'll be on the ten o'clock Acela."

"The Stafford. Private dining room. One o'clock. Come alone."

He hung up without saying goodbye, which was not rudeness but efficiency, and which I respected even when it irritated me, which was always.

I stood in my bedroom for a moment. Through the door, I could hear Sophie pretending not to listen, which she did by typing more loudly on her phone, as though the percussive force of her thumbs could disguise the fact that she was holding her breath.

"Sophie."

She appeared in the doorway instantly, which confirmed she'd been listening from approximately two feet away.

"Cancel Thursday. Clear the week."

"Kessler?"

"Kessler."

Her eyes changed. Not excitement, exactly. Something more complicated, the specific alertness of a young hawk that's spotted movement below and doesn't yet know if it's prey or predator. I'd seen that look on another face, in another life, and it never stopped making me catch my breath.

"Book me on the Acela," I said. "Ten o'clock. And Sophie?"

"Yeah?"

"Pack a bag. Not for you—for me. Enough for a week, warm climate. I don't know where I'm going yet, but when Kessler calls like that, it's never local."

She nodded and was gone, phone already to her ear, and I stood in my bedroom and looked at the bed I'd shared with a man whose name I should have remembered and didn't, and I felt the thing I always felt when the phone rang and the work arrived and the world opened up its terrible, irresistible mouth.

Relief.

Because the truth about me, the truth I carry like a scar beneath my clothes, visible only to those who've been allowed close enough to see, is that I am better at saving other people's lives than I am at living my own. I am sharper in crisis. I am calmer under fire. I am more myself when the stakes belong to someone else, because when the stakes are mine, I hesitate, and hesitation is the thing I cannot forgive.

But that's a story for later. Maybe. If you earn it.

I dropped the robe and got dressed for the most powerful man in Washington, which required the same calculation it always required: look expensive enough to belong in the room, understated enough to disappear from memory, and strong enough that when I walked in, Martin Kessler would remember why he called me and not someone else.

Black trousers, silk blouse, the good blazer. My mother's ring. The Cartier. Heels that I could run in if I had to, because you never know, and because the one time I'd worn shoes I couldn't run in, I'd promised myself never again.

I checked the mirror one last time. I looked like a woman who had her life together. This is the most elaborate lie I tell, and I tell it every single day, and I have gotten so good at it that sometimes I almost believe it myself.

Almost.

CHAPTER TWO

THE CALL – *Washington, D.C.*

The Stafford Hotel is the kind of place that Washington runs on and nobody outside of Washington has ever heard of. It sits on Sixteenth Street, a block from the White House, and it has the deliberate anonymity of a building that exists specifically so that powerful people can meet without being seen meeting. No lobby bar. No scene. Just quiet hallways and private dining rooms and the particular hush of money that doesn't need to announce itself.

I arrived at 12:55. I am always five minutes early to meetings with Martin Kessler, because Kessler is always ten minutes early to everything, and there is a specific power dynamic in being the person already seated when the most important person in the room walks in. Kessler knows I do this. He does it anyway. We've been performing this small choreography for four years, and neither of us has ever acknowledged it, which is its own kind of intimacy.

The private dining room was on the second floor. Wood-paneled, no windows, a table set for two with the kind of china that suggests someone once cared deeply about this room and now it just exists, a relic of a Washington that did its business over brandy instead of text messages. A waiter in a white jacket brought me sparkling water without being asked, which meant Kessler had briefed the staff, which meant he'd been here long enough to brief the staff, which meant this was worse than his voice had suggested.

I sat with my back to the wall. Force of habit. The agency trains it into you and then you spend the rest of your life doing it in restaurants and feeling slightly ridiculous, like a woman who brings a parachute to a dinner party. But the one time you don't do it is the one time it matters, and I'd made my peace with being the kind of person who always knows where the exits are, even in a room with only one.

Kessler appeared at exactly one o'clock. He came through the door with the controlled momentum of a man who is always moving toward the next decision, and for a moment—just a flash, before the professional mask settled—I saw something I'd never seen on Martin Kessler's face.

Fear.

Not panic. Kessler doesn't panic. But fear, the real kind, the kind that lives beneath competence, the kind that says I have a problem I'm not sure I can solve. I'd seen that look exactly twice before in my career: once on a station chief in Baghdad the night before an operation went sideways, and once in my own mirror.

He sat down across from me, unbuttoned his jacket, and did not smile.

"Thank you for coming on short notice."

"You said it was the most serious call you'd ever made to me. I cleared my week."

"You may need to clear your month."

The waiter reappeared. Kessler ordered coffee, black, no food. I ordered the same, because this was not a lunch. This was a briefing, and the absence of food was its own kind of information: whatever he was about to tell me, it was the kind of thing that makes people forget to eat.

He waited until the waiter left. Then he placed a phone on the table between us. Not his usual phone, I noticed, but a burner, the kind you buy at a gas station and throw away after one conversation. Martin Kessler, the Chief of Staff to the President of the United States, was carrying a burner phone. The implications of that alone were enough to make me sit up straighter.

He opened the phone to a photograph and slid it across the table.

I looked.

A terrace. Night. Two people kissing. The image was crisp—professional lens, good angle, the kind of shot that required patience and planning. The woman was beautiful in a way that photographed well: dark hair, olive skin, a dress that moved like water. The man was younger than her, tall, with the particular grooming of someone who'd grown up around cameras.

I recognized him immediately, because every person in America would recognize him immediately. I just didn't want to.

"That's Cole Hartwell," I said.

"Yes."

"The President's son."

"Yes."

"Who's the woman?"

Kessler's jaw tightened. It was a small movement, the kind most people would miss. I don't miss small movements. It's one of the few things I'm unreservedly good at, and it's kept me alive more than once.

"Her name is Gabriela Montero. She's Colombian. Thirty-four years old. Educated at the Sorbonne, speaks four languages, sits on the board of a children's literacy foundation in Bogotá." He paused. "She's also married to Andrés Salcedo."

The name took a moment to land, and when it did, it landed like a stone dropped into still water. The impact was small, but the ripples went everywhere.

"Salcedo," I said. "As in—"

"As in. Yes."

Andrés Salcedo. I didn't know much about him yet. I would, soon, in the way I eventually know too much about everyone who enters my professional orbit. But I knew the name. Salcedo ran one of Colombia's newer cartels, the kind that doesn't make headlines because it's too smart for headlines. Diversified, sophisticated, ruthless when necessary and polished when it served. He was reportedly charming, reportedly brilliant, and reportedly responsible for a distribution network that moved product through Central America and the Caribbean with the quiet efficiency of a Fortune 500 supply chain.

The President's son had slept with a cartel boss's wife. In a photograph. Taken by someone.

I looked at Kessler and saw the full shape of his fear, and I understood it, because it was the kind of problem that has no good solution, only a choice between various catastrophes.

"Tell me everything," I said. "From the beginning. And Martin—don't edit. I can't help you if you manage the information."

He nodded. He knew this about me. It was one of the reasons he called me instead of someone else. Not because I was the most discreet (I was), or the most connected (I wasn't), but because I was the one person in his professional life who required the full truth as a precondition for engagement. Most people in Washington would take whatever version of reality you offered them and work with it. I wouldn't. It had cost me clients. It had also kept me alive.

"Cole was in St. Barts last week," Kessler began. "Vacation. Personal trip. He rented a villa on Flamands Bay—his money, not ours, nothing from the campaign or the party. He met Gabriela Montero at the bar at Eden Rock. They had a three-day affair."

"How three-day? Dinners and conversation, or—"

"The photograph answers that question."

It did. The kiss on that terrace was not a first kiss. It was the kiss of two people who had already been everywhere with each other and were running out of time. I could see it in the angle of her body toward his, in the way his hand rested in her hair with the familiarity of someone who'd been given permission more than once.

I felt a pang. Not for Cole, for Gabriela. For the woman on the terrace who'd kissed a man knowing it was the last time, because the life she was going back to didn't include the freedom to want what she wanted. I recognized that. I recognized it more than I cared to examine at 1:15 on a Tuesday afternoon in a wood-paneled room in Washington.

"Who took the photograph?" I asked.

"A man named Rafael Herrera. Former Colombian military: special forces, discharged in 2016, now a private security contractor with ties to the Cartagena underworld. Not cartel, but cartel-adjacent. The kind of man who works the spaces between legitimate and illegitimate."

"How did you identify him?"

"We haven't, officially. This is all off-book, Catherine. There is no file. There is no briefing. There is no interagency response. The Secret Service doesn't know. The FBI doesn't know. The only people who know about this photograph are sitting in this room."

The weight of that settled on me. The Chief of Staff to the President of the United States was sitting in a private dining room with a burner phone, telling me something he hadn't told the Secret Service. That meant this was beyond embarrassing. This was existential.

"What does Herrera want?"

"His brother." Kessler reached into his jacket and produced a thin file folder, actual paper, no digital trail. He slid it across the table. "Miguel Herrera. Currently serving a thirty-year sentence at FCI Coleman in Florida. Drug trafficking conspiracy. Convicted in 2018 as part of a DEA operation called Bright Horizon."

I opened the file. Miguel Herrera's booking photograph looked back at me—a man in his late thirties with the flat, exhausted eyes of someone who'd already given up. I scanned the summary. Major trafficking operation. Multi-defendant case. Cooperating witnesses. Thirty years with no possibility of parole.

"Rafael's demand," Kessler continued, "is that the President secure Miguel's release. Commutation, pardon, compassionate release—he doesn't care about the mechanism. He wants his brother out. And if he doesn't get it within ten days, he sends the photographs to the Salcedo cartel."

There it was. Not blackmail against the President, exactly. Something worse. A threat aimed at the President's son's life, using the President's power as the ransom.

"If Salcedo finds out his wife was sleeping with Cole Hartwell—" I began.

"Cole is dead," Kessler said flatly. "Not probably dead. Not potentially dead. Dead. Salcedo doesn't tolerate humiliation, and the President's son sleeping with his wife is the kind of humiliation that demands a response. And the response won't be quiet. It will be public, because that's how these men operate. They make examples."

I sat with this for a moment. The waiter returned with coffee. I wrapped my hands around the cup and felt the heat and thought about the architecture of the problem, which is what I do. I think about problems the way other people think about buildings, looking for load-bearing walls and structural weaknesses and the places where, if you apply pressure just right, the whole thing shifts.

"The pardon is off the table," I said. It wasn't a question.

"Completely. The President can't pardon a convicted drug trafficker to protect his son from a cartel. If it ever came out, and it would come out, it would end the presidency and potentially trigger criminal investigations. Not to mention that it would signal to every cartel in the hemisphere that the President's family is a pressure point. We'd be getting demands like this weekly."

"So you need the threat neutralized without giving Rafael what he wants."

"I need someone to go to the Caribbean, find Rafael Herrera, and make this problem disappear. No official footprint. No connection to the White House. No violence—we cannot have the President's office connected to anything that looks like an operation against a Colombian national, even a criminal one." He looked at me across the table, and in that look was everything he wasn't saying: I have tried to think of another way. There isn't one. You're it.

"Where is Herrera now?"

"We believe he's returned to Cartagena. He has family there, contacts, a network. He'll feel protected."

Cartagena. Salcedo's territory. I'd be operating in the backyard of the man whose wife had caused this entire mess, looking for a blackmailer who was using that man's capacity for violence as his primary weapon. The degree of difficulty was extraordinary.

I loved it.

I hated that I loved it, which is a feeling I've stopped trying to analyze and started simply accepting, the way you accept that your body craves sugar even though you know it's bad for you. Some people are built for quiet lives. I am not one of them, and pretending otherwise is a waste of the limited honesty I have left.

"The fee," I said.

Kessler named a number. It was twice my usual rate. I kept my face neutral, which required effort, because twice my usual rate from

Martin Kessler meant this was not just serious. It was the kind of serious that keeps Chiefs of Staff awake at night staring at the ceiling of the White House residence, calculating how many careers end if this goes wrong.

"Budget for operational expenses?"

"Unlimited. No receipts. No documentation. A wire to whatever account you specify, replenished as needed."

"Ten days."

"Ten days. That's Rafael's deadline. After that, the photographs go to Salcedo, and I'm making a phone call to Cole Hartwell that no father should ever have to make."

Something in his voice when he said that—a fracture so small you'd need a seismograph to register it—told me that this was not entirely professional for Kessler. He'd watched Cole grow up. The Hartwells weren't just his principals; they were, in whatever limited way power allows, his people. This was a man trying to save someone he cared about, using the only tool he had: me.

I should have found that touching. Instead I found it useful. A client with emotional stakes is a client who won't second-guess your methods, and Kessler second-guessing my methods was the last thing I needed in Cartagena.

I closed the file folder and slid it back across the table.

"Keep the paper. I've read it." I had a photographic memory for documents, not the parlor-trick kind, but the operational kind, the kind the agency trains into you until reading a page once means you've read it forever. It's useful and occasionally inconvenient, because there are things I've read that I'd very much like to forget.

"I need to talk to Cole," I said. "In person. Before I go to Cartagena."

"He's still in St. Barts. I told him to stay put until this is resolved. His security detail thinks it's a vacation extension."

"St. Barts first, then. I'll want to see the villa, trace the photographer's position, talk to Cole about everything—and I mean everything—that happened with Gabriela. Then Cartagena."

Kessler nodded. "What do you need from me?"

"Stay by your phone. Don't contact Cole directly. From this point forward, all communication goes through me. And Martin?" I leaned forward slightly, just enough to close the distance between us by six inches, which in the grammar of power meetings is the equivalent of grabbing someone by the collar. "If there's anything else—anything you've left out, anything you think is too sensitive or too embarrassing or too politically complicated to share—tell me now. Because if I find out later that you managed the information, I walk. And you don't get a second call."

He held my gaze. Martin Kessler is one of the few men I've met who can hold my gaze without it becoming a contest, and that's because he's not trying to win. He's trying to calculate, which is different and more dangerous.

"That's everything," he said.

I believed him. Not because I trusted him. I don't trust anyone, which is either my greatest professional asset or the reason I'll die alone, depending on the time of day you ask me. But because the fear I'd seen on his face when he walked in was genuine, and genuine fear is the one emotion that makes powerful people honest.

I stood. He stood. We did not shake hands, because we never shake hands, because the formality would imply a distance that doesn't exist between us. What exists is something more specific and less comfortable: the understanding that he will call me with the worst problems of his professional life, and I will solve them, and neither of us will ever fully trust the other, and that's fine, because trust is overrated and results are not.

"Catherine," he said as I reached the door.

I turned.

"Bring him home."

It wasn't an order. It was the closest Martin Kessler would ever come to begging. I filed it away, not to use against him, but to remember, later, when the case got hard and the options got ugly, that at the center of this particular mess was a man who wanted to save a boy he'd watched grow up. That mattered. Not strategically. Just humanly.

"I'll call you from St. Barts," I said.

I walked out of the Stafford Hotel into the February gray of Washington, D.C., and stood on the sidewalk for a moment, breathing cold air and feeling the weight of what I'd just agreed to settle into my body the way it always does, not as anxiety but as architecture, the case assembling itself in my mind, walls and doors and corridors, a structure I would walk through over the next ten days, looking for the room where the answer lived.

I called Sophie from the cab.

"Change of plans. I need a flight to St. Barts tomorrow morning. The first available. And book the Sofitel Legend Santa Clara in Cartagena for after. Suite. Open-ended."

"St. Barts and then Colombia?" A pause. "This is a Kessler case."

"This is a Kessler case."

"How bad?"

I watched Washington scroll past the cab window—the monuments, the marble, the magnificent architecture of a government that functions on the belief that enough rules and enough columns can hold back the chaos of human nature. I'd believed that once. Now I knew better. The chaos doesn't stop at the columns. It lives inside them.

"Pack the Louboutins," I said. "The ones I can run in."

Sophie understood. She always understood. It was one of the things that made her indispensable and one of the things that terrified me, because the last person who understood me that well without being told was her father, and understanding me is not, historically, a safe occupation.

She didn't say be careful. She never said be careful. Instead she said, "I'll have the bag at your apartment by six," and hung up, and I sat in the back of a cab on Constitution Avenue and thought about a woman on a terrace in St. Barts and a man with a camera and a brother in a federal prison, and I felt the familiar hum in my chest, the one that says this is going to be dangerous, and the one that says good.

CHAPTER THREE

THE ISLAND — *St. Barts*

The thing about St. Barts is that it's so beautiful it makes you angry.

Not immediately. First it makes you breathless—the descent into Gustaf III, which is less an airport and more a flat spot between two hills where small planes perform controlled acts of faith, drops you over a ridge and suddenly the whole island is there: green hills, white sand, water so blue it looks like someone adjusted the saturation on reality and forgot to turn it back down. You see it and your first thought is this can't be real. Your second thought is I don't deserve this. Your third thought, if you're me, is who does.

The taxi from the airport took twelve minutes. The driver was a sun-darkened Frenchman who drove a vintage Mercedes with the casual fatalism of someone who'd made peace with the island's narrow roads and their relationship with gravity. He didn't try to make conversation, which I appreciated, because I was working. Not visibly—I was looking out the window like any other tourist arriving in paradise. But I was cataloging. The roads. The sightlines. The density of buildings near the harbor, the sparseness as we climbed toward Flamands. Where you could see and where you could hide. Where a man with a long lens could set up and wait.

The agency never leaves you. It just changes what you look at.

Cole Hartwell's villa sat above Flamands Bay on a hillside that had no business being that green in February. It was the kind of property that doesn't appear on rental websites. You had to know someone, and the someone had to decide you were worth knowing, which in St. Barts meant either your net worth or your last name opened the right doors. Cole had both.

A gate. A gravel drive lined with oleander. A house that was all white walls and natural wood and floor-to-ceiling glass, designed to make the boundary between inside and outside feel philosophical rather than architectural. The infinity pool caught the light and threw it back in shifting patterns that played across the ceiling of the open-air living room, and beyond it the bay stretched out in that impossible turquoise, and I stood in the driveway for a moment and thought: this is where you come to forget that consequences exist.

Which is, of course, exactly what had happened.

Cole's security detail was two men in dark polos who looked ex-military and bored, the specific kind of bored that comes from protecting someone who doesn't go anywhere and doesn't do anything and who you've been told is extending a vacation for reasons no one has explained. They checked my ID—the clean one, the Catherine Sloane who consults on international risk, which has the advantage of being true if incomplete—and waved me through with the professional disinterest of men who'd decided I wasn't a threat. I probably wasn't. Probably.

Cole met me on the terrace.

I recognized it immediately: the railing, the view, the angle. This was the terrace from the photograph. This was where he'd kissed Gabriela Montero while a man in the darkness below captured everything. Standing here now, in daylight, with the bay sparkling and a light breeze carrying the smell of salt and frangipani, it looked like a postcard. It looked like the least dangerous place on earth. But I'd spent enough of my life in beautiful places to know that beauty is just camouflage. The most dangerous rooms I've ever been in were all stunning.

Cole Hartwell was not what I expected.

I'd prepared for a certain type. The president's son as tabloid shorthand: entitled, careless, the kind of man who mistakes access for accomplishment and treats other people's lives as collateral damage to his appetites. I'd seen the type a hundred times in Washington, in New York, in every city where wealth and power produce children who grow up believing the world is a room that was decorated for them.

Cole wasn't that. Or if he was, he'd been scared out of it.

He was tall, taller than he looked in photos, with the lean build of a man who ran or rowed or did something that required discipline rather than vanity. Brown hair that needed cutting, pushed back from a face that was handsome in a forgettable way, the kind of face that would age into distinguished if he lived long enough. He wore a linen shirt and shorts and no shoes, and he looked like he hadn't slept in days, which he probably hadn't.

His handshake was firm and brief and slightly damp, which told me more than his face did. You can control your expression. You can't control your palms.

"Ms. Sloane. Thank you for coming."

"Cat."

"Cole." A pause. "Did Kessler tell you everything?"

"Kessler told me what Kessler knows. I need you to tell me what you know. All of it. Including the parts you didn't tell him."

Something flickered across his face—surprise, maybe, or the small relief of being seen through by someone who wasn't pretending. He nodded and led me inside to a living room where the furniture was white and the art was abstract and the air conditioning was set to a temperature that suggested someone was spending money without thinking about it. He offered me water, coffee, wine. I took water. It was 11 AM, and I don't drink when I'm working unless drinking is the work.

We sat across from each other, me on a low sofa, him in a chair he'd pulled to face me directly, which I noted. People who sit at angles are trying to keep their options open. People who face you straight on have decided to commit to the conversation, for better or worse. Cole had committed.

"Start at the beginning," I said. "Eden Rock."

He took a breath. "I was at the bar. Late afternoon. I'd been on the island for two days and I was bored, which is a stupid thing to be in a place like this, but there's only so much swimming and reading you can do before your own company starts to feel like a sentence."

I understood that more than I wanted to.

"She was at the end of the bar, alone. Reading a novel. I asked what it was about." He almost smiled. "Which is the most unoriginal thing a man can say to a woman in a bar, and I knew it, and I said it anyway because something about her made originality feel unnecessary."

"What did you know about her?"

"Nothing. She said her name was Gabriela. She said she was from Colombia. She didn't mention a husband. She didn't mention a last name."

"When did you learn she was married?"

"The second night. We were on this terrace—" he gestured behind him without looking, the way you gesture at a place that's become a wound—"and she told me she had to go back to a life that didn't include choices. I asked what that meant. She said, 'It means I'm married to a man I can't leave, and this is the freest I've felt in years, and tomorrow it's over.' She didn't say his name. I didn't ask."

"But you didn't stop."

"No."

He said it without defensiveness, without the self-justifying performance that most people in his position would deploy—the she came on to me, the I didn't know, the it just happened. He said "no" and let it sit there, bare and honest, and I found myself respecting him for it even as I cataloged it as a liability.

Because here's what I know about men like Cole Hartwell—men who are smart and privileged and fundamentally decent, who have spent their lives inside a system that tells them they're special while simultaneously controlling every aspect of who they're allowed to be —what I know is that the thing they want most in the world is to feel real. Not presidential. Not strategic. Not curated for public consumption. Real. And the most dangerous version of that desire is when it meets a woman who makes them feel it, because then they'll do anything, risk anything, burn any number of carefully constructed futures for another hour of feeling like a person instead of a position.

I knew because I'd done it myself. Not with a president's son, and not on a terrace in St. Barts, but the impulse was the same. The reckless, intoxicating surrender to being known by someone, even briefly, even at a cost you can't calculate. I'd paid that cost. I was still paying it.

But I didn't say any of that. I was working.

"Tell me about the last night," I said. "Every detail. Where you were standing, what you could see, what you heard."

He walked me through it. The terrace. The sunset. The conversation. The kiss that the camera caught. He was precise: good memory, organized mind, the Georgetown MBA training showing in the way he sequenced events and flagged what he wasn't sure about. I asked about the villa's sightlines, about the hillside below, about whether he'd heard anything, seen anything, noticed any unfamiliar faces on the island in the days before.

He hadn't. He'd been in a bubble—the specific bubble of new desire, where the entire world contracts to the size of one person and everything else becomes scenery. I'd been in that bubble. It's warm and it's beautiful and you can't see a goddamn thing.

"The photograph arrived the next morning," he said. "Seven fourteen AM. She'd already left. I'd been standing right here—" he pointed to the railing, and I could see it in his face, the exact moment replaying —"watching the sunrise, feeling sorry for myself in the way you do when someone leaves and the place they were still smells like them. Then the phone buzzed."

"What did you do?"

"For about ten minutes, I couldn't do anything. I sat down and stared at it. Then I called Kessler, because Kessler is the person I call when the world is ending. He's been that person since I was sixteen and got arrested for underage drinking in Georgetown and my father was in a debate prep and couldn't be reached." A small, sad smile. "Kessler has been fixing my messes for half my life. I just never thought I'd make one this big."

"Did you know who Gabriela was married to? Then, or now?"

"Kessler told me. After." Cole's face went still. "Andrés Salcedo. I looked him up. Read everything I could find. And then I understood why Kessler sounded the way he sounded on the phone."

"How do you feel about that?"

He looked at me like the question surprised him. Maybe no one had asked. "Terrified," he said. "Of what he'll do to me if he finds out. But also—" He stopped.

"Also?"

"Terrified of what he might do to her."

That landed. It landed because it was real. Not rehearsed, not strategic, not the thing you say to make the fixer sympathize with you. He was afraid for Gabriela. The woman he'd spent three days with. The woman he'd held on this terrace. He was sitting in a five-bedroom villa that cost more per night than most people earn in a month, and the thing keeping him awake wasn't his own safety. It was hers.

I'd been in this business long enough to know that most clients lie, and the ones who don't lie omit, and the ones who don't omit shade. Cole Hartwell was doing none of those things. He was sitting in front of me with his whole stupid, reckless, genuine heart on the table, and the hell of it was that his heart was the very thing that had gotten him into this mess, and it was also the thing that made me want to get him out of it.

"I have one more question," I said. "And I need the truth."

"You've had the truth."

"Did you love her?"

He didn't answer immediately, which was itself an answer. A lie comes fast. The truth has to find its way past everything you've built on top of it.

"I loved being with her," he said finally. "I loved who I was when I was with her. I don't know if that's the same thing. I think maybe it's worse."

I stood up. I'd heard enough. Not just the facts—those I'd gotten from Kessler. I'd heard the emotional architecture, which is what I actually needed, because you can't solve a problem built on human desire without understanding the desire. Cole Hartwell had wanted to feel alive in a world that had spent thirty-two years keeping him safe from his own life. Gabriela Montero had wanted to feel free in a world that had locked every door. They'd found each other for three days, and now that recklessness had a price, and the price was denominated in blood, and I was the one who'd been hired to renegotiate the terms.

"Stay on this island," I said. "Don't leave the villa. Don't contact Gabriela—not a text, not a call, nothing. If Rafael or anyone else reaches out, you don't respond, you call me immediately. This number." I wrote it on a card and handed it to him. "I'm going to fix this, Cole. But I need you to do something very difficult."

"What?"

"Nothing. Sit here. Wait. Let me work."

He nodded. It was the nod of a man who was used to action, used to solving problems with spreadsheets and phone calls and the vast machinery of being a Hartwell, and who was now being told that the best thing he could do was absolutely nothing. It was, I suspected, the hardest instruction he'd ever received.

I walked back through the living room, past the security detail, and out into the driveway where the rented Jeep I'd picked up at the airport was baking in the sun. I sat behind the wheel and didn't start the engine for a moment. The villa was beautiful. The bay was beautiful. The whole island was a jewel set in an ocean that didn't care what happened to the people who floated on its surface.

I thought about Gabriela Montero, back in Colombia now, in whatever gilded cage Andrés Salcedo had built for her. Did she know about the photographs? Did she know that the three days she'd stolen for herself had been captured by a man with a camera and a desperate brother and turned into a weapon? Did she lie awake at night and think about the terrace, about Cole's hand in her hair, about the last kiss and the silence after?

I thought about David. I always thought about David at the worst possible moments: in the middle of cases, in the middle of the night, in the middle of a thought about someone else's ruined love. David, who'd loved me the way Cole loved Gabriela, with his whole self, recklessly, in defiance of everything the world they'd built demanded. David, who'd eventually stopped. Not because he stopped loving me. Because I'd made it impossible for him to reach me, and there's only so long a man can stand on the other side of a wall before he goes home.

I started the Jeep. I had work to do. A photographer's vantage point to find, a blackmailer to trace, a clock ticking down to something I was not going to let happen.

The island shimmered in the heat as I drove back toward the harbor, and I let it be beautiful without flinching, because that's a skill too—being in paradise and remembering that you're there to work, not to want, not to feel, not to stand on a terrace with someone and pretend the world has stopped. I was very good at that skill. I'd been practicing it my entire adult life.

Some days I almost believed it was enough.

CHAPTER FOUR

THE TRAIL – *St. Barts*

I drove back to the villa alone that afternoon with the photograph on my phone and the hillside in my sights.

The image told a story if you knew how to read it. Not the obvious story—the kiss, the terrace, the doomed romance—but the operational one underneath. The angle was upward, maybe fifteen degrees. The focal length was long—300mm at least, probably 400—which meant the photographer had been close enough to get sharp resolution but far enough to stay invisible. The lighting said dusk, and the shadow cast by the railing said the lens was positioned south-southwest of the terrace, which meant the hillside below the villa's garden wall. And the framing was patient. Centered. Composed. This wasn't a lucky shot grabbed by a paparazzo on a scooter. This was a man who'd chosen his position, settled in, and waited.

I parked the Jeep on the road below the villa, where the manicured landscaping gave way to wild scrub and the kind of volcanic rock that makes Caribbean hillsides look like they're designed to break your ankle. I was wearing the wrong shoes for this—leather flats, fine for a client meeting, idiotic for fieldwork—but I'd done worse in worse shoes in worse places, and vanity has never been the thing that stops me. Stupidity has, on occasion. But not vanity.

The hillside was steeper than it looked from the road. I picked my way down through scrub brush and sea grape, following the angle I'd calculated from the photograph, checking my phone every few meters to compare the terrace's position against the image. The Caribbean opened up below me—Flamands Bay, obscenely blue, a sailboat cutting a white line across the water like someone drawing on glass—and I ignored it, because beauty is a distraction and I was looking for something ugly.

I found it twenty meters down the slope.

A flat spot in the scrub, about two meters square, where the vegetation had been pushed back and the ground was packed harder than the soil around it. Someone had sat here. Recently. There were two shallow impressions where knees or a tripod base had pressed into the dirt, and a scuff mark on a rock where a bag had rested. The sightline to the terrace was clean—unobstructed, slightly elevated from the garden wall, with a natural blind of sea grape that would make the position invisible from above.

Professional. This man knew how to set up an observation post. Military training, almost certainly—the position was textbook. Good cover, clear egress down the slope to the road, sight lines that gave him the terrace and the pool and most of the interior living area through those floor-to-ceiling windows. He could have watched Cole and Gabriela for hours without being seen. He probably had.

I crouched in the spot and held up my phone, framing the terrace through the camera. The angle matched. The villa's railing cut across the upper third of the frame exactly the way it did in the blackmail photograph. I was sitting where Rafael Herrera had sat, seeing what he'd seen, and for a moment I felt the specific discomfort that comes from occupying someone else's vantage point—the awareness that watching is its own kind of intimacy, and that the man who'd sat here had watched two people fall in love and seen only leverage.

I took photos of the position, the sightlines, the scuff marks. Then I climbed back up to the road, scraped volcanic dirt off my shoes, and called Ezra.

Ezra Munn picked up on the sixth ring, which for Ezra was practically sprinting to the phone.

"Boss." His voice had the slightly unfocused quality of a man who was already doing three things when the call came in and had no intention of stopping any of them. In the background, I could hear what sounded like Icelandic electronica at a volume that would constitute noise pollution in most European capitals. Ezra lived in a converted warehouse in Lisbon that I'd visited exactly once and that looked like a server farm had detonated inside a mid-century furniture showroom. He was twenty-eight years old, hadn't set foot in the United States in four years for reasons I'd never asked about and he'd never explained, and he was, without qualification, the most talented digital intelligence operative I'd ever worked with. Including the ones at Langley. Especially the ones at Langley.

"I need you to find someone," I said.

"Time zone?"

"Caribbean, maybe South American. Start with St. Barts in the last ten days."

"St. Barts." A pause. "You're in St. Barts and you didn't bring me? I'm offended. I'm hurt. I'm also deeply jealous, but mostly hurt."

"Ezra."

"Right. Person. Go."

"Rafael Herrera. Former Colombian military, special forces, discharged 2016. Now private security, based in or around Cartagena. He was on this island within the last week. I need to know when he arrived, where he stayed, how he got here, what devices he was carrying, and where he went when he left. I also need his full background—service record, associates, financials, family."

The music in the background dropped by half, which was Ezra's version of giving something his full attention.

"Former special forces doing private security work in the Caribbean," he said. "So we're looking at a guy who knows how to stay invisible. Fun. Anything else?"

"He has a brother. Miguel Herrera. Currently at FCI Coleman, Florida. Thirty-year sentence, drug trafficking, convicted 2018. DEA operation called Bright Horizon. I need everything on that case—the conviction, the co-defendants, the evidence, the informants. Especially the informants."

"You're asking me to pull federal case files."

"I'm asking you to find federal case files. How you find them is between you and your conscience."

"My conscience charges time and a half for federal databases."

"Bill me."

"Already billing you. Give me four hours for Herrera, longer for the DEA files. Those systems are annoying. Not hard—annoying. There's a difference, and the difference is mostly about how much ramen I eat while I'm waiting for their terrible servers to respond."

"Call me when you have something."

"Boss?"

"Yeah."

"Is this a Kessler thing?"

I hesitated. Ezra had never met Kessler, would never meet Kessler, existed in a completely separate compartment of my operational world. But he'd worked enough Kessler cases to recognize the shape of them—the urgency, the budget, the specific gravity that attached to anything connected to that particular phone number.

"It's a Kessler thing."

"Cool. So, high stakes, morally ambiguous, probably going to ruin your week. My favorite kind."

He hung up without saying goodbye, which was a habit he shared with Kessler and which I suspected both of them would be horrified to know they had in common.

I had four hours to kill and an island to learn, so I drove.

St. Barts is eight square miles. You can cross it in twenty minutes if you're in a hurry, and nobody on St. Barts is ever in a hurry, because hurrying would suggest that wherever you are isn't exactly where you want to be, and every inch of this island is designed to make you feel like you've arrived at the place you've been trying to reach your entire life. The roads are narrow and absurdly steep, switchbacking through green hills dotted with white villas, and around every curve is another view that makes you want to pull over and stare and question every decision that's led to a life where you don't wake up to this every morning.

I drove through Gustavia, the main harbor town, which was all red roofs and designer boutiques and yachts moored so close together their masts looked like a bare forest. Hermès. Louis Vuitton. Cartier. A jewelry store that didn't have prices in the window because if you had to ask, you'd already lost. I parked near the harbor and walked, because you can't know a place from inside a car—you need to feel the streets under your feet, smell the salt air mixing with boulangerie bread, hear the particular frequency of a town where French is the first language and money is the second.

I bought a croque monsieur from a café on Rue de la République and ate it standing up, watching the harbor. A megayacht was backing into the quay with the slow, careful arrogance of a vessel that cost more than most countries' GDP. Two women in resort wear and improbable hats were photographing each other in front of a bougainvillea wall, performing the kind of effortless beauty that requires enormous effort. A stray cat—ginger, indifferent, clearly the actual owner of the street—threaded between their ankles and they shrieked, which ruined the shot and improved the moment considerably.

I smiled. I don't always remember to notice things like this: the small, unscripted moments that make a place real instead of scenic. The agency trained me to see threats. The work trained me to see angles. But underneath all of that, before all of that, I was a woman who loved cities and waterfronts and the specific chaos of strangers living their lives in public. I'd been good at noticing before I'd been good at anything else. The tragedy, and I use the word carefully, is that the skill that makes me love the world is the same skill that makes me dangerous in it.

I drove on. Shell Beach, where the shore was made of millions of tiny white shells that crunched underfoot and glowed pink in the afternoon light. Colombier, at the end of a dirt road, where the water was so clear you could see the sandy bottom thirty feet down and where three boats floated in a bay that looked like it had been painted by someone who'd never been sad. Saline, the long white beach on the south side, backed by salt ponds where herons stood in the shallows with the absolute stillness of creatures who have figured out that patience is a form of power.

I could understand why Cole Hartwell had come here to forget himself. I could understand why Gabriela Montero had let herself be found. This island was a conspiracy against caution—every view, every breeze, every glass of cold rosé on a terrace above an impossible sea was an argument that the life you'd built on the mainland didn't matter, that consequences were a fiction, that the only real thing was right now and the warmth of a hand on your skin.

The island was wrong, of course. Consequences are not a fiction. They're just patient.

But God, it was beautiful. And I was alone in it, which was its own kind of information about my life that I filed away under the heading of things I'll think about later, which is a file that has gotten very large and that I never open.

Ezra called back in three hours and forty-two minutes, which was eighteen minutes ahead of schedule and which meant he'd found something that excited him. Ezra excited was indistinguishable from Ezra bored to anyone who didn't know him, except that when he was excited he talked slightly faster and forgot to eat, which in Ezra's case was the equivalent of a normal person jumping on a table and shouting.

I was sitting on a low wall above Gustavia harbor, watching the sun drop toward the water, when the phone buzzed.

"Rafael Herrera," he said without preamble. "Forty-one years old. Born in Buenaventura—that's Pacific coast, Colombia, for the geographically incurious. Colombian Army, 2005 to 2016, assigned to the Joint Special Operations Command, which is their Tier 1 unit. Sniper qualified. Counternarcotics operations, mostly in Nariño and Putumayo. Discharged in 2016 under conditions that the official record describes as 'voluntary separation' and that my slightly less official sources describe as 'asked to leave before we make you leave.'"

"Why?"

"Unclear. Could be discipline, could be politics, could be that he looked at someone the wrong way. The Colombian military isn't great about documenting the difference between those things. After discharge, he went private. Security consulting, executive protection, the usual menu for a guy with his skill set. Based in Cartagena for the last five years. Works the legitimate-adjacent space—bodyguard work for wealthy Colombians, security assessments for corporate clients, the occasional job that nobody puts in writing."

"Cartel ties?"

"Not directly. He's careful. But in Cartagena, careful doesn't mean clean—it means you know which lines not to cross and who's watching. He orbits the Salcedo organization without touching it. Some of his clients have Salcedo connections. Some of his associates are former cartel security. He's in the ecosystem without being in the food chain."

"That's a narrow ledge."

"It is. And now for the part that explains why he's standing on it." Ezra's voice shifted—marginally, almost imperceptibly, but I'd been listening to this man for two years and I knew what his voice did when the data turned from interesting to significant. "Miguel Herrera. Younger brother by three years. Same hometown, same trajectory up to a point. Miguel didn't go military—he went the other direction. Low-level trafficking operation, mostly moving cocaine through Central American corridors. Got rolled up in 2018 by the DEA's Operation Bright Horizon. Multi-defendant conspiracy case. Miguel was a mid-tier player—not a boss, not a foot soldier. A logistics guy. The kind of person who makes the machine run without ever touching the product."

"Thirty years for a logistics role seems heavy."

"Very heavy. The mandatory minimums in these cases are brutal, but even by those standards, Miguel got hammered. Two co-defendants who were arguably more senior got twenty and twenty-two. Miguel got thirty. No parole."

"Why the disparity?"

"That's the interesting question, and I don't have the interesting answer yet. The case file has the usual architecture—cooperating witnesses, intercepted communications, physical evidence. But some of it's sealed. There's a confidential informant designated CI-7 who provided the key testimony linking Miguel to the conspiracy's leadership tier. Without CI-7, Miguel's a twenty-year case at most. With CI-7, he's the connective tissue that holds the whole prosecution together."

"Who's CI-7?"

"Sealed. I'm working on it, but federal informant files are genuinely difficult—not annoying-difficult, actually-difficult. Give me time."

I sat with this for a moment, watching the harbor lights come on one by one as the sky went from blue to lavender. A couple walked past me on the seawall, hand in hand, her head on his shoulder, and I felt the smallest twist beneath my sternum. Not jealousy, exactly, but the recognition of something I used to want and had trained myself to stop reaching for.

"So we have a former special forces sniper," I said, "whose little brother got a disproportionately harsh sentence in a federal drug case, possibly on the basis of questionable informant testimony. And he's using compromising photographs of the President's son to try to force a release."

"That's the shape of it."

"He's not doing this for money."

"No. His financials are modest—he lives well by Colombian standards but he's not wealthy. No offshore accounts, no unexplained income. This is personal. He wants his brother back."

I closed my eyes. The breeze off the harbor was warm and smelled like salt and diesel and someone's dinner, and I thought about Rafael Herrera sitting on that hillside in the dark, watching two strangers kiss on a terrace, patient as a heron, and I understood him. Not approved of him—understood. Because I knew what it was like to have one person in the world whose safety mattered more than your own, and I knew what you'd do—what you'd become—to bring them home.

Kessler had said the same thing to me yesterday. Bring him home. Two men, on opposite sides of this mess, driven by the same impulse: save the person you love. The symmetry was almost elegant. It was also the kind of thing that makes cases like this so dangerous, because when both sides are operating from love, nobody backs down, and somebody gets destroyed.

"Where is he now?" I asked.

"Back in Cartagena. He flew St. Barts to San Juan, San Juan to Bogotá, Bogotá to Cartagena. Arrived three days ago. His phone's been pinging towers in the Manga district—that's old money Cartagena, residential, quiet. He's staying with family or friends. He feels safe."

"For now."

"For now," Ezra agreed. "Boss, one more thing. The phone he used to send the photographs to Cole Hartwell—it's a burner, obviously, but he made one other call from it before he ditched it. A number in Bogotá. I traced it to a law office. García, Restrepo & Vidal. Criminal defense firm, specializes in narcotics cases."

"He's already talked to a lawyer about Miguel's case."

"Which means the blackmail isn't his first move. It's his last one. He tried the legal route and it didn't work, so he went to the only leverage he had."

A desperate man. Not a monster, not a mercenary—a brother who'd exhausted every legitimate option and was now holding a match over a powder keg because nobody had given him a door. That didn't make him less dangerous. Desperate people are the most dangerous kind, because they've already decided they have nothing left to lose, which means the normal calculus of risk and consequence doesn't apply. You can't negotiate with someone's floor when they've already hit it.

But you can build them a new one. If you're fast enough. If you're smart enough. If you can find the thing they actually need and give it to them before the match hits the fuse.

"Keep digging on CI-7," I said. "And Ezra—the Bogotá law firm. Find out exactly what they told Rafael about Miguel's options. I want to know what he thinks is possible and what he's given up on."

"On it. Try to enjoy the island. You sound like you're forgetting to breathe, which is medically inadvisable and professionally counterproductive."

"Goodnight, Ezra."

"Goodnight, Boss. Eat something. And not from a minibar."

He hung up. I sat on the wall a moment longer, watching the last light drain from the sky and the harbor transform into a constellation of reflected mast lights and restaurant candles. The air was warm. The evening was perfect. And somewhere in Cartagena, a man with a camera and a brother in a cage was counting down the days, and I was the only person standing between his desperation and somebody else's destruction.

Eight days left.

I got in the Jeep and drove back to my hotel through the dark, and the island was even more beautiful at night—the road winding through black hills under a sky so thick with stars it looked like the universe was showing off—and I let myself feel it, just for a moment, the way you let yourself feel a song that reminds you of someone you've lost. Then I put it away and thought about Cartagena.

CHAPTER FIVE

THE BALCONY – *St. Barts*

The hotel was called Le Toiny, and it sat on the southeastern coast of the island in a collection of private bungalows that climbed the hillside like white birds nesting. Each one had its own plunge pool and its own terrace and its own particular angle on the Caribbean, and they were spaced far enough apart that you could forget anyone else existed, which was either the appeal or the danger depending on who you were and what you were running from.

My bungalow was at the top. I'd checked in that morning, dropped my bag, and left immediately for Cole's villa. Now, twelve hours later, I stood in the doorway for the first time and actually looked at the place where I'd be sleeping. White linen. Dark wood. A bed that was wider than any reasonable person needed, made up with the kind of sheets that have a thread count high enough to qualify as a personality trait. The French doors were open to the terrace, and through them the evening air came in warm and salt-heavy and carrying the sound of tree frogs beginning their shift.

I set the Jeep keys on the nightstand. Kicked off the leather flats that had betrayed me on the hillside and would never be the same. Stood barefoot on cool tile and felt the day leave my body in stages—first the tension in my shoulders, then the ache in my calves from the slope, then the particular exhaustion that comes not from physical effort but from hours of sustained attention, of reading a frightened man and a photograph and a hillside for information that would keep someone alive.

I was good at this part—the work, the focus, the architecture of a case assembling itself in my mind. What I was less good at was the part that came after, when the focus had nowhere to go and the evening stretched ahead of me like a road with no destination.

I poured a glass of wine from the bottle the hotel had left—a white Burgundy, cold, probably expensive, definitely wasted on a woman who was going to drink it standing up in a bathrobe. But the first sip was good—clean and mineral and faintly floral—and I took it out to the terrace and sat in the low chair and let St. Barts do what St. Barts does at this hour.

The sun was dropping into the sea.

Not setting—dropping. There's a difference. A sunset implies something gentle, gradual, photogenic. What the Caribbean does at dusk is more dramatic than that. The sun hits the water and the whole horizon catches fire—golds and corals and a deep, saturated pink that has no business existing outside of a painting—and then it's gone, swallowed, and what's left is a sky that moves through violet into indigo into black so quickly you feel like you've witnessed something private. An ending that wasn't meant for an audience.

I watched it alone. I watch most beautiful things alone. This is a fact about my life that I have learned to hold without squeezing, the way you hold something fragile—not examining it, not turning it over to find the crack, just letting it sit in your palm and acknowledging that it's there.

The wine helped. Not enough to blur anything—I don't drink to blur, I drink to soften the edges just enough that I can sit with myself without the constant narrator, the woman in my head who is always assessing, always calculating, always three moves ahead. She's useful, that woman. She's kept me alive. But she's exhausting company, and sometimes I need her to go quiet so I can feel the air on my skin without it being tactical.

The air on my skin.

I became aware of it the way you become aware of music that's been playing for a while. Not all at once but gradually, the way warmth registers first as temperature and then as something closer to touch. The Caribbean evening was seventy-eight degrees and humid enough that my skin had a sheen to it, the kind of warmth that makes fabric feel like an argument. I was still in the clothes I'd worn to meet Cole—linen trousers, a silk shell, the blazer long since abandoned on the bed. The trousers were wrinkled from the hillside. The silk was damp at the small of my back. I felt rumpled and salt-sticky and alive in a way that had nothing to do with the case and everything to do with the fact that I was a body in a warm place with nothing to do and nowhere to be, and my body, freed from purpose, was reminding me it existed.

I finished the wine. Went inside. Drew a bath.

The bathtub was a deep, freestanding thing with claw feet, the kind of tub that takes ten minutes to fill and that nobody puts in a hotel room unless they understand that luxury is not about things. It's about time. The time to fill a bathtub. The time to lie in it. The time to do absolutely nothing and feel no guilt about it, which is the most expensive commodity in the world and the one I almost never purchase.

I undressed slowly. Not for anyone, there was no one, but slowly because the act of undressing alone in a beautiful room is its own kind of permission. I peeled the silk shell over my head. Stepped out of the trousers. Unhooked my bra and felt the relief of it—that small, specific liberation that every woman knows and that men will never fully understand, the way your body changes shape when it's no longer being held. I caught my reflection in the bathroom mirror—not looking for it, just catching it the way you catch a stranger's eye on the street.

Forty-seven years old. I looked at her—at me—the way I'd look at a document I needed to assess. Not critically. Not admiringly. Just honestly. The body that had carried me through a career, through a marriage, through a firefight in Fallujah, through the particular battlefield of being a woman in rooms full of men who thought they were more dangerous than I was. Long legs that still worked. Shoulders that carried more than they should. The scar on my left side, below the ribs

—a pale, puckered line that started just under my breast and curved toward my hip like a parenthetical, like the body's way of enclosing a thought it didn't finish. I touched it, briefly, the way I sometimes do. Not to remember. To acknowledge.

The rest of me was holding up. Not the way it held at thirty—the skin looser at the inner thigh, the waist thicker by degrees I noticed even if no one else did, the particular softness at the belly that no amount of running would undo and that I'd stopped fighting because fighting your own body is a war with no armistice, and I'd fought enough wars. But strong. Capable. A body that knew what it could do and had stopped apologizing for what it couldn't.

I stepped into the bath.

The water was perfect. Just past the border of too hot, the temperature where your skin protests for a moment and then surrenders. I sank down until it reached my collarbones and closed my eyes and felt the heat open me in stages. Muscles first. Then joints. Then something deeper. A loosening in the chest, in the jaw, in the place behind my sternum where I store everything I don't let anyone see.

I lay there for a long time. The tree frogs outside. The water cooling around me by degrees. The specific silence of being the only person in a room with no expectations.

And then, because my body is honest even when the rest of me isn't, I became aware of a warmth that had nothing to do with the bath.

It started the way it always starts, not as a thought but as a pulse, a low hum somewhere between my hips that the hot water and the wine and the sheer animal fact of being naked and unobserved had coaxed to the surface. I'd been working for twelve hours. I'd been professional and controlled and sharp and careful, and now I was in a bathtub in the Caribbean and my body was doing what bodies do when you finally stop telling them to be quiet.

I didn't think about Brian-or-Ryan. I didn't think about David. I didn't think about anyone specific, which was the point—or maybe the problem, I could never decide which. My hand moved under the water and I let it, the way you let yourself reach for something you've been denying. Not urgent. Not desperate. Slow. The way the sunset had dropped. The way the evening had arrived. I had nowhere to be and nothing to do and no one to perform for, and for once—just this once—I let the want be about nothing but sensation.

The water moved against my skin. The warm air came through the open door and mixed with the steam. I found the rhythm my body wanted—not the efficient rhythm, not the taking, but something slower and more honest, the difference between feeding yourself and actually tasting the food. My breath changed. My back arched against the porcelain. I let the feeling build the way the sky had built its colors—not forced, just allowed, layer over layer, warmth deepening into heat.

I thought about hands. Not anyone's hands—just hands. The idea of being touched by someone who wasn't me, who didn't know my name or my history or the architecture of my damage, who would just put their hands on my body and want nothing except to make me feel this. The fantasy was almost unbearably simple. Not a scenario, not a face, not a story. Just touch. Just someone. Just not alone.

When I came it was different from the other night. Not sharp. Not taken. It moved through me like a wave—slow and deep and aching, starting at the center and spreading outward through my hips, my thighs, the soles of my feet. I made a sound I wouldn't have made if anyone were listening—quiet, involuntary, the sound of a woman who has let herself feel something without controlling how it ends. The water rocked gently against the sides of the tub. The tree frogs sang their indifferent song. And for maybe twenty seconds I was not Cat Sloane, not a fixer, not an ex-wife, not a woman with a scar and a dead partner and a file full of things she'll think about later. I was just a body in warm water in a beautiful place, and the world was the size of my own skin, and that was enough.

Twenty seconds. Then it receded, the way pleasure always recedes, leaving me clean and warm and very slightly hollowed out, like a bell after it's been rung. I lay in the bath until the water went tepid, until the stars appeared through the open door, until my fingers pruned and the wine was a fading warmth in my chest. Then I pulled the drain and stood up and wrapped myself in a towel so thick it felt like forgiveness and went out to the terrace with wet hair and bare feet and looked at the Caribbean under a sky that was more stars than dark.

I could give myself this. I was good at this. The sensation, the release, the specific competence of knowing my own body well enough to make it sing. I'd been doing it since I was fifteen years old, since before any man had touched me, since before I'd learned that the world would try to make my body about something other than my own pleasure. I was good at it the way I was good at everything I could control.

But the afterward. The standing on the terrace with wet hair. The looking at the sea with no one beside me. The twenty seconds of grace already fading into the familiar architecture of my solitude—the quiet apartment, the too-wide bed, the phone calls that start with how are you and end with I'm fine. That was the part I couldn't fix. That was the part no amount of competence could reach.

I can give myself pleasure. What I can't give myself is the part that comes after—the arm that pulls you close, the chest that rises and falls beside you in the dark, the particular peace of being a body next to another body with nothing between you but trust and the mutual agreement that for tonight, at least, neither of you has to be brave.

I wanted that. Standing on a terrace in St. Barts, clean and warm and alone under a sky so vast it made my solitude feel geological, I wanted it so badly it frightened me. Not the sex—I could get that anywhere, with anyone, any night I chose. The other thing. The thing I didn't have a word for. The thing that Brian-or-Ryan couldn't give me and David had given me once and I'd broken.

The tree frogs didn't care. The stars didn't care. The Caribbean turned and breathed and broke against the shore the way it had been doing for millennia, before anyone was here to ache at it, and it would keep doing it long after I was gone, and there was something almost comforting in that—the reminder that my loneliness was not important, not in the scale of things. Just specific. Just mine.

I went inside. I dried my hair. I set my alarm for six AM and got into the too-wide bed and pulled the white sheets up to my chin like a child, which is a thing I do when I'm tired and alone and have stopped pretending I'm not, and I lay in the dark and listened to the tree frogs and the sea and the sound of my own breathing, and I thought: eight days. Find Rafael Herrera. Neutralize the threat. Save the president's son. Go home.

Go home to what, I didn't let myself answer.

I slept. I dreamed about hands.

CHAPTER SIX

THE PROBLEM — *St. Barts*

I woke at six to the sound of tree frogs surrendering their shift to the birds, and for three seconds I didn't know where I was, which is a feeling I've had in enough hotel rooms to recognize as a kind of freedom—the brief, disorienting grace of being nobody, nowhere, unburdened by the architecture of your own life. Then the case reassembled itself in my mind, the way it always does, and I was Cat Sloane again, in St. Barts, with seven days left and no solution.

I made coffee with the machine in the kitchenette—a Nespresso, which is what hotels give you when they want you to feel cared for without actually caring—and took it to the terrace with my laptop and the notes I'd made after Ezra's call. The Caribbean was doing its morning routine: flat, silver, the light not yet warm enough to turn the water that obscene blue. A pelican dove into the shallows and came up with something silver thrashing in its bill. Efficient. I respected the pelican. It knew what it wanted and it went and got it and it didn't agonize about the methodology.

I opened the case file and started building the problem on paper, because I think better when I can see the architecture, and because screens lie to you. They make information feel manageable by fitting it into windows, when the truth is that some problems are bigger than any frame you put around them.

The problem had three walls and no door.

Wall one: Rafael Herrera had photographs that would get Cole Hartwell killed. He would release those photographs to the Salcedo cartel in seven days unless his brother Miguel was freed from federal prison. This was not a bluff. Ezra's profile confirmed it—Rafael was former special forces, patient, methodical, and motivated by the only thing that makes patient, methodical men dangerous: love. He would do exactly what he said he would do, on exactly the timeline he'd specified, because his brother's life was worth more to him than anyone else's.

Wall two: the presidential pardon was impossible. Kessler had been clear, and Kessler was right. A president cannot pardon a convicted drug trafficker to protect his own son from the consequences of an affair with a cartel boss's wife. The sentence contained so many impeachable clauses it read like a law school exam designed to make students cry. Even if the pardon could be executed in secret—which it couldn't, because pardons are public record—the political fallout would end the presidency, invite criminal investigation, and signal to every hostile actor on earth that the President's family was a pressure point. Kessler would sooner resign than recommend it. The President would sooner lose a son than lose the republic.

I wrote that down and then stared at it, because there was something monstrous in the calculation, and something honest, and the place where those two things met was the place where people like me did our work.

Wall three: violence was off the table. I could, theoretically, find Rafael in Cartagena and neutralize the threat through coercion. Steal the photographs, destroy his copies, make him understand that pursuing this further would have consequences. I'd done harder things. But Kessler had been explicit: no operation that could connect to the White House. And Rafael was a trained sniper with a network in his home city. Coercing him risked escalation, exposure, and the very real possibility that he'd kept copies in places I couldn't reach. If I tried force and failed, he wouldn't wait seven days. He'd send the photographs immediately, and Cole Hartwell would be dead before I landed back in the States.

Three walls. No door. The coffee was getting cold.

I stood up and walked to the railing and looked at the water and did the thing I'd been trained to do when the obvious paths are all closed: I stopped looking at the walls and started looking at the floor.

Rafael wanted his brother free. That was the demand. But demands are not the same as needs, and the gap between what someone asks for and what they actually require is where solutions live. Rafael had asked for a presidential pardon. What he needed was Miguel out of prison. Those were not the same thing. A pardon was one mechanism—the most dramatic, the most politically visible, the one Rafael had fixated on because it was the only tool powerful enough to cut through a thirty-year sentence.

But what if the sentence itself was the problem?

Ezra had flagged it: Miguel's thirty years was disproportionate. Co-defendants with arguably greater culpability had received twenty and twenty-two. The sealed informant—CI-7—had provided the key testimony that elevated Miguel from mid-tier logistics to connective tissue for the entire conspiracy. Without CI-7, Miguel was a twenty-year case. With CI-7, he was doing thirty with no parole.

I didn't know yet whether CI-7's testimony was legitimate. I didn't know if the conviction was clean. But I knew that Rafael had already consulted a criminal defense attorney in Bogotá before turning to blackmail, which meant the legal route had been explored and apparently exhausted. The question was whether it had been explored well enough, or whether a Colombian lawyer working narcotics cases had simply looked at a US federal conviction and seen a wall where someone with better resources might see a crack.

It was thin. It was the thinnest thread I'd ever considered building a strategy on. But it was the only thread in the room, and in my experience, thin threads are the ones that hold—because nobody else thinks to pull on them, which means nobody has tested whether they'll bear weight.

I needed more information. I needed the full case file—not the summary Kessler had given me, but the actual prosecution record, the sealed documents, the informant file. I needed to know whether Miguel Herrera's conviction had a weakness that a good attorney could exploit. And I needed to get to Cartagena, because Rafael was there, and the clock was there, and the only way to solve this was to be in the same city as the man holding the match.

I called Kessler.

He picked up on the first ring, which meant he'd been waiting, which meant he hadn't slept. I recognized the texture of his voice—the controlled exhaustion of a man who'd spent the night running scenarios and finding the same dead ends I had. We were, for once, in the same position: two people who were paid to see solutions staring at a problem that didn't have one. At least not an obvious one.

"Martin. I've completed my assessment."

"Tell me."

"The pardon is impossible. You already knew that. Force is too risky. Rafael is trained, careful, and operating on his home ground with copies of those photographs in locations we can't identify. If we try coercion and miss, he accelerates the timeline and Cole is dead. Negotiation on his current terms is a dead end. He doesn't want money and he won't accept less than his brother's freedom."

Silence on the line. The silence of a man hearing his worst assessment confirmed.

"However."

The silence changed quality. Hope is a sound, even when it's trying to be quiet.

"Miguel Herrera's sentence is disproportionate. Thirty years for a logistics role in a multi-defendant conspiracy where more senior players received less. The conviction rests heavily on sealed informant testimony—a confidential informant designated CI-7 whose identity and credibility I haven't been able to verify. Rafael already consulted a defense attorney before resorting to blackmail, which tells me two things: he'd prefer a legal solution, and the legal solution he was offered wasn't good enough."

"You think the conviction is flawed."

"I think the conviction might be flawed. There's a difference, and the difference is about six weeks of legal work and access to sealed federal documents. But if the informant testimony was compromised—if CI-7 was unreliable, or coerced, or had a deal that taints the evidentiary chain—then Miguel has a legitimate path to appeal. Not a pardon. Not a political favor. An actual legal challenge that could reduce or overturn the sentence."

"And you could offer that to Rafael."

"I could offer him something better than blackmail. A real chance to free his brother through a courtroom instead of through a back door. It's legitimate, it's permanent, and it doesn't require the President to do anything except not interfere with the judicial process."

Another silence. I could hear him thinking—the specific frequency of a political mind weighing options against consequences, running the scenario through every possible failure mode. Kessler didn't make decisions quickly because quick decisions are what destroy administrations. He made decisions thoroughly, and then he made them once.

"What do you need?" he said.

"Access to the full prosecution file for Operation Bright Horizon. The sealed informant records. Everything the DEA has on CI-7. And I need it through channels that don't lead back to the White House."

"That's DOJ and DEA. I can't touch either without leaving fingerprints."

"You can't. I know someone who can."

David. I didn't say his name. I didn't need to. Kessler knew about my ex-husband the way everyone in Washington's inner circle knew—not the details, not the wound, just the fact that Cat Sloane had once been married to a man who was now the CIA's Deputy Director, and that they still talked, and that the relationship occupied a space too complicated for gossip to fully map.

"The Deputy Director of the CIA pulling DEA case files," Kessler said carefully. "That's not without risk."

"David owes me a favor." This was not true. David owed me nothing. What David had was guilt, and a residual tenderness, and the specific willingness of a man who had left a woman he loved to do almost anything she asked if it meant he could still be useful to her. I wasn't proud of knowing this. I wasn't above using it.

"What else?"

"I need to go to Cartagena. Rafael is there. The clock is there. I can't negotiate from an island in the French Caribbean—I need to be in his city, understand his network, find the approach that doesn't spook him. And I need to do it without anyone connecting me to this case or to the White House."

"Cartagena is Salcedo territory."

"Yes."

"You'll be operating in the backyard of the man whose wife started this entire situation."

"Yes."

A pause. Then: "Budget?"

"Unlimited. Same terms. No receipts, no documentation, no connection to your office. I'll use a local contact—someone who knows Cartagena's power structure, someone with access to the circles where Rafael operates. I have a name. A former Colombian intelligence officer who does private security consulting. Lucía Vega."

"I don't know her."

"You wouldn't. She's not in your world. She's in mine."

Kessler was quiet for a moment, and in that quiet I heard the calculation completing—the moment when a man who controls the levers of the most powerful office on earth accepts that the best he can do is hand the problem to a woman he can't control and hope she's as good as he thinks she is.

"Go," he said. "Find another way. And Catherine—"

"I know. Seven days."

"Six. You lost one getting here."

He was right. The clock didn't pause for reconnaissance. It didn't pause for bathtubs or sunsets or the small, private collapse of a woman alone in a hotel room. It just kept counting, the way clocks do, indifferent to everything except the next second and the one after that.

"Six days," I said. "I'll call you from Cartagena."

I hung up and sat on the terrace for one more minute, watching the Caribbean turn from silver to blue as the sun climbed high enough to unlock the color. Somewhere out there, past the horizon, past the chain of islands that curved south toward the Venezuelan coast, Colombia waited. Cartagena waited. A man with a camera and a countdown and a brother he loved enough to burn the world for.

I had six days to give him a reason not to light the match.

I closed my laptop. Packed my bag. Left the bungalow key on the nightstand and the half-empty bottle of Burgundy on the counter, and I didn't look back at the terrace or the plunge pool or the view that I'd watched alone last night while the stars did their indifferent work above me. You can't afford to fall in love with the places you pass through. They'll be there when you leave, unchanged, and you'll be different, and the distance between those two facts is the loneliest math I know.

I drove to the airport and bought a ticket to Cartagena.

CHAPTER SEVEN

THE PREP — *In Transit*

I made three phone calls from the airport in St. Barts, sitting on a plastic chair in a departure lounge the size of a living room while small planes taxied past the window with the cheerful recklessness of toys. The first call was logistics. The second was intelligence. The third was the one I'd been putting off, which is always the one that matters most, which is why I put it off, which is a pattern I'm aware of and have no intention of fixing.

Sophie first.

She picked up before the first ring finished, which meant she'd been sitting with the phone in her hand, which meant she'd been waiting since my text two hours ago that said only: Moving to Cartagena. Stand by. Sophie was not a woman who stood by well. She stood by the way a border collie sits—technically still, vibrating with the effort of not moving, every muscle coiled toward the door.

"Sofitel Legend Santa Clara," I said. "Suite. Open-ended reservation, starting tonight. The hotel is a converted seventeenth-century convent in the old walled city, which means thick walls and unreliable Wi-Fi, and I'll need you to arrange a portable hotspot through the concierge before I arrive."

"Already booked."

I paused. "How did you already book it?"

"You said warm climate and Kessler case. I looked at where the case connects and booked the two most likely cities. Cartagena and Bogotá. I'll cancel Bogotá."

There are moments when Sophie's competence makes me want to promote her and moments when it makes me want to lock her in a room where nothing can hurt her. This was both. She was thinking ahead of me. She was thinking the way I'd taught her to think, or the way her father had wired her to think before I'd ever met her, and the difference between those two things was a question I didn't let myself ask because the answer involved a man who bled to death in the back of a Humvee while I drove.

"Good," I said, instead of any of that. "I also need you to reach out to a contact. Lucía Vega. Former Colombian intelligence, now private security consulting. She's in Cartagena. I'll send you the encrypted contact. Tell her I need a meeting tomorrow morning, and tell her it's paying work, not a favor. Lucía doesn't do favors."

"Background?"

"She's the best local fixer on the Caribbean coast. Knows every power player in Cartagena, legitimate and otherwise. She was Colombian military intelligence before she went private, which means she understands both sides of the table. She's cool, she's careful, and she doesn't ask questions she doesn't need answered."

"Sounds like someone I know."

"Lucía is better dressed."

Sophie almost laughed. I could hear it—the exhale, the nearly-sound—and I held onto it the way I hold onto all the small human moments between us, because they are the proof that underneath the operational choreography we've built, there are two women who might, under different circumstances, simply be friends. Under different circumstances. In a world where I hadn't let her father die.

"Anything else?" she asked.

"Check in with Ezra. He's running background on a DEA operation called Bright Horizon and a sealed federal informant. Make sure he's eating."

"Ezra always eats."

"Ezra eats ramen. I mean food."

"I'll text him. He'll ignore me. I'll text him again with a threat involving his server access. He'll eat a vegetable."

"That's the spirit."

I hung up and sat for a moment, watching a twin-engine prop plane land with the aggressive optimism of an aircraft that had clearly made a personal decision about the relationship between runway length and physics. Then I called Ezra.

He answered on the third ring this time, which meant he was between tasks, or that I'd caught him during the brief daily window when the Icelandic electronica was between albums.

"Boss. I was about to call you."

"You never call me. You wait until I call you and then claim you were about to call me. It's one of the least convincing lies in our professional relationship."

"That's hurtful. Also accurate. What do you need?"

"I'm moving to Cartagena. Today. I need you operational on Colombian infrastructure—cell networks, surveillance systems, anything you can access remotely. Can you work there the way you work in the Caribbean?"

A long exhale. The sound of a man doing math in real time. "Colombian telecom infrastructure is—how do I put this diplomatically—it's fine. It's workable. The major carriers are penetrable, the surveillance architecture is about ten years behind what the US has, which actually makes it easier in some ways because older systems have more holes. Cell tower data, I can get. Financial transactions, I can get. Government databases, depends on which ones. The National Police systems are surprisingly robust. The military systems are less robust and more paranoid, which is a combination that makes my job annoying."

"Scale of one to ten."

"Seven. I can do seven without leaving my apartment. Eight if you give me forty-eight hours to set up some local access points. Nine if you want me to fly to Bogotá, which I don't, because the last time I was in South America I had a disagreement with some people about some servers, and the statute of limitations on that particular disagreement is ambiguous."

"Seven is fine. Stay in Lisbon. I need you tracking Rafael Herrera's movements in real time once I'm on the ground. Phone, known associates, any communications. And keep working the CI-7 angle—if that informant file is the crack in Miguel's conviction, I need to know before I sit across from Rafael."

"On it. One thing, though."

"Yeah?"

"Cartagena is Salcedo's city. The Salcedo cartel owns about forty percent of everything worth owning on the Caribbean coast, and the other sixty percent has a polite understanding with them. If you're operating there without the cartel knowing, that's difficult. If you're operating there and the cartel finds out, that's—"

"Dangerous."

"I was going to say spectacularly inadvisable, but sure, dangerous works. Be careful, Boss. I'm not in a position to hire a replacement for you, and the job market for morally flexible former CIA officers with good taste in shoes is surprisingly thin."

"I'll be careful."

"No you won't. But it was nice of me to say."

He hung up. I stared at the phone for a moment, smiling at a screen in an airport in the Caribbean, which is not something I do often enough, and which Ezra would be mortified to know he'd caused. He was, in his way, the simplest relationship in my life—no history, no guilt, no subtext. He solved the problems I gave him, he said things that made me almost laugh, and he never asked me to be anything other than the woman who called him with impossible tasks. It was the closest I came to an uncomplicated human connection, and the fact that it existed entirely through encrypted channels and had involved exactly three face-to-face meetings said something about my life that I chose not to examine.

I looked at my phone. One call left.

David.

I've done harder things than call my ex-husband. I've driven through a firefight with shrapnel in my side. I've sat across from men who would have killed me if they knew who I really was and smiled and ordered wine. I've walked into Langley for the last time and sat in my car in the parking lot for twenty minutes and then driven away from everything I'd ever been. All of those things were, objectively, harder than dialing a phone number I still know by heart.

None of them made my stomach feel like this.

David Aldridge picked up on the second ring. His voice was the same as it had always been—warm, measured, the voice of a man who processes everything twice before he lets it out. Some people found David reserved. I'd always found him careful, which is different, and which I'd loved about him, and which had eventually become one of the things that made it impossible for us to survive. Because careful people are patient, and patient people wait, and David had waited for me to come back from Iraq whole, and I hadn't, and he'd waited for me to heal, and I hadn't done that either, and eventually the patience ran out, not because he was weak but because patience is a form of hope, and you can't hope forever without it breaking something.

"Cat." He always called me Cat. He was the last person left who had known me before I was anyone, when I was just a young case officer in Amman who thought the world was a puzzle she was smart enough to solve, and his use of my name carried all of that—the before, the during, the after.

"David. I need a favor."

"You always need a favor." But he said it gently, and I could hear the quiet rearrangement of his attention: the sound of a door being closed, a chair being adjusted, a man creating privacy in whatever room at Langley he'd been occupying. The Deputy Director of the CIA, making space for his ex-wife's phone call. I tried not to think about what that meant. I failed.

"A DEA operation called Bright Horizon," I said. "2018. Multi-defendant drug trafficking conspiracy. I need the full prosecution file—especially the sealed informant records. There's a confidential informant designated CI-7 whose testimony was pivotal, and I need to know who they are and whether the testimony holds up."

A pause. Not Kessler's pause—Kessler paused to calculate. David paused to understand. He was reading the request the way he'd once read me—looking for the thing I wasn't saying, the shape of the problem behind the ask.

"Bright Horizon was a DEA operation," he said. "Not agency. You're asking me to pull files from a sister service."

"I'm asking you to access files that the CIA would have legitimate interagency reason to review. Bright Horizon intersected with Colombian counternarcotics operations that the agency was monitoring. There's a paper trail that justifies the request. I'm not asking you to steal anything, David. I'm asking you to look."

"You're asking me to look in a very specific direction, which means you already know what you expect to find."

He was good. He'd always been good. It was one of the things that had made us work—two people who could read each other without effort, who could sit in a room and communicate in half-sentences and silences. It was also one of the things that had made us impossible, because you can't hide from someone who sees you that clearly, and hiding was the only thing I knew how to do after Iraq.

"I think the conviction of a defendant named Miguel Herrera may have been built on compromised informant testimony," I said. "I think CI-7's credibility may not survive scrutiny. I think a thirty-year sentence for a mid-tier logistics player in a case where more senior co-defendants got twenty is disproportionate enough to suggest something went wrong in the prosecution. And I need to know if I'm right, because someone's life depends on it."

"Whose life?"

"I can't tell you that."

"Kessler?"

I didn't answer, which was an answer. David knew about Kessler the same way Kessler knew about David—as a name attached to a relationship they couldn't fully map, someone who occupied a part of my life they weren't invited into. My world was compartmentalized the way the agency had taught me to compartmentalize—everyone had a piece, nobody had the whole picture, and I was the only person standing in the middle where all the pieces met. It was exhausting. It was safe. Those two things were, for me, the same.

David was quiet for a long moment. I could hear him weighing it—the request, the risk, the fact that he was the Deputy Director and I was asking him to use that position for something that wasn't official and wasn't clean and wasn't something he could easily explain if it surfaced.

"I'll look," he said finally. "Give me forty-eight hours."

"Thank you."

The silence that followed was the particular silence that exists between people who were once everything to each other and are now something they don't have a word for. Not friends—that's too casual. Not colleagues—that's too cold. Something warmer and sadder and more careful than either. The silence of two people who know where all the bruises are and have agreed, by unspoken contract, not to press them.

"Cat."

"Yeah."

"Are you okay?"

He always asked. Every phone call, every conversation, no matter the subject. Are you okay. Not how are you—that's a greeting, a formality, a thing you say when you don't want the real answer. Are you okay is different. Are you okay is a man who remembers finding his wife on the bathroom floor at three in the morning, silent, staring at nothing, still wearing her coat from a flight she'd landed twelve hours earlier. Are you okay is a man who knows that I lie about this, and asks anyway, because the asking is the point.

"I'm fine, David."

"You're always fine."

"I'm always fine."

Another silence. Then, softly: "Be careful. Whatever this is."

"I will."

I hung up before he could say anything else, because if he said one more kind thing I was going to feel something I didn't have time to feel, and feelings are a luxury I don't allow myself on a clock. I'm aware that this is not a healthy way to live. I'm aware that the therapist I saw three times in 2019 before I stopped going would have something to say about it. I'm aware that the fact I stopped going is itself the thing she'd have something to say about.

I put the phone in my bag. My flight was boarding—a small plane to Sint Maarten, then a connection to Bogotá, then Cartagena by evening. Six hours of travel. Six days on the clock. And somewhere in my chest, in the place where I file the things I don't look at, a new entry: the sound of David's voice saying are you okay, and the specific weight of lying to the one person who would have believed the truth.

I boarded the plane. The Caribbean tilted below me as we climbed —turquoise and impossible, an entire ocean pretending that the world was beautiful and nothing was wrong—and I thought about Cartagena, and Rafael, and a brother in a prison in Florida, and a sealed file that might hold the key to all of it.

And underneath all of that, quieter than thought, the voice I don't let anyone hear: David. I'm not fine. I'm not fine and I haven't been fine in a very long time, and the only thing keeping me upright is the next problem, the next case, the next city, the next version of myself I put on like the good blazer—expensive, tailored, hiding everything underneath.

But that's not what I said. What I said was I'm fine, and the plane flew south, and the ocean didn't care.

CHAPTER EIGHT

THE CITY – *Cartagena*

Cartagena hit me like a wall of sound.

Not a metaphor, a physical fact. I stepped out of the airport into air so thick and hot it felt like the city was breathing on me, and underneath the heat was a sound that had no single source: car horns and cumbia and the chatter of vendors and the low diesel growl of buses painted in colors that shouldn't work together but did—turquoise and orange, pink and gold, the palette of a city that had decided centuries ago that restraint was for other places.

The taxi driver talked the entire way to the old city. I understood about seventy percent of it. My Spanish is good, but Colombian coastal Spanish is its own dialect, faster and more musical than what I'd learned in Mexico City, the words running together like notes in a song where you feel the meaning before you catch the lyrics. He told me about the weather. He told me about the traffic. He told me about his daughter, who was studying medicine in Bogotá, and the way he said it—turning half around in his seat, one hand on the wheel, grinning—I understood something about this city before I'd seen a single street of it. Cartagena was a city where people led with love. Where the first thing you told a stranger was who you loved and why.

I envied that. I also filed it.

We crossed the modern city first: Bocagrande, the high-rise district, which could have been Miami if you squinted and ignored the fruit sellers and the military checkpoints and the particular way Colombian light made everything look like a photograph someone had saturated by ten percent. Then the road curved and the wall appeared.

The wall.

I'd seen photographs. Photographs don't prepare you. The wall that surrounds Cartagena's old city is four hundred years old, forty feet high in places, built of stone that the Spanish forced enslaved Africans and indigenous people to quarry and carry and stack, and it runs for seven miles around a city that has been besieged, sacked, burned, rebuilt, besieged again, and eventually declared too beautiful to destroy. It's the color of sand at sunset—warm, golden, pockmarked by centuries of weather and war—and when the taxi passed through the gate at the Clock Tower and I entered the old city for the first time, I felt what I imagine people felt four hundred years ago when they arrived by ship and saw these walls rising from the Caribbean: that I was entering a place that kept its secrets behind stone.

Inside the walls, Cartagena changed again. Narrower. Older. The streets were cobblestone, the buildings colonial—two and three stories, painted in faded blues and yellows and pinks and corals that the humidity had softened to watercolors. Wooden balconies hung overhead, dripping with bougainvillea so dense and vivid it looked like the buildings were bleeding flowers. Brass door knockers shaped like lions' heads. Wrought iron gates that opened onto courtyards you could glimpse through the bars—a fountain, a mango tree, a woman in a yellow dress crossing in shadow. Every street turned and every turn revealed something: a cathedral, a plaza full of pigeons and men playing dominoes, a woman balancing a basket of fruit on her head with the posture of a queen.

I cataloged all of it: the sightlines, the choke points, the fact that these narrow streets were both beautiful and tactically difficult, easy to get lost in and easier to be followed through. Professional habit. But underneath the assessment, something else. Something that had nothing to do with the case. Cartagena was gorgeous, and it was gorgeous in a way that asked something of you—not to admire it from a distance but to participate, to let the heat and the color and the sound into your body and become part of it.

I am a woman who has been trained to resist exactly that kind of invitation. I am also a woman who is tired of resisting, which is a dangerous combination in a city this seductive.

The Sofitel Legend Santa Clara stood on the Plaza de San Diego, a quiet square where old men sat on benches under almond trees and children chased pigeons in the late afternoon light. Sophie had booked me a suite on the third floor, which meant she'd specified a high floor, which meant she'd been thinking about sightlines, which meant I'd trained her better than I intended to or she'd trained herself, and either way the thought made me feel the particular vertigo of watching someone you love become capable of things that could get them killed.

The hotel was a converted convent. The lobby was cool and dim, with stone arches and terracotta floors and the kind of silence that buildings hold when they've been praying for four hundred years. My suite had high ceilings, white walls, dark wood furniture, and a balcony that looked out over the rooftops of the old city toward the cathedral dome and, beyond it, the Caribbean. The nuns who'd lived here would have seen the same view. They would have stood where I was standing and looked at the same water and the same sky, and they would have been thinking about God, and I was thinking about a man with a camera and a six-day deadline and a brother in a prison in Florida, and the distance between those two kinds of devotion was not as far as you'd think.

I unpacked. I showered. I put on a clean white shirt and dark trousers and sat on the bed and called Lucía Vega.

She arrived at seven, crossing the hotel's courtyard restaurant with the walk of a woman who had never in her life hurried for anyone and wasn't going to start now. Lucía Vega was somewhere between forty and fifty, I couldn't tell and suspected she'd engineered it that way. Tall, dark-haired, dressed in black linen that moved like it cost more than my flight. Silver jewelry. No makeup that I could detect, which in her case wasn't austerity but confidence—the face was enough. She had the bone structure of a woman whose ancestors had been making conquistadors nervous for centuries, and eyes that did the same thing mine did: they entered a room and read it before they settled on anyone.

She saw me. She didn't smile. She inclined her head one degree, which in Lucía's economy of expression was the equivalent of a warm embrace.

"Catherine."

"Lucía."

She sat down, ordered a gin and tonic without looking at the menu, and studied me for three seconds with the frank, clinical gaze of someone who had once debriefed captured FARC operatives and had therefore seen every kind of human deception and wasn't interested in any of them.

"You look tired," she said.

"I flew from St. Barts through Sint Maarten and Bogotá. I've been in four airports in ten hours."

"That's not why you look tired."

I liked Lucía. I had liked her since the first time we'd worked together—a situation in Medellín three years ago that involved a kidnapped tech executive and a ransom negotiation that went sideways. Lucía had been the local contact, and she'd done two things in the first hour that earned my permanent respect: she'd told me I was wrong about my approach, and she'd been right. In my world, people who tell you the truth about your mistakes are more valuable than people who tell you how brilliant you are, and Lucía had never once told me I was brilliant.

"I have a situation," I said. "It involves someone in this city. I need local knowledge, access to social circles I can't enter alone, and your honest assessment of the landscape. Paid work. My terms."

"Your terms are always interesting. Continue."

I gave her the version she needed—enough to work, not enough to compromise the client. A blackmail situation. A man named Rafael Herrera, former military, operating in Cartagena, holding leverage over a client whose identity I couldn't disclose. The blackmail involved photographs. The target's demand was the release of his brother from an American prison. I needed to find Rafael, understand his network, and negotiate an alternative resolution—all without escalation, exposure, or violence.

Lucía listened without interrupting. She drank her gin and tonic with the patience of a woman who understood that the first version of any story was never the complete one.

"Rafael Herrera," she said, when I'd finished. "Former Fuerza Especial. Discharged in 2016. I know the name. He does private security—corporate clients, some personal protection work, occasionally something less legitimate. He's not cartel, but he operates in cartel-adjacent spaces, which in this city means he has understandings with people you don't want to misunderstand."

"What kind of understandings?"

"The kind where you don't step on certain business and certain business doesn't step on you. Cartagena has a particular ecosystem, Catherine. It's not like Medellín, where the violence is closer to the surface. Here, everything is polite. The money is clean on its second washing. The parties are elegant. The people who control the city smile at you and offer you champagne and the whole time they are calculating exactly what you're worth to them, alive or otherwise."

She set down her glass and looked at me with an expression I'd learned to recognize: Lucía preparing to say the thing you didn't ask about but needed to hear.

"You said the photographs involve someone's wife."

I hadn't said that. I'd said the blackmail involved photographs. Lucía had extrapolated, and she'd extrapolated correctly, and the fact that she'd done it in the space of a gin and tonic reminded me why I'd come to her.

"Yes."

"Whose wife?"

I weighed it. Lucía needed enough information to be useful. She also needed to understand the level of danger, because if she was working for me, her safety was my responsibility, and I don't take that lightly. I'd lost one person I was responsible for. The cost of that was a scar and a lifetime and a twenty-four-year-old woman in New York who didn't know the truth about her father's death. I wouldn't lose another.

"Gabriela Montero," I said.

Lucía's hand paused. Not a dramatic pause—she wasn't a dramatic woman—but a pause nonetheless. The kind of pause that happens when new information changes the weight of everything that came before it.

"Gabriela Montero," she repeated. "Wife of Andrés Salcedo."

"Yes."

Lucía picked up her gin and tonic again and took a slow sip, and I watched her recalculate the entire situation—the danger, the fee, the question of whether this was worth the risk—in the time it took the ice to shift in her glass.

"Andrés Salcedo," she said, and her voice had dropped half a register, the way voices do when they're talking about someone who commands a certain kind of gravity. "Let me tell you about Andrés Salcedo."

She leaned back. Crossed her legs. The courtyard around us was filling with the evening crowd, tourists and wealthy Colombians, and the particular international class of beautiful people who seem to exist in every warm city, all of them laughing and drinking and being gorgeous under the bougainvillea. Lucía lowered her voice just enough that I had to lean in, which was deliberate, because Lucía understood that information delivered intimately is information received differently.

"Andrés Salcedo is the most powerful man on the Caribbean coast. Not the richest—that's a telecommunications family in Barranquilla who made their money legally, or legally enough. Not the most politically connected—that's a former governor who has lunch with the President. But the most powerful, because Andrés controls the thing that everyone else needs and no one else can provide: safe passage. His organization moves product through the Caribbean corridor—cocaine, primarily, but also people and weapons and anything else that needs to travel without being seen—and he does it with an efficiency and a discretion that makes him indispensable to every other criminal enterprise operating in this hemisphere."

She paused. Not for effect. To choose her next words with care.

"But here is the thing about Andrés. He is not what you expect. He is not a thug in an expensive suit. He is educated—Bogotá first, then two years at the London School of Economics, which he actually attended, not as a front, but because he wanted to understand how legitimate money works so he could make his money look legitimate. He speaks four languages. He collects art. He funds a children's literacy foundation that is not a money-laundering operation—or if it is, it's also a real foundation that actually teaches children to read, which makes him either a philanthropist or the most sophisticated hypocrite in Colombia. Probably both."

I was listening carefully, and not just to the facts. I was listening to Lucía's tone. The way she described Salcedo with a precision that sat somewhere between professional respect and personal wariness, the tone of a woman who knew the exact distance you should keep from a man like this and had measured it with instruments.

"And his wife?" I asked.

"Gabriela is thirty-two. She was a model in Bogotá before she married Andrés six years ago. She is beautiful in the way that women in this world are required to be beautiful—maintained, curated, always dressed as if someone is photographing her, which someone usually is. She is not happy. Everyone knows she is not happy. Andrés knows she is not happy. And yet the marriage continues, because in this world, marriage is not about happiness. It is about architecture. It is about the structure that holds everything else in place."

I thought about David. I stopped thinking about David.

"If those photographs exist," Lucía continued, "and if they show what I think they show, then the man who took them is either very brave or very stupid. Andrés is not a violent man by nature. He is a controlled man. A strategic man. The most polite man in Colombia. He will pour you a glass of wine and ask about your family and listen to your answer with genuine interest. And then, if you have crossed him, he will have you killed with the same thoughtfulness he applied to the wine selection. He does not enjoy violence. He simply does not let it stop him."

The most polite man in Colombia who will also kill you without hesitation. I turned the description over in my mind and felt something I shouldn't have felt—not fear, though the fear was there, but curiosity. Interest. The particular pull I feel toward people who are more complicated than they should be, which is the pull that has led me into most of the best and worst decisions of my life.

"Does Rafael have a relationship with Salcedo?"

"Not directly. Rafael operates at the edges of Salcedo's territory. He would know who Salcedo is—everyone in Cartagena knows who Salcedo is—but they don't move in the same circles. Rafael is working class. Military. Buenaventura-born. Salcedo is aristocracy, or the cartel version of it. They would not have occasion to meet."

"Which means Rafael's leverage isn't access to Salcedo. It's the photographs themselves."

"Correct. And those photographs, in the wrong hands, would not just end a marriage. They would humiliate Andrés Salcedo publicly. In this culture, in this world, that is worse than a business loss. That is an attack on his identity. And Andrés would respond accordingly."

"Meaning the man in the photographs—"

"Would be dead within the week. And Gabriela—" She paused. "Gabriela's situation would depend on whether Andrés is the man I think he is or the man his business requires him to be. Those are not always the same person."

I filed that. Two versions of Andrés Salcedo: the man and the enterprise. The gap between them might be the space I needed to navigate.

"I need to get close to Rafael's world without approaching him directly," I said. "I need to understand his network, his pressure points, what matters to him beyond his brother. And I may need access to Salcedo's circle—not to approach him, but to understand the terrain. If the photographs are the weapon, I need to understand what happens if they're fired."

Lucía studied me. Those dark, assessing eyes, reading something in my face that I wasn't sure I was showing.

"There is a gathering tomorrow night," she said. "A private cocktail event at a restored mansion in San Diego. The guest list is a cross-section of Cartagena's elite—business, politics, culture, and the less visible economy. It is the kind of event where you can learn more in two hours of conversation than a month of surveillance. I can get you in."

"Will Salcedo be there?"

"Andrés attends everything. He considers it operational. Social gatherings are where he takes the temperature of the city—who is worried, who is spending, who is looking over their shoulder. He treats every party like an intelligence briefing. You would like him." She looked at me. "Which is part of the problem."

I didn't respond to that. I didn't need to. Lucía and I understood each other in the way that women who operate in dangerous spaces understand each other—the specific dangers, the specific calculations, the fact that a woman who is good at this work is also, inevitably, a woman who is drawn to the kinds of men this work puts in her path. It wasn't a weakness. It was a feature of the landscape, like the heat, like the bougainvillea, like the ancient walls. You navigated it. You didn't pretend it wasn't there.

"Get me in," I said. "And Lucía—double your rate. This is Salcedo-level risk and I want you compensated for it."

The almost-smile. The single degree of inclination. "I'll send the details in the morning. Dress code is cocktail. In Cartagena, that means weapons-grade elegance. I trust you have something appropriate?"

"Sophie packed the Louboutins."

"Then you're ready."

She finished her drink, stood, touched my shoulder once—the only physical contact Lucía Vega would initiate—and walked out of the courtyard with the same unhurried stride she'd walked in with, leaving the faint scent of something clean and expensive and a silence that felt, for the first time since I'd arrived, like the silence before a door opens.

I stayed in the courtyard until the candles were lit and the evening deepened and the air cooled from brutal to merely warm. Then I went upstairs, poured a glass of water, and stepped onto the balcony.

Cartagena at night.

The old city lay below me like a map drawn by someone who believed that beauty and danger were the same thing. The rooftops were terra-cotta and shadow. Church domes caught the last light. The wall curved away toward the sea, its battlements lit by floods that turned the stone from gold to amber. Music rose from somewhere below—a trumpet, playing something slow and sad and Colombian in a courtyard I couldn't see—and the sound mixed with the sound of voices and laughter and the distant rhythm of the Caribbean breaking against the wall the way it had been breaking for four hundred years, wearing the stone down by degrees so slow they were invisible but accumulating all the same.

Five days.

In five days, Rafael Herrera would send photographs to Andrés Salcedo's organization, and a man I'd met on a terrace in St. Barts—frightened, honest, in love with someone he shouldn't love—would be dead. And Gabriela Montero, the woman who'd kissed him in the Caribbean moonlight, who'd been reckless enough to reach for something real in a life that didn't allow it, would face whatever Andrés Salcedo decided she deserved, from a man who was either capable of mercy or merely capable of its simulation.

I had five days, an unlimited budget, a tech genius in Lisbon, a fixer who didn't smile, a possible weakness in a federal conviction, and a cocktail party tomorrow night where I would walk into a room full of people who could help me or destroy me and smile and drink champagne and try to find the thread that would unravel this before the clock ran out.

I also had, somewhere in the back of my mind, the image Lucía had painted of Andrés Salcedo—a man who poured wine and asked about your family and listened with genuine interest and then, if necessary, had you killed with the same thoughtfulness he'd applied to the wine selection. I should have felt only wariness. Wariness was the appropriate, professional, survival-oriented response.

But I have never been a woman who feels only the appropriate thing. I felt wariness, yes. And underneath it, threaded through it like the trumpet music threading through the Cartagena night, something else. Something that had nothing to do with the case and everything to do with the particular weakness I have for complicated, dangerous men who are smarter than they should be, kinder than they have any right to be, and capable of things I should want no part of.

Curiosity. Interest. The warm pull of wanting to meet a person and measure him against the legend.

I'd been warned. By Lucía, by my own instincts, by the entire history of my life, which is essentially a record of what happens when a woman who knows better follows her curiosity into rooms she shouldn't enter. I'd been warned, and I was going anyway, and I stood on the balcony of a converted convent in the most beautiful city I'd ever seen and let the warning sit beside the wanting and didn't try to resolve the contradiction, because the contradiction was the truest thing about me.

Five days. A cocktail party. A man I hadn't met yet.

The trumpet played. The city breathed. The clock ran.

I went inside and chose what I'd wear tomorrow.

CHAPTER NINE

THE HUNT BEGINS – *Cartagena*

Lucía arrived at nine the next morning with a laptop, two cafés con leche from a place she refused to name—"my supplier," she said, as if the man frothing milk on a corner in Getsemaní were a state secret—and a map of Cartagena that she'd annotated by hand in a script so precise it looked like calligraphy. The map wasn't the kind you buy at a tourist shop. It was military-grade, printed on heavy paper, and covered in Lucía's notations: names, addresses, circles of influence, arrows indicating relationships I wouldn't have seen without ten years of local knowledge. She spread it across the desk in my suite like a general opening a campaign, and in a sense that's exactly what it was.

"Cartagena has three cities," she said, standing over the map with her coffee untouched, which in Lucía's economy meant this was serious enough to postpone caffeine. "The first is the one tourists see—the old city, the walls, the restaurants, the plazas. Beautiful. Expensive. Designed to make you feel like you're inside a postcard. The second is the one residents live in—Bocagrande, Manga, Crespo, the neighborhoods where the money lives when it's not performing for visitors. And the third is the one nobody talks about unless they're inside it—the network underneath, where the real power moves. You need to understand all three, because Rafael Herrera exists at the intersection of the second and the third."

She pointed to a neighborhood on the southeastern curve of the bay. Manga. On the map it looked like a finger of land extending into the water, connected to the mainland by a bridge. In Lucía's annotation, it was circled in red with three names written beside it, one of which was Rafael's.

"Manga is old money and new money pretending to be old," she said. "Large houses. Gated. Quiet streets with mango trees and security cameras. It's where the cartel-adjacent professionals live—the lawyers, the accountants, the logistics people who make the business run without ever touching the product. Rafael has an apartment there. Third floor of a building on Calle del Bouquet. He's been there for eighteen months."

"How do you know that?"

"The building is owned by a holding company that I've been watching for three years for entirely different reasons. Rafael's name isn't on any lease. He pays through a security firm registered in Buenaventura that also handles corporate protection contracts for two shipping companies. The shipping companies are legitimate. The security firm is a ghost."

I looked at Lucía across the map and felt the specific gratitude I feel for people who are better at something than I am, which is a feeling I experience rarely enough to recognize it when it arrives. Lucía wasn't just a fixer. She was an intelligence officer who had never stopped being an intelligence officer, even after she'd officially stopped. The map in front of me was the product of years of quiet, methodical work—relationships cultivated, patterns tracked, a city read the way I read individual people. I read rooms. Lucía read the city.

"So Rafael is insulated," I said. "Professional infrastructure. Cutouts between him and anything traceable. He's not operating like a desperate man."

"He's operating like a man who was trained," Lucía said. "Former special forces don't lose their discipline when they leave the military. They apply it to whatever comes next. Rafael's next is private security, which in Cartagena means he provides services to people who need discretion, and in return he receives the protection of their network."

"Whose network?"

Lucía picked up her coffee. Took one slow sip. Set it down. The gesture of a woman who was about to name the thing in the room that everyone could smell but nobody wanted to identify.

"That," she said, "is where it gets complicated."

I called Ezra while Lucía laid out the network map. He picked up with the sound of keyboard activity in the background and what I was reasonably certain was the same Icelandic electronica album he'd been playing three days ago, which meant either the album was very long or Ezra had developed a relationship with it that I wasn't qualified to evaluate.

"Rafael's phone," I said. "Please tell me you have it."

"I have it, I've had it since yesterday, and it's been sitting in Manga for the last fourteen hours, which either means he's sleeping in or the phone is and he's not. He's using a Colombian prepaid SIM on the Claro network, which has the security posture of a screen door, so I've got cell tower triangulation giving me a position accurate to about forty meters. He's in that building on Calle del Bouquet that your fixer identified, which is nice because it means our two data streams agree, which happens less often than you'd think."

"Call patterns?"

"Three regular contacts in the last week. One is a Bogotá number registered to the law firm we already identified—his brother's attorney. One is a local Cartagena number that traces to a security company called Grupo Escudo, which does corporate protection and event security and is, I suspect, about as legitimate as a three-dollar bill. The third is interesting."

"How interesting?"

"The third is a phone that doesn't want to be found interesting. It's routed through a VoIP service based in Panama, bounced through two relay servers, and the call duration is always under ninety seconds.

Whoever's on the other end doesn't want the conversation recorded and doesn't want the call traced. I can't get a location yet. Give me another day."

I filed the third number. A phone that didn't want to be found was, in my experience, either someone doing something illegal or someone doing something secret, and in Cartagena those categories had a Venn diagram that was practically a circle.

"What about his movements?"

"From the phone data: he leaves the apartment between eight and nine most mornings. Goes to a gym in Bocagrande—I've got him pinging off a tower near the Hilton for about ninety minutes. Then back to Manga. In the evenings, he moves around the old city—restaurants, bars, the usual pattern of a man who has a social life or is maintaining the appearance of one. He went to the fish market in Bazurto twice this week, which is either a cover meeting location or the man really likes ceviche."

"Or both."

"Or both. Colombia is a country where the most dangerous conversations happen over the best food. It's honestly one of the more civilized approaches to organized crime."

I almost laughed. Ezra had a gift for making the operational feel absurd, which was either a coping mechanism or a genuine worldview, and I'd stopped trying to determine which because the answer probably involved a level of psychological complexity that neither of us wanted to examine.

"Keep tracking him," I said. "I want a full pattern-of-life over the next forty-eight hours. Every location, every contact, every deviation from routine. And work the third number. If you can crack that relay, I want to know who he's talking to."

"On it. One other thing—Grupo Escudo, the security company? They provide event staffing for private parties in the old city. Guest list vetting, personal protection, that sort of thing. High-end clients. The kind of parties where the champagne costs more than my rent and the guest list is curated like an art exhibition."

"Why does that matter?"

"Because one of their regular clients is hosting a cocktail gathering tomorrow night at a mansion in San Diego. And the guest list includes some names that you and your fixer would find very interesting."

I looked at Lucía. She was already looking at me. The almost-smile.

"I know about this party," she said.

"Of course you do."

Lucía spent the next hour teaching me Cartagena.

Not the city—I'd seen the city, driven through it, felt its heat and heard its music and let its beauty do its work on me. What Lucía taught me was the system. The invisible architecture that held the beautiful city together, the way a skeleton holds a body—unseen, structural, and absolutely essential.

She started with the legitimate economy. Cartagena was a port city, a tourist destination, and increasingly a hub for international business conferences and real estate investment. Foreign money was pouring in —American, European, Middle Eastern. New hotels, restored colonial properties, luxury condominiums on Bocagrande's waterfront. The city was booming, and the boom attracted the particular species of wealth that prefers places where regulations are flexible and questions are optional.

"The legitimate economy and the other economy are not separate," Lucía said. "They are the same economy at different altitudes. A restaurant in the old city serves tourists and launders money. A real estate developer builds condominiums with clean financing and dirty financing in the same project. A shipping company moves containers of textiles and containers of cocaine on the same vessel. The line between legal and illegal is not a line. It's a gradient. And most people in Cartagena live somewhere in the middle, not because they're criminals but because the middle is where the city works."

I understood this. Not theoretically—I'd spent a career in a profession that operated in exactly this gradient, where the legal and the necessary and the technically-prohibited existed in a constant negotiation that nobody ever resolved and everybody pretended was clear. The CIA had taught me that the world was not divided into good and evil. It was divided into useful and not useful, and the moral architecture was something you built afterward to justify the choices you'd already made.

Lucía moved to the power structure. At the top: a handful of families who had controlled Cartagena's economy for generations—old money, political connections, legitimate on the surface and unknowable beneath. Below them: the business class, the developers, the hoteliers, the professionals who made the city function. Below that: the cartel-adjacent layer, the people who provided services to organizations they understood without naming. And at the bottom, invisible and essential: the organizations themselves. The Salcedo operation was the largest, but not the only one.

"Andrés Salcedo operates at every level," Lucía said. "That is what makes him exceptional and what makes him dangerous. He has dinner with the governor. He funds the arts festival. His wife sits on the board of a children's hospital. And beneath all of that, his organization moves cocaine through the Caribbean corridor with an efficiency that the legitimate shipping industry would envy. He is not hiding in the shadows. He is standing in the light, and the light is so bright that nobody can see what's behind him."

She paused. Looked at me with those dark, assessing eyes.

"Rafael Herrera is in the layer below Salcedo. He provides services —security, surveillance, occasionally something more direct—to people who operate in Salcedo's territory. He doesn't work for Salcedo directly. He works for the ecosystem that Salcedo controls. The distinction matters, because it means Rafael has autonomy. He chose to take those photographs. He chose the blackmail. The question is whether he chose alone."

"You think someone told him to do it?"

"I think," Lucía said carefully, "that in Cartagena, very few things happen at Rafael's level without someone at a higher level knowing. Whether that means permission, instruction, or simply awareness—I can't tell you. Not yet."

I turned that over. If Rafael was operating independently—a desperate brother making a desperate play—then the problem was containable. Find him, negotiate, solve. But if someone above him knew about the photographs, knew about the blackmail, had approved or even orchestrated it—then the problem was bigger than Rafael, and the solution would have to be bigger too.

I didn't have enough information to answer the question yet. But I could feel it forming at the edges of the case, the way you can feel weather changing before you see the clouds—a pressure shift, a sense that the landscape was larger than what I'd mapped so far.

"The party tomorrow night," I said. "Who's hosting?"

"A woman named Carmen de la Vega—no relation to me, though we share an ancestor somewhere four centuries back, as does half of Cartagena. Carmen is old city society. She hosts quarterly gatherings that are part salon, part intelligence exchange, part theater. Everyone comes: business, politics, culture, and the less visible economy. It's the room where the city talks to itself."

"Will Salcedo be there?"

"Andrés never misses Carmen's parties. For him, they're operational. He reads the room the way you and I read the room—for information, for temperature, for the small shifts that tell you what's about to change before it changes."

"Will Rafael's people be there?"

"Grupo Escudo provides the security staffing. So yes—not Rafael himself, but his employees. His eyes."

I stood up and walked to the balcony. The old city stretched below me—rooftops and cathedral domes and the wall curving toward the sea. Somewhere in Manga, Rafael Herrera was in his apartment, forty meters from where Ezra's cell tower data said he was, making calls on a phone with a security posture of a screen door and one encrypted line that led somewhere I couldn't yet see. Somewhere in this city, the party was being prepared—champagne ordered, guest lists finalized, a room being set where the powerful and the dangerous and the beautiful would gather and perform their intricate dance. And I was going to walk into that room with nothing but a cocktail dress and twenty years of training and try to learn something that would keep a man alive.

Five days. The clock was patient but it wasn't kind.

"Get me into that party," I said.

Lucía was already reaching for her phone. "You're already in. I made the call last night."

I looked at her. She looked at me. The almost-smile became, for the first time, an actual smile—brief, sharp, the smile of a woman who had been two moves ahead of me since she walked into this hotel and wasn't going to apologize for it.

"You're good," I said.

"I know," she said. And finished her coffee.

CHAPTER TEN

THE PARTY – *Cartagena*

There is a ritual to dressing for a room you intend to own, and like most rituals, it begins with an honest assessment of what you have to work with.

I stood in front of the bathroom mirror at six-thirty in the evening with my hair wet and my face bare and looked at the woman who would walk into Carmen de la Vega's party in ninety minutes. Dark hair, still thick, still the deep brown that people sometimes mistake for black until they see it in sunlight, where it shows the auburn my mother gave me. I'd inherited her coloring—olive skin that tans without burning, the kind of complexion that reads as Mediterranean or Latin or vaguely exotic depending on the continent, which has been professionally useful my entire career and personally disorienting in the way that belonging everywhere means belonging nowhere. High cheekbones from my father's side—Irish-Polish, all angles—and his gray eyes, which are the feature men mention first and the feature I trust least, because eyes that look like honesty are the best tool a liar ever had.

I was forty-seven. The mirror was honest about this, even if I wasn't always. Fine lines at the corners of my eyes that I'd earned and didn't resent. A jawline that was still sharp but softer than it had been at thirty, the way a blade gets after years of use—still functional, just less cruel. My mouth was good. I'd always known my mouth was good, in the way that women learn early which features are currency and which are overhead, a calculation so automatic that we barely notice we're making it, and that men would find horrifying if they understood how constant it is.

What the room would see tonight: a tall woman in her late forties, well-maintained, expensively dressed, with the specific confidence that comes from either wealth or competence or both. An American, probably—the coloring was ambiguous but the posture was not, and Americans carry themselves differently abroad, a looseness in the shoulders that reads as either ease or arrogance depending on your politics. The room would see a woman who belonged. That was the objective. Not to stand out. To be plausible.

I dried my hair. Applied makeup with the efficiency of a woman who learned long ago that the goal is not beauty but architecture—the right shadow to sharpen the cheekbones, the right color on the lips to draw attention upward toward the eyes, which are where I do my best work. I kept it minimal. In Cartagena, at this kind of party, the local women would be immaculate—perfect hair, perfect nails, the specific polished glamour of Latin American society women who understand that presentation is a language and fluency is non-negotiable. I couldn't compete with that, and competing would mark me as trying, so I went the other direction: understated, clean, the elegance of less. European, almost. Which, in a room full of Colombian beauty, would register as either refreshing or cold, and I could work with either.

The dress was black. It was always going to be black. Sophie had packed three options and I'd chosen the simplest—a fitted sheath that ended just above the knee, silk crepe, high neck in front and open back, the kind of dress that looks like nothing on a hanger and everything on a body. It covered the scar. It left my arms bare, which was a choice: arms are where you read a woman's age and her strength, and mine showed both. The Louboutins—the ones I could run in, because old habits—and a thin gold chain at the wrist. No earrings. No clutch. I needed my hands free, because hands are the first thing that betrays you when you're performing, and I was about to perform.

I looked at the finished product in the mirror. She looked like a woman who had her life together, which was, as I'd noted on a morning in New York that felt like a year ago, the most elaborate lie I tell. But it was a good lie. Convincing. Expensive. The kind of lie that opens doors and pours champagne and makes people want to tell you things they shouldn't.

I picked up my phone, dropped it in the invisible pocket Sophie had sewn into every dress I owned—the girl was operational even about fashion—and went downstairs to meet Lucía.

The mansion was on a corner in the San Diego neighborhood, three blocks from my hotel—a colonial house that had been restored to the particular standard of Cartagena's old money: original stone walls, polished hardwood, ironwork balconies dripping with jasmine, and a central courtyard that had been transformed for the evening into something between a garden party and a stage set. Candles floated in a stone fountain. A string quartet played something by Piazzolla in the corner—tango, which was Argentine, not Colombian, but nobody seemed to mind, which told me the hostess valued sophistication over nationalism. Interesting.

The courtyard was already full. Sixty people, maybe seventy, dressed in that specific register where money meets taste and the result is a room that looks casual but cost someone a fortune to produce. The women were exactly what I'd predicted—stunning, polished, the kind of beauty that requires a team and a schedule and the particular discipline that beautiful women in powerful circles understand is not vanity but survival. The men were in linen and lightweight wool, tanned and silver-haired or dark-haired and young, and they moved through the room with the ease of people who had never once doubted their right to be anywhere.

I cataloged the security without looking like I was cataloging. Two men at the entrance in black suits—Grupo Escudo, Rafael's company. One positioned near the courtyard's rear exit. Another on the second-floor balcony with a sightline over the entire space.

Professional setup. Discreet but present. Rafael's eyes, just as Lucía had said.

Lucía materialized beside me with two glasses of champagne and the air of a woman who had been born in this room. She was wearing deep green tonight—silk, draped, the kind of garment that announces taste without raising its voice. She handed me a glass and inclined her head one degree toward the far corner of the courtyard.

"Carmen de la Vega," she said. "The woman in red. I'll introduce you in twenty minutes, after she's finished performing for the governor's wife. To your left, the man in the gray suit with the young woman on his arm is Julio Restrepo—shipping, construction, sits on the board of three banks. Behind him, the woman laughing too loudly is Patricia Lloreda, who runs the largest art gallery in the old city and knows everyone's secrets because they tell her while she's appraising their collections. Useful, but indiscreet."

"And Salcedo?"

"Not here yet. He's usually late. And I should warn you—I don't have a recent photograph. He's careful about that. No social media, no press shots in the last five years. I know his face because I've seen him in person, but I haven't been able to give you an image to work from. When he arrives, I'll point him out."

I filed this. An intelligence gap I didn't love—walking into a room knowing a man would be there but not knowing which man he was. In my experience, the people who control their image that carefully are either paranoid or strategic, and in Salcedo's case it was probably both.

"I need to make a few introductions on the other side of the room," Lucía said. "Stay visible. I'll find you when he's here."

She disappeared into the crowd with the fluidity of a woman who had been navigating rooms like this for decades. I sipped the champagne. It was excellent—dry, cold, French—and I let myself be a woman at a beautiful party in a beautiful city for exactly thirty seconds before the operational part of my brain reasserted itself and I began to work the room.

I spent the next hour being Catherine Sloane, private consultant, in Cartagena for a client whose interests required discretion. It was close enough to the truth to be sustainable and vague enough to be interesting, which is the sweet spot for cover stories—you want people curious, not suspicious. I talked to a real estate developer about waterfront properties. I talked to a university professor about Colombian literature. I talked to a woman who ran a sustainable fashion label and who told me, with the unselfconscious passion of someone who actually cared, about the weavers in Mompox whose techniques were six hundred years old. I listened more than I spoke, because listening is the most powerful tool in any room, and because Cartagena's elite, like elites everywhere, were more interested in being heard than in hearing.

I kept one eye on the entrance. Lucía hadn't signaled. Salcedo hadn't arrived, or he had and she hadn't reached me yet, or he'd decided not to come, which would make the evening a pleasant waste of operational time. I was mid-conversation with the professor—he was explaining something about Gabriel García Márquez and magical realism that I actually wanted to hear, which was inconvenient because I was also tracking the security rotation and waiting for Lucía's signal—when I became aware of someone standing near the fountain, watching me.

Not staring. Watching. There's a difference. Staring is clumsy, aggressive, the blunt instrument of men who haven't learned subtlety. Watching is something else—patient, intelligent, the focused attention of someone who has chosen you out of a room full of choices and is taking his time about it. I felt it before I saw it, the way you feel someone's eyes on your back, the particular electricity of being observed by someone who is paying real attention.

I turned.

He was tall. That was the first thing. Six-one, maybe six-two, leaning against the stone column nearest the fountain with a glass of something amber in his hand and the ease of a man who owned every room he walked into, or at least rented it at a rate he found acceptable. Dark navy suit, no tie, white shirt open at the collar. His hair was dark, threaded with gray at the temples in a way that looked like it had been designed by someone who understood that aging, on the right man, is not deterioration but emphasis. Late forties. The face was angular, lived-in, the kind of face that gets better with time because the bones were always the story and time just clears away the distractions.

He was looking at me. Not at the room, not at the party, not at any of the stunning women who populated every corner of that courtyard. At me. And his expression wasn't the appraising look I get from men who are calculating whether I'm worth the effort—it was something closer to interest. Genuine interest. The look of a man who has seen something that doesn't fit the pattern and wants to understand why.

I looked back. Half a second too long. Then I turned away, because looking away first is a signal—it says I noticed you and I'm choosing not to pursue it, which in the grammar of attraction is the equivalent of an engraved invitation. I knew this. I did it anyway.

I turned back to the professor and said something about Márquez that I don't remember.

He found me ten minutes later. I was standing near the fountain, alone for the first time all evening—Lucía was still on the far side of the room, working her own agenda—and he materialized beside me with the ease of a man who had been navigating rooms full of interesting people his entire life and had long ago stopped pretending it was coincidental.

"You're not from Cartagena," he said.

His voice. That was the second thing that caught me off guard, after the height. It was low, unhurried, accented in a way that told me his English was learned in London, not Los Angeles—the consonants precise, the vowels rounded, a voice that made you lean in not because it was quiet but because it was worth leaning toward. He spoke English the way some people play piano: fluently, musically, with an awareness of the instrument.

"What makes you say that?" I said.

"You've been watching the room for an hour. Not the way a guest watches—the way an architect watches a building. You're reading the structure, not admiring the decoration."

I should have been alarmed. A stranger at a party identifying my operational behavior should have triggered every professional instinct I had. Instead, I felt something I hadn't felt in a long time, something that had nothing to do with danger and everything to do with the rare, electric pleasure of being in a conversation with someone who was exactly as smart as I was.

"Maybe I'm an architect," I said.

"You're not. Architects look at walls. You look at people. And you look at exits, which tells me you're either very cautious or very interesting, and in my experience those are usually the same thing."

He extended his hand. "Andrés."

Just the first name. In Colombia, at a party like this, that wasn't unusual—first names were intimacy, last names were formality, and the space between them was where you negotiated how much of yourself you wanted to reveal. I noted the omission without reading anything into it. Half the people I'd spoken to tonight had introduced themselves the same way.

"Catherine."

His handshake was warm, firm, and lasted exactly the right amount of time—not the dominance grip of a man proving something, but the confident touch of a man who had nothing to prove. I felt the heat of his palm against mine and I filed it and I didn't let go a millisecond early because that would have been its own kind of signal, and this man was reading signals the way I was.

We talked. I don't know how long. That's not something I say often —I am a woman who tracks time the way a pilot tracks altitude, constantly, automatically, because losing track of time is how you lose track of everything else. But with Andrés, the clock went somewhere I couldn't reach it, and I was left in a conversation that moved like the best conversations move: fast, surprising, layered, each exchange building on the last so that by the time you pause to breathe, you've covered territory you didn't know existed.

He asked what I did. I gave him the cover: private consulting, discretion required. He smiled—not a social smile but something sharper, more private—and said, "That could mean anything from mergers and acquisitions to hiding bodies. I choose to believe it's somewhere in between."

I laughed. I actually laughed, which I don't do at parties, which I barely do anywhere, and the sound of my own laughter startled me the way an unexpected reflection startles you—a glimpse of someone you'd forgotten you could be.

"What about you?" I asked.

"Investments," he said. "Logistics. I move things from places where they exist to places where they're wanted. Supply and demand, the oldest story in the world."

The irony was invisible to me. I heard a businessman describing his work with the wry self-awareness of a man who understood that all business, at some level, is the same story told in different currencies. I liked that. I liked him. And the liking arrived not slowly but all at once, like a door opening onto a room I hadn't known was there.

He asked about New York. I told him about the city in winter—the cold that makes you feel like the world is made of edges, the way the light comes through the buildings at four in the afternoon in January and turns everything gold for exactly seven minutes before it's gone. He listened the way very few people listen—not waiting for his turn to speak but actually receiving what I was saying, holding it, considering it. And then he said, "Cartagena is the opposite. Here the light is generous. It gives you everything all day and expects nothing in return. It's the only honest thing about this city."

I noticed: the way his shirt collar sat against his neck. The particular shade of his skin, which was the brown of old wood, of something that had been in the sun for a long time and was better for it. His hands when he gestured—large, precise, the hands of a man who built things, or at least understood how things were built. A scar on his right hand, faint, between the thumb and forefinger. I wanted to ask about it. I didn't.

The sentences were getting shorter. I could feel it happening—the rhythm of my own thoughts quickening, the details sharpening, the analytical distance narrowing. I knew what this was. I'd felt it before. The body recognizing something before the mind gives it permission, the way a tuning fork vibrates when it finds its frequency.

I didn't want this. Not here. Not now. Not in the middle of a case, not in a city I'd be leaving in days, not with a man I'd met thirty minutes ago at a party where Rafael Herrera's security team was standing twenty feet away.

I didn't want this. I stayed.

The party swirled on around us, but I'd lost the thread of it. An hour, maybe more—I couldn't say. At some point Andrés excused himself briefly. "A phone call I can't ignore. Two minutes. Don't go anywhere." He touched my arm—just his fingertips, just for a second—and disappeared through a doorway toward the rear courtyard. I watched him go and felt the absence of him like a change in temperature.

I used the minutes. Found Lucía near the bar, deep in conversation with a woman in white whose jewelry could have funded a small government. Lucía extracted herself with the graceful efficiency I'd come to expect and guided me three steps away, her voice low.

"Salcedo was here," she said. "I spotted him about forty-five minutes ago. Tall, navy suit. He spoke with Carmen and a few others, worked the room for maybe half an hour, and I saw him moving toward the rear courtyard about ten minutes ago. I think he's left—he does that sometimes. Makes an appearance and disappears before anyone can pin him down. I'm sorry—I tried to get to you, but I was across the room and by the time I looked again he was heading out."

Tall. Navy suit. The description was half the men in the room. I felt a flicker of professional frustration—I'd come to this party specifically to get eyes on Salcedo, and he'd come and gone like smoke while I'd been distracted. I thought about the last hour, the conversations I'd had, and tried to remember if anyone I'd spoken to had matched the profile: powerful, educated, the kind of man who controlled a room. But the truth was that I'd spent most of the last hour talking to one person, and that person was not a cartel boss. He was a man named Andrés who worked in logistics and had learned his English in London and was, at this moment, making a phone call in a rear courtyard.

"Did you get a good look at him?" I asked.

"Briefly. He was moving through the crowd. I saw his face but not for long—he was heading toward the back of the house when I last spotted him."

Heading toward the back of the house. Gone before Lucía could reach me. I felt the professional frustration of a missed opportunity — I'd come to this party for Salcedo, and he'd slipped through without my ever getting a look at him. But the night wasn't wasted. I'd mapped the room, met Carmen, watched Grupo Escudo's security in action. And there was still Andrés, somewhere behind me, making his phone call, and the thought of him returning was doing something to my focus that I chose not to examine.

"We'll get another chance," I said. "He can't be invisible in his own city."

Lucía gave me a look I couldn't quite read—appraising, maybe, or simply noting something she chose not to say. "You seem like you're having a good evening."

"The champagne is excellent."

"Mm-hmm," she said, in a tone that was becoming a theme among the women in my life. She drifted back toward the bar, and I was alone for approximately thirty seconds before I heard his voice behind me.

"I'm back. Did you miss me?"

I turned. Andrés. His jacket slightly rumpled from whatever doorway he'd leaned against to take his call. His eyes warm and focused entirely on me. And I felt something I had no business feeling in the middle of a case in the middle of a foreign city with four days left on a clock that didn't care about my personal life: relief. Simple, uncomplicated relief that he'd come back.

"Terribly," I said. "I almost spoke to someone else. It was a close call."

He laughed. A real laugh, quick and surprised, and I thought: I want to keep making this man laugh. Which was a dangerous thought and an honest one and I let it stay because the night was warm and the champagne was good and somewhere in the back of my mind, in the part that should have been working, a small voice said: Salcedo has left the building. The operation can wait until tomorrow. You are allowed this.

I was not, in fact, allowed this. But I didn't know that yet.

The party thinned around us the way weather changes—gradually, then all at once. People left in couples and clusters, trailing laughter and perfume and the particular satisfied energy of an evening well spent. The candles guttered in the fountain. The staff moved through the empty chairs like ghosts. And we stayed, standing near the fountain, then drifting to the base of the staircase, then—his suggestion, casual as breathing—to the balcony on the second floor, where the view was better and the night was ours.

The balcony was narrow, wrought iron, barely wide enough for two people standing close. The old city fell away below us in a tumble of rooftops and shadows and distant light. The cathedral dome was lit from below, golden against the dark. The wall traced its ancient line toward the sea. Somewhere below, a trumpet was playing—or maybe Cartagena just kept a trumpet playing at all times for moments exactly like this, which would have been the most strategically romantic thing a city had ever done.

"Tell me something true," he said.

We'd been standing on the balcony for a few minutes in a silence that was not uncomfortable but alive—the kind of silence between two people who are aware that the next thing said will change the register of the conversation. The party sounds had faded to a murmur below. The air was warm and smelled of jasmine and salt and the specific sweetness of a tropical city at night.

"Something true," I repeated.

"We've spent two hours being clever. I've enjoyed it. I suspect you have too. But I'm more interested in what you sound like when you're not performing."

The wry distance dropped. Just like that. Not because he'd asked for it but because he'd named it—he'd seen the performance and called it, gently, without judgment, the way you'd point out a mask to someone who'd forgotten they were wearing it. And the thing about having your mask identified by someone who is clearly wearing one of his own is that it creates a strange, vertiginous intimacy—two performers acknowledging the stage.

"I'm in Cartagena because someone's life depends on me being here," I said. "I don't know yet if I can save them. I'm good at what I do, and I'm not sure that's enough, and the not-knowing is the part I handle worst."

He was quiet. The city breathed below us.

"That," he said, "is the most honest thing anyone has said to me in a very long time."

"Your turn."

He looked out over the rooftops. In profile, his face was different—less charming, more serious. The face underneath the face he showed the room. I watched it the way I watched everything—closely, carefully—but for the first time tonight I wasn't reading him for information. I was just looking.

"I built everything I have," he said. "From nothing. From a place that most people in this room would never visit and couldn't survive. And I am very good at what I've built. But there are nights—not many, but some—when I stand on a balcony like this one and look at a city like this one and I wonder if the thing I built is the thing I actually wanted, or if I just built what I was capable of building and called it enough."

I looked at him. He looked at me. The trumpet played. The city held its breath, or I held mine, or both.

"I know that feeling," I said. And I meant it. God help me, I meant it completely, because the thing he'd described—building something impressive and wondering if it was the right thing—was the architecture of my own life rendered in someone else's voice. And the recognition was so precise, so specific, that for a moment I forgot to be careful, forgot to calculate, forgot that I was a woman on a case in a dangerous city talking to a man I'd met three hours ago. I was just a person who had been understood by another person, and the rarity of that was so acute it almost hurt.

He smiled. Not the party smile. Something quieter. Something that lived in the space between the man and the mask.

"Catherine," he said. "I would very much like to see you again."

I should have said no. Every piece of training I'd ever received, every professional instinct, every lesson the agency and the years and the damage had taught me—all of it said no. Do not get involved. Do not blur the lines. Do not let a stranger in a beautiful city make you feel something you'll have to carry when you leave.

But Salcedo had gone. The operation was on hold until morning. And this man—this Andrés with no last name and London English and a scar on his hand I wanted to trace with my finger—this man was not part of the case. He was the opposite of the case. He was the thing I never let myself have: a human being, standing in front of me, offering an uncomplicated evening.

"Yes," I said.

Below us, the old city slept, and the trumpet played, and the Caribbean broke against the wall the way it had for four hundred years, and I stood on a balcony with a man whose last name I didn't know and whose first name I'd remember for the rest of my life, and I let myself feel the thing I'd been running from since a bathtub in St. Barts: the terrifying, exhilarating, absolutely inadvisable pull of wanting to be known.

Five days left. And everything was about to get more complicated.

CHAPTER ELEVEN

THE FIRST NIGHT — *Cartagena*

We were the last ones on the balcony.

The party had emptied below us in stages—first the couples leaving early, then the clusters of friends spilling into the street with promises to meet tomorrow, then Carmen de la Vega herself sweeping through the courtyard with the satisfied air of a woman whose evening had gone exactly as designed. The candles guttered in the fountain. The staff moved through the empty chairs like ghosts. And we stayed, leaning against the iron railing two feet apart, not touching, looking at the city as if neither of us wanted to be the one to break the spell by suggesting we leave it.

"Walk with me," he said.

It wasn't a question. It wasn't a command. It was something in between—an invitation made by a man who understood that the best invitations leave the other person room to decline, which is what makes them impossible to refuse.

"Where?"

"Anywhere. The old city is best at this hour. When the tourists are asleep and the city belongs to itself again."

We went downstairs and out through the heavy wooden doors into the street. The night was warm and the air tasted like salt and jasmine and something I couldn't name that I would later learn was Cartagena itself—the city's particular perfume, the accumulated scent of four centuries of stone and sea and human desire baked into the walls.

We walked. There is no other word for what we did, though walk is too simple for what it contained. We moved through the old city's streets the way you move through a museum after hours—slowly, attentively, as if each turn revealed something that had been waiting to be discovered. The streets were narrow and cobblestoned and lit by wrought-iron lamps that threw pools of gold onto the stone. Bougainvillea cascaded from balconies overhead. A cat watched us from a doorway with the disinterested authority of a creature that had seen a thousand years of humans doing exactly this and was not impressed.

He told me about the buildings. Not like a tour guide—like a man who loved a city and couldn't help himself. This church was built by Jesuits in 1603 and the stone came from a quarry on the island of Tierra Bomba. This house had been a merchant's residence, a hospital, a convent, and was now a hotel, and if the walls could talk they'd tell four centuries of stories that would scandalize every person sleeping inside. This courtyard was where a viceroy's wife had kept a garden so beautiful that her husband had the gardener killed when they were reassigned to Lima, because he couldn't bear the thought of anyone else walking through it.

"That's either the most romantic or the most horrifying thing I've ever heard," I said.

"In Cartagena, those are usually the same story."

His arm brushed mine. Not deliberately. The street was narrow and we were walking close and the contact was the kind that happens when two bodies share limited space. But the brush of his forearm against my bare skin sent something through me that had nothing to do with accident and everything to do with the particular electricity that builds between two people who are pretending not to want what they obviously want.

I was aware of him the way you become aware of a sound that's been playing so long you forgot it was there and then suddenly can't stop hearing it. The rhythm of his stride. The scent of his cologne—

something warm, cedar or sandalwood, worn lightly, the kind of scent you only catch when the wind shifts or when he turns his head and you're too close. The way his hand moved when he gestured toward a building, the sleeve of his jacket riding up just enough to show the bones of his wrist.

I wanted to touch that wrist. The thought arrived without permission and settled in with no intention of leaving.

We turned into the Plaza de Santo Domingo. The church rose above us, massive and pale in the lamplight, and the plaza was empty except for a Botero sculpture of a reclining woman, voluptuous and absurd and beautiful in the way that only Botero is beautiful—generously, unapologetically, without asking anyone's permission to take up space.

"I like her," I said, nodding at the sculpture.

"Everyone does. She's the most honest woman in Cartagena. She doesn't pretend to be anything other than what she is."

"Is that a comment on the city or on women?"

"It's a comment on honesty. Which is the rarest thing in any city and the most attractive quality in any woman." He looked at me. "You were honest on that balcony. I'm still thinking about it."

His hand found mine. Not a grab. Not a fumble. His fingers slid between mine with the quiet confidence of a man who knew exactly what he was doing and was giving me every opportunity to stop him. I didn't stop him. His hand was warm and large and his thumb settled against the base of my palm in a way that was not sexual but was more intimate than anything sexual, because it was deliberate and unhurried and it said: I am choosing to hold your hand in an empty plaza at midnight and there is nowhere else I would rather be.

We walked like that. Through the plaza, down a street I didn't know, past darkened doorways and sleeping balconies and the occasional burst of music from a bar two blocks away. His thumb moved against my palm in a slow, absent rhythm that I felt in places his thumb was not touching. I was aware of the heat of his skin, the way his grip tightened slightly when the cobblestones were uneven, the way he shortened his stride to match mine without being asked.

The conversation changed. Or rather, it dropped—below the clever register we'd established at the party, below the mutual performance of intelligence and wit, into something lower and quieter. He asked me if I was happy. Not in general—right now, tonight, walking through this city in the dark. I said yes, and it was true, and the truth of it was so simple and so surprising that it made me want to cry, which I did not do, because I don't cry, but the impulse was there, lodged in my throat like a fishbone, and I swallowed it the way I swallow everything that threatens to be real.

We were near my hotel. I knew this because I always know where I am, even when I don't want to, even when the knowing interrupts something I'd rather not interrupt. The Sofitel was two blocks away. We were running out of street.

"This is me," I said, which was absurd, because we were standing in the middle of a block and there was no entrance, no lobby, nothing to indicate that this was anything. But what I meant was: this is the moment. The hinge. The point where we say goodnight and I go back to my room and lie in the dark and think about the bones of your wrist, or—

He stopped walking. He turned to face me. The lamplight caught one side of his face and left the other in shadow, and I thought: this is how I'll remember him. Half-illuminated. Half-hidden. Which was, I would later understand, the most accurate portrait anyone could have drawn.

"Catherine," he said. Just my name. Nothing after it. The sentence complete.

I kissed him.

Not the other way around. I need that to be clear, because later—when everything I thought I knew about this man turned to ash in my hands—I would need to remember that I chose this. He didn't seduce me on a dark street. I crossed the distance. I put my hand on the side of his face and felt the roughness of his jaw beneath my palm and I pulled his mouth to mine and I kissed him with everything I had, which was considerable, because what I had at that moment was twenty years of loneliness and the first real hunger I'd felt in longer than I wanted to count.

He tasted like champagne and something darker. His mouth was warm. His hands came to my waist—both hands, pulling me against him with a certainty that sent heat from my ribs to the base of my spine—and he kissed me back the way a man kisses a woman he has been thinking about kissing all night: thoroughly, without rush, as if the kissing itself were the destination and not a stop on the way somewhere else.

We stayed like that. In the street. Under a lamp. His body against mine. His hands on my waist, my hips, the small of my back. I could feel him—all of him—through the thin fabric of my dress, and the knowledge of how much he wanted me was a drug more potent than anything I'd felt in years.

I pulled back just enough to speak. My mouth was an inch from his. His breath on my lips.

"My hotel is two blocks from here."

"I know," he said. And something about the way he said it—not smug, not triumphant, just certain, the way you're certain about gravity—made me laugh against his mouth, and then we were both laughing, and then we were kissing again, and then we were walking.

The lobby of the Sofitel was marble and candlelight and the specific hush of a luxury hotel at midnight, when the staff is trained to see everything and acknowledge nothing. I walked past the front desk with Andrés beside me and the night porter didn't blink. The elevator was small and mirrored and we didn't touch inside it, which was its own kind of foreplay—standing two feet apart, watching each other in the mirrors, the anticipation building like a wave that hasn't crested yet but you can feel it gathering, you can feel the ocean pulling back, and you know what's coming and the knowing is almost better than the arrival. Almost.

I unlocked the door. We went inside. The room was dark except for the light from the courtyard below, coming through the French doors in a wash of gold, and the air conditioning had been running and the room was cool after the warm night and I felt goosebumps rise on my arms and couldn't tell if it was the temperature or him.

He kissed me in the doorway. Slower this time. His hands in my hair, tilting my head back, his mouth on the curve of my neck, the hollow of my throat. I closed my eyes and my world contracted to the size of his mouth on my skin, the scrape of his jaw against my collarbone, the way his fingers tangled in my hair with a gentleness that was more devastating than roughness would have been, because gentleness requires attention, and attention requires presence, and presence was the thing I craved more than any physical act.

I pulled his jacket off his shoulders. He let it fall. I unbuttoned his shirt with fingers that were steady because I am a woman who has undressed men before and knows how to do it well, but my steadiness was a performance covering a tremor that I felt all the way to my wrists, because this was different. This was not the nameless man in New York. This was not controlled. This was not a system.

His chest. His skin against my palms. The heat of him. The muscle beneath the skin—not the sculpted gym body of a younger man, but the solid, lived-in body of a man in his late forties who was strong because his life had required strength. I ran my hands across his shoulders and down his arms and felt the specific weight of a body that wanted mine, and the wanting was in every tightened muscle, every caught breath, every place where his skin was warmer than the air.

He found the zipper at the back of my dress. Drew it down slowly—so slowly that I felt every tooth release, felt the dress loosen around my ribs, my waist, and then his hands were on my bare back and his fingers traced the line of my spine from the base of my neck to the curve above my hips and I heard myself make a sound that I didn't recognize, low and involuntary and honest in a way I am almost never honest.

The dress fell. I let it. I was standing in the dim golden light in nothing but black silk and the Louboutins and his eyes moved over me with an expression that was not the appraising look I'd received from a hundred men in a hundred rooms but something else—something closer to recognition, as if he were seeing not my body but me, the actual me, the one who lives inside the body and almost never comes to the door.

"You're extraordinary," he said. Not beautiful. Extraordinary. The word choice undid me more than his hands had.

I stepped out of the shoes. Lost three inches. Looked up at him. Put my hand flat against his chest and felt his heart hammering beneath my palm, and the knowledge that this man—this composed, commanding, unhurried man—had a heart going at a hundred and twenty because of me was a power I didn't want to examine too closely because examining it would mean acknowledging how much I wanted it and acknowledging want is the thing I'm worst at.

We fell onto the bed. Not gracefully. Not like a movie. The real way—his knee between mine, my back on cool white sheets, his weight settling over me and then shifting because he was too careful to crush me, his forearm braced beside my head, his mouth finding mine again while his free hand traced a path from my jaw to my throat to the silk at my hip.

He touched me through the silk first. His fingers against me, patient, learning, pressing just enough to make my hips lift toward him before pulling back, and the tease of it was exquisite and maddening and I heard my own breathing change and didn't care. He slid the silk down my legs. Slowly. His mouth following his hands—a kiss on my hip bone, my inner thigh, the crease where my leg met my body—and I was shaking. Actually shaking. My hands in his hair. My body a single exposed nerve.

He knew what he was doing. That's the thing about men who pay attention—they listen with their hands, they read your body the way a musician reads a score, and Andrés read mine with a fluency that made me arch off the bed and grip the sheets and say his name in a voice that didn't sound like my voice, a voice with no armor in it, no wit, no distance, just the raw and desperate honesty of a woman who was being taken apart by someone who understood exactly which pieces to move.

His mouth between my thighs. His hands holding my hips. The slow, deliberate devastation of a man who was in no rush because the undoing was the point. I came with his name in my mouth and my hand fisted in the sheet and my back arched and my eyes open, staring at the ceiling of a hotel room in Cartagena, seeing nothing, feeling everything, the wave cresting and breaking and cresting again because he didn't stop, he kept going, reading my body's signals with a precision that was almost frightening, and the second time was deeper and slower and pulled something out of me that I hadn't known was stored there—a sound, a surrender, the last locked door swinging open.

Then I pulled him up. I needed him above me. I needed his weight, his mouth, his skin against mine with nothing between us. He reached for his wallet—a question in his eyes—and I said "yes" and he was careful and quick and then he was inside me and we both went still.

That moment. The first moment. Before either of you moves. When two bodies are joined and the world stops and you can feel your own pulse in places you didn't know had a pulse and the man above you is looking at you with an expression that is not lust but something closer to awe—that moment is the most honest thing sex offers, and I have had enough sex in my life to know how rare it is and how impossible it is to manufacture.

We moved together. Not fast—not yet. He set a rhythm that was steady and deep and I matched it and we found the place where two bodies stop being two bodies and become a single system, a single engine, and the pleasure built in layers—each stroke deeper than the last, each breath harder, his forehead against mine, my legs wrapped around him, his hand cradling the back of my head as if I were something precious, which no one had treated me as in so long that the tenderness almost hurt more than the pleasure.

The rhythm accelerated. His breathing ragged against my neck. My nails on his back. The specific beautiful violence of two people trying to get closer than physics allows, the wanting so acute that every nerve ending was a live wire and the slightest shift in angle sent shockwaves through both of us. I pulled his mouth to mine. His hand slid between us, finding me again, and the dual sensation—him inside me, his fingers on me, his mouth swallowing every sound I made—was too much and not enough and I came again, harder this time, and felt him follow seconds later, his whole body shuddering, his grip tightening, his breath broken against my throat.

We stayed tangled. Neither of us moved. His weight on me, which I didn't want him to shift. His heartbeat against my ribs, decelerating. My hand on the back of his neck, my fingers in his hair. The room reassembling itself around us—the golden light, the courtyard sounds, the ceiling fan turning slowly above us. The world coming back, the way the world always comes back after you've left it.

He propped himself on his elbow and looked at me. I looked back. We were lying on our sides in the ruined bed, and the light from the courtyard painted him in gold and shadow, and I thought: I should memorize this. Not his face—I already had his face—but this particular configuration of light and skin and the way his eyes looked when they were soft, when the intelligence and the alertness stepped back and let something warmer take the stage.

"Stay," I said. Not a question. Not a demand. The same register he'd used when he said walk with me—the space between asking and telling, the space where honesty lives.

He stayed.

We talked in the dark. The kind of talking that only happens after—when the performance is impossible because your body has already told every truth you have, and the only thing left is the voice, and the voice has nowhere to hide. He told me about Buenaventura, where he grew up—the Pacific coast, poor, beautiful, violent, a city that the rest of Colombia tried to forget existed. He told me about his mother, who cleaned houses and read poetry and told him that the difference between surviving and living was that surviving happens to you and living is something you choose. He told me about leaving at seventeen with nothing and building everything from nothing and the particular loneliness of people who come from nowhere and end up somewhere and can never fully belong to either.

I told him about the agency. Not specifically—I said government work, international, the kind of career that gives you the world and takes your life. I told him about David, though I didn't use his name. A man I'd loved who'd loved me back and we'd still failed, because loving someone and being able to live with them are two different skills and I was only good at one. I told him about leaving—walking out of a building in Langley for the last time with a box of personal effects and the sudden, nauseating freedom of a person who has been defined by their work and now has no work to be defined by.

I didn't tell him about Jimmy. I didn't tell him about the forty-seven minutes. Some doors stay locked even when the rest of the house is open.

He traced a line on my shoulder with his finger. Absentminded. Intimate. The touch of a man who was thinking about something and letting his hand think along with him.

"You carry something," he said. "I can feel it. I don't need to know what it is. But I can feel the weight of it."

Nobody had ever said that to me. Not David, who knew the weight and its source. Not Sophie, who was part of the weight without knowing it. No one had ever identified the thing I carried without asking me to name it. He just felt it. The way you feel a current in the ocean—not visible, but undeniable.

"Everyone carries something," I said.

"Yes. But not everyone carries it as well as you do."

I put my head on his chest. His arm came around me. The ceiling fan turned. The courtyard was quiet. Somewhere in the old city, the trumpet had finally stopped.

This is the part I need to tell you about. Not the sex—though the sex was the kind that rearranges your understanding of what your body is capable of wanting. The part that mattered was this: lying in the dark with my head on the chest of a man whose last name I hadn't asked, listening to his heartbeat, feeling his arm around my shoulders and his thumb moving slowly on my skin, and experiencing something I hadn't experienced in so long that I'd stopped believing it was real.

Peace.

Not the empty peace of the St. Barts balcony—the peace of solitude, which is really just loneliness with better lighting. This was the other kind. The kind that requires another person. The kind where your body is warm and your mind is quiet and you don't need to perform or protect or plan because someone else is in the room and their presence is enough.

I lay there and I let myself feel it. For twenty minutes, or thirty, or whatever the number was—I wasn't counting, and not counting was itself a miracle—I let the peace sit inside me without interrogating it, without analyzing it, without bracing for its departure. I just felt it. The way a person who has been cold for a very long time feels the first warmth and doesn't move because moving might break the spell.

He fell asleep. I knew the moment it happened because his breathing changed and his arm got heavier and the thumb on my shoulder stopped its slow rhythm. I stayed very still. I listened to him breathe. And I thought: this is the most dangerous thing that has happened to me in Cartagena, and I am not talking about the case.

Because the case I could handle. The danger I could calculate. But this—a man's arm around me in the dark, the sound of his breathing, the warmth of his chest beneath my cheek—this was the kind of danger that doesn't announce itself, the kind that arrives disguised as comfort, the kind that you don't recognize until you're already inside it and the doors have locked behind you.

I closed my eyes. I didn't sleep—I almost never sleep beside someone, not really, not the deep sleep that requires trust I don't have—but I rested. I let my body soften into his. I let the night be what it was.

And I thought, in the last conscious moment before something like sleep arrived: if this is a mistake, it's the best mistake I've made in years. And if it's not a mistake—if this is the real thing, the thing I've been pretending I don't need—then I am in more trouble than I know.

I was in more trouble than I knew.

CHAPTER TWELVE

MORNING – *Cartagena*

I woke to an empty bed and a piece of paper on the pillow.

The light in the room was different from the night before—the golden courtyard glow replaced by the flat white of early morning coming through the French doors, the kind of light that doesn't flatter anyone and doesn't lie. The sheets were tangled. One pillow still held the impression of his head. The air conditioning hummed. And on the pillow beside mine, folded once, a piece of hotel stationery with handwriting I'd never seen before and would recognize anywhere now.

Dinner tonight? I know a place in Getsemaní. 8pm. I'll find you.

No name. No phone number. No explanation for leaving before I woke, which could have been courtesy or could have been strategy, and I didn't have enough data to determine which and wasn't sure I wanted to. Below the words, a single line drawn with the pen—not a signature, just a mark, the casual gesture of a man who assumes you'll know who wrote it. I did.

I held the note for a moment. The paper was warm from the pillow, or I imagined it was, which amounts to the same thing. Then I set it on the nightstand and lay back in the ruined bed and let myself feel good.

Twenty minutes. That's what I gave myself. Twenty minutes to lie in the wreckage of the previous night and not think about the case, the clock, the photographs, Rafael Herrera, the thirty-year sentence, or the fact that I'd slept with a man whose last name I still didn't know in a city where I was supposed to be working, not accumulating the kind of complication that gets people killed.

Twenty minutes to be a woman in a bed who'd been well loved the night before.

It was enough. It wasn't enough. Both things were true in the way that contradictions always are when you're forty-seven and you've spent your life building walls and someone has walked through one as if it weren't there.

I stretched. My body felt different. Not sore—used. Thoroughly, specifically used, in the way that only happens when the other person is paying attention to you as a particular body and not as a generic one. There was a tenderness at my hip where his grip had tightened. A faint rawness on my chin from his jaw. Small evidence. Temporary marks that would be gone by afternoon. I pressed my fingers to the spot on my hip and felt the ghost of his hand and allowed myself one more minute of being a person to whom something good had happened.

Then I got up.

The shower was hot and the water pressure was excellent and I stood under it for longer than I should have, letting the heat work the remaining ache from muscles that had been asked to do things they hadn't done in a while. I washed my hair. I scrubbed the night off my skin and immediately missed it—the scent of him, cedar and warmth, that had been on my throat and my shoulders and the insides of my wrists. Gone now. Down the drain with the soap and the steam and whatever version of myself had existed between midnight and dawn.

I toweled off. Wrapped my hair. Stood in front of the same mirror where I'd assembled myself for the party twelve hours ago, and the woman looking back was different in ways I couldn't quite locate. Same face. Same gray eyes. Same fine lines. But something behind the eyes had shifted—a softness, or the memory of softness, that hadn't been there yesterday. A crack in the armor that I could either repair or leave open, and I didn't yet know which was the braver choice.

My phone buzzed on the marble counter. Sophie.

I picked up. "Morning."

"It's seven-fifteen your time, which means you're already up, which means you're already thinking, which means you need coffee before you talk to anyone, but I'm calling anyway because Ezra has something and he's been texting me since five a.m. my time, which means he was up at ten a.m. Lisbon time, which for Ezra is practically dawn, and when Ezra is awake before noon it means either the internet is broken or he found something important."

Sophie in her morning mode. A river of words, precise and warm and carrying exactly the information you needed plus ten percent more context than you asked for. I could hear New York behind her—traffic, a horn, the particular acoustic signature of a woman talking on her phone while walking east on a Manhattan sidewalk. I felt a pang of something that might have been homesickness if I had a more conventional relationship with the concept of home.

"What did he find?"

"The third phone number. The VoIP line that routes through Panama. He hasn't cracked the relay yet, but he's found a pattern in the call timing. Rafael calls that number every day between six and seven p.m. Cartagena time. Same window, never misses. The calls are always under ninety seconds. And the interesting thing—" She paused. I heard her dodge something on the sidewalk. "The interesting thing is that on three occasions in the last month, after Rafael makes his call, the same VoIP endpoint initiates an outbound call to a number in Bogotá that Ezra is still tracing. So the Panama relay isn't just receiving Rafael's reports. It's passing them up the chain."

"Chain of command," I said.

"That's what Ezra thinks. Rafael calls someone. That someone calls someone else. Classic cell structure. He's not freelancing, Cat. He's reporting."

I stood in the bathroom in a towel with water still dripping from my hair and felt the case shift beneath me like tectonic plates—the same surface, the same landscape, but the ground underneath rearranging itself into a configuration I hadn't mapped yet. Rafael reporting to someone. The blackmail not a solo operation but part of a structure. A chain that extended upward, through a relay in Panama, to a number in Bogotá that we couldn't yet see.

The twenty minutes were over. The woman in the bed was gone. The woman in the mirror was back.

"Tell Ezra to prioritize the Bogotá number," I said. "And pull everything he can on Grupo Escudo—the security company. Financials, contracts, client lists. If Rafael is reporting to someone, the money will show us who."

"Already on it. Ezra anticipated you'd want that. He said to tell you—and I'm quoting—'the internet in this country is seven out of ten but the corporate registry is a masterpiece of incompetence, which makes my job either very hard or very easy depending on whether they're incompetent about security too.'"

I almost smiled. "Anything from David?"

"He called yesterday. Said he's working the DEA angle but it's slow. The CI-7 file is sealed at a level that requires approvals he's not sure he can get without raising flags. He said—" Another pause. "He said to tell you he's trying."

David trying. David careful and methodical and pulling strings quietly in a building where everyone watches everyone else and loyalty is a currency that depreciates the moment you spend it. I thought about calling him. I didn't.

"Anything else?" Sophie asked.

"No. I'll check in this afternoon."

"Cat?"

"Yeah."

"You sound different this morning."

I looked at the woman in the mirror. The crack. The softness behind the eyes. Sophie heard everything, the way her father had heard everything, and the resemblance in that particular skill was the kind of thing that could undo me on a Wednesday morning in a hotel bathroom if I let it.

"Bad connection," I said.

"Mm-hmm," Sophie said, in the tone of a woman who didn't

believe me and was choosing not to press it, which was either kindness or strategy, and with Sophie it was usually both.

I hung up. Got dressed. White linen shirt, dark trousers, flats. Working clothes. A woman with a case, a deadline, and the particular clarity that comes from compartmentalizing so effectively that you can file away an entire night of extraordinary sex and focus on the task at hand. I was very good at compartmentalizing. It was one of my finest skills. It was also, I was beginning to suspect, one of the things that was making my life progressively unlivable, but that was a realization for a woman with more time and fewer deadlines, and today I had neither.

I ate breakfast on the hotel terrace. Café con leche, fruit, an arepa with cheese that was better than anything I'd eaten in New York, which I would never admit to Sophie. The terrace overlooked the small courtyard garden where nuns had once walked in contemplation, and the morning light fell through the bougainvillea in patterns that shifted when the breeze moved. It was beautiful and calm and I was reviewing Ezra's overnight intelligence reports on my phone and not seeing any of it.

A woman crossed the courtyard below me. Young, maybe thirty, in a yellow sundress, carrying a child on her hip. The child was maybe two—dark curls, brown skin, the compact roundness of a toddler's body. The woman shifted the child to her other hip with the practiced ease of someone who does this a hundred times a day, and the child laughed—a sound that carried up through the courtyard to where I sat, clear and delighted and entirely free of the complications that would come later, because children laugh like that before the world teaches them not to.

I watched them for longer than I should have. The woman kissed the child's forehead. The child grabbed a fistful of her hair. She laughed too, and the sound of her laughter layered over the child's, and I felt the thing I'd spent fifteen years learning not to feel—the specific, precise, anatomically sourced grief of a woman whose body had been damaged in a way that closed a particular door permanently. The shrapnel that had given me the scar on my left side had done other things too—things the surgeons explained in careful language in a hospital in Germany while I stared at the ceiling and understood that the word never, applied to your own body, is a sound you hear in a room but feel in your bones. I was thirty-two. I had not yet decided whether I wanted children. The decision was made for me, by a piece of metal the size of a shirt button, in a place I'd gone because I was following orders and a man I loved was dying and I was forty-seven minutes too late to save him and just in time to catch the blast that would save my life and end a possibility I hadn't yet learned to want.

I don't grieve this every day. I need you to know that. It's not a wound I carry in my hands. It's a wound I carry in the architecture—in the way I flinch when someone asks if I have kids, in the silence between David and me that grew into a canyon and eventually became the reason he left, in the way I watch Sophie with an intensity that is not entirely professional and not entirely healthy and is the closest I will ever come to knowing what it feels like to raise someone you'd die for. It's there. It's always there. Most days it's a room in a house I don't enter. Some mornings—a courtyard, a child's laugh, yellow sundress, bougainvillea—someone opens the door and I stand in it for a moment before I close it again.

I closed it. I went back to Ezra's reports. The arepa was getting cold. The light shifted. The courtyard was empty.

By nine o'clock I was working. The note from Andrés was in the nightstand drawer. The sheets had been changed by housekeeping. The room smelled like cleaning products and air conditioning and nothing at all like cedar or warmth, and the night might as well have happened in another country, except that it hadn't, and I knew it hadn't, and every time I shifted in my chair I felt the fading tenderness at my hip and remembered his hands and had to refocus.

Compartmentalize. Work the case. Five days left.

I opened my laptop and began to build the map that Lucía had started and Ezra was feeding with data—the network around Rafael Herrera, the financial architecture, the call chains, the connections between Grupo Escudo and the broader ecosystem of Cartagena's power structure. I worked methodically, the way I always work—one thread at a time, following each one as far as it would take me before picking up the next, building the picture the way you build a mosaic: piece by piece, stepping back periodically to see what the pieces are becoming.

The picture was becoming complicated. Rafael's security company had contracts with four private clients and two corporate entities. One of the corporate entities was a real estate development firm that was renovating colonial properties in the old city. The development firm's investors included a holding company registered in the Cayman Islands. The Cayman holding company was a shell. Beyond the shell: nothing. A wall. The kind of wall that costs money to build and exists for one reason: to keep people like me from seeing what's behind it.

I'd seen walls like this before. In my experience, what they protected was never as complicated as the wall itself. The wall was the performance. Behind it was usually a person, or a handful of people, who had something straightforward to hide and were willing to spend a fortune to hide it. The question was whether the person behind this wall was Rafael's handler, and whether that handler was the same voice on the other end of the VoIP line that routed through Panama.

I worked. The morning passed. The heat built outside the windows. Cartagena went about its business—horns, music, the clatter of construction, the endless productive chaos of a city that never stopped moving.

At noon, I took a break. Walked to the balcony. Looked out at the city that was becoming, against my better judgment and professional training, a place I didn't want to leave. The old city's rooftops were baking in the sun. The cathedral dome blazed. The wall traced its line to the sea.

Somewhere in this city, a man who had held me in the dark was going about his day, and I didn't know where he lived or what he did for a living or whether his last name would mean anything to me if I heard it. What I knew was the sound of his breathing when he slept and the way his hand felt in my hair and the thing he'd said on the balcony about building something and wondering if it was the right thing. I knew the weight of his body and the warmth of his mouth and the scar on his right hand between his thumb and forefinger that I still hadn't asked about.

I knew enough. I knew too much. I knew nothing at all.

I went back inside and returned to the map and worked until the afternoon light went gold and the city cooled and it was time to think about what to wear to dinner in Getsemaní with a man named Andrés who knew a place and would find me.

Something had shifted. The crack was there, hairline but real, running through the architecture of the life I'd built. I could repair it. I could reinforce it. I could pretend it wasn't there and add another layer of professional discipline and personal distance and carry on the way I'd been carrying on for fifteen years.

Instead, I chose a dress. Something softer than last night. Something that said: I'm not performing. Something that said: this is what I look like when I'm not wearing armor.

When the day ended, there'd be four days left. And the crack was widening.

CHAPTER THIRTEEN

THE ANGLE – *Cartagena*

I sat in my hotel room with three laptops, two phones, the remnants of a room service breakfast I'd barely touched, and the growing conviction that this case was not what it appeared to be.

Not the Andrés part. That part was exactly what it appeared to be —a woman falling for a man in a foreign city, which is the oldest story in the world and one I'd told myself I was too smart to star in. I was wrong about that, but I wasn't ready to examine how wrong. The part that was bothering me was Rafael Herrera.

Ezra had delivered overnight. The Bogotá number—the one the Panama VoIP relay had been calling after each of Rafael's check-ins—traced to a law firm called García, Mendoza & Prieto. Legitimate. Well-regarded. Specializing in criminal defense with a sideline in international human rights cases. The kind of firm that represented narcos and political dissidents with equal conviction and charged both of them handsomely.

But here was the thing that made my coffee go cold: the same firm had been communicating directly with Rafael on his Claro phone. Different number than the VoIP line—this was an open, traceable connection. Weekly calls, fifteen to twenty minutes, going back four months. Rafael was talking to his brother's lawyers. Regularly. Openly.

And separately from whatever he was doing on the encrypted line through Panama.

Two channels. One encrypted and passed through a relay. One open and direct. That was the structure of a man who was conducting two different operations simultaneously—one that required secrecy and one that didn't. The open channel was the legal campaign to challenge Miguel's conviction. The encrypted channel was something else.

I called Ezra.

"The law firm," I said. "García, Mendoza & Prieto. What do we know?"

"Founded in 1994. Three partners, twelve associates. Main office in Bogotá, satellite in Medellín. They've handled some significant cases—two former paramilitary commanders, a senator who was acquitted of bribery charges that everyone knows were valid, and, relevantly, three drug trafficking appeals in the last five years. Two of those appeals were successful. The third is pending."

"The successful ones—what was the basis?"

"That's where it gets interesting. Both appeals challenged the reliability of confidential informant testimony. Both argued that the DEA's source—designated in the case files as CI-7—provided tainted information that formed the basis for prosecution. In one case, the court found that CI-7's testimony was inconsistent with physical evidence. In the other, the defense demonstrated that CI-7 had a personal financial incentive to fabricate. Both convictions were overturned."

I set my coffee down. The mug left a ring on the desk that I stared at while the architecture of the case rearranged itself in my head.

CI-7. The same informant designation, in the same DEA operation, used to convict multiple defendants. Two of those convictions already overturned on the grounds that the informant was compromised. And Miguel Herrera—Rafael's brother, the man whose thirty-year sentence was the stated motivation for the blackmail—had been convicted on testimony from the same source.

"The operation," I said. "What was it called?"

"Operation Bright Horizon. DEA-led, 2016 through 2018. Targeted cocaine trafficking networks on the Caribbean coast. Resulted in fourteen convictions, mostly mid-level operators. CI-7 was the linchpin—

the informant whose testimony corroborated the surveillance evidence in almost every case. Without CI-7, most of those convictions would have been circumstantial at best."

"And two have already fallen."

"Two confirmed overturned. The third is the pending appeal I mentioned. And here's the detail that kept me up last night: Miguel Herrera's conviction was the largest of the fourteen. Thirty years, the maximum sentence, handed down by a judge who cited CI-7's testimony as—and I'm quoting from the sentencing transcript—'the most compelling and detailed account of the defendant's direct involvement in trafficking operations.' If CI-7 is compromised in two other cases from the same operation, there is a legitimate legal argument that Miguel's conviction is built on the same rotten foundation."

There it was. The angle. Not a pardon—Cat Sloane doesn't deliver pardons. A legal challenge. A legitimate path to overturning Miguel's conviction through the courts, using the same argument that had already succeeded twice. Rafael didn't need the President to free his brother. He needed a lawyer to demonstrate that the informant who put Miguel away was the same informant whose testimony had already been discredited.

Except Rafael already had a lawyer. The Bogotá firm was already working this angle. The open-channel calls, four months of them—Rafael and García, Mendoza & Prieto were already building the appeal.

So why the blackmail?

If Rafael had a legal path, why risk everything on a desperate play against the President of the United States? Why put Cole Hartwell's life in danger? Why trigger the kind of crisis that would bring someone like me to Cartagena?

The answer was either that Rafael didn't trust the legal process—which was plausible; the Colombian and American judicial systems had not been kind to the Herrera family—or that the legal challenge wasn't enough. Maybe the appeal was stalling. Maybe the DEA was blocking access to the CI-7 files. Maybe Rafael needed pressure from above—presidential pressure—to force the sealed records open and give his lawyers the ammunition they needed.

Or maybe there was something else entirely going on, something I couldn't see yet, and the blackmail and the legal challenge were two halves of a picture that only made sense when you put them together.

I filed the question. I didn't have enough to answer it yet, but I could feel it sitting at the edge of the case like a door I hadn't opened—not locked, just waiting for me to decide whether I wanted to see what was behind it.

"Ezra. The CI-7 files from Operation Bright Horizon. Are they accessible?"

"Sealed by the DEA under national security provisions. The court records reference CI-7 by designation only. The actual identity of the informant is classified. Even the defense attorneys in the successful appeals didn't get the name—they challenged the testimony without knowing who gave it. To get the identity, you'd need someone inside the intelligence community with high-level clearance and a willingness to access files that are very clearly marked as do-not-touch."

I knew someone. I'd been married to someone.

"Keep working the Bogotá firm," I said. "I want to know everything about the pending appeal. And pull the court transcripts from the two successful cases—I want to see exactly how they discredited CI-7."

"Already downloading. You'll have them by lunch."

"Ezra?"

"Yeah."

"You're very good at your job."

"I know. It's a burden I bear with remarkable grace. Talk later."

He hung up. I stared at the coffee ring on the desk and thought about David.

There are phone calls you plan and phone calls you postpone and phone calls you make because the case requires it and your personal feelings about the person on the other end are irrelevant, which is a lie you tell yourself so effectively that you almost believe it's true.

I called David at two in the afternoon, which was noon in Washington, which was the hour David took his lunch at his desk—a sandwich from the cafeteria, an apple, a black coffee—because David was a man of routine in the way that people who work in chaos cling to the small things they can control. I knew his routine the way I knew my own breathing. The marriage ends. The knowledge doesn't.

He picked up on the second ring. "Cat."

Just my name. The way he said it—careful, warm, a word he was handling gently because it still meant something to him, or because he knew it still meant something to me, or both—was enough to make me close my eyes for a second before I spoke.

"I need an update on the DEA files," I said. Professional. Direct. The voice of a woman who had not spent the previous two nights in bed with a stranger in a foreign city and was not currently experiencing the specific cognitive dissonance of asking her ex-husband for help while the scent of another man's cologne was still, faintly, on her pillowcase.

"I've been working it," he said. "Operation Bright Horizon. It's a mess, Cat. Bigger than I expected."

"Tell me."

"The operation ran for two years and produced fourteen convictions. Solid work on the surface. The DEA was proud of it—it was a career-maker for the agents involved. But the foundation was CI-7. Everything traces back to one informant whose testimony corroborated the surveillance in every major case. Without CI-7, most of those convictions are circumstantial."

"Two convictions have already been overturned," I said.

A pause. "You know about that."

"My tech person found it. The Bogotá law firm handling the appeals—García, Mendoza & Prieto—successfully challenged CI-7's testimony in two cases. They're working a third."

"Right. And that's what's making the DEA nervous. If CI-7 is discredited in enough cases, the entire operation unravels. Fourteen convictions. Some of those people are serving twenty, twenty-five, thirty years. If the informant was compromised, every one of those sentences is challengeable. The DEA is sitting on a potential scandal that would make the headlines for weeks."

"Which is why the files are sealed."

"Which is why the files are sealed. And not just sealed—compartmented. CI-7's identity is classified at a level that requires separate authorization from the DEA's Office of Professional Responsibility. I can confirm that the informant existed, that the testimony has documented inconsistencies, and that there's internal concern about the integrity of the operation. But the name—"

He stopped. I heard him take a breath. The particular breath David takes when he's weighing professional risk against personal obligation and trying to find a line he can walk without falling off either side.

"The name is behind a wall I can't get through without triggering every alarm in the building. The access logs for that file are monitored in real time. If I pull it, people will know. People whose attention I can't afford. Not because of my career—because it would raise questions about why the CIA Deputy Director is accessing sealed DEA informant files, and those questions would eventually lead back to you, and I won't do that to you."

I won't do that to you. Five words that carried the entire weight of our history—the marriage, the divorce, the residual tenderness that neither of us had been able to kill no matter how hard we tried. David wasn't protecting his career. He was protecting me. And the fact that he could still do that—still put me first after everything I'd done to make that impossible—was a kindness I didn't deserve and couldn't afford to feel.

"So I have the shape but not the name," I said.

"You have the shape. CI-7 existed. The testimony is questionable. There are documented inconsistencies that would support a legal challenge to any conviction that relied on it, including Miguel Herrera's. If his lawyers are good—and from what you're describing, they are—they don't need the name. They need the pattern. Two overturned convictions from the same operation, based on the same informant's testimony, establish a pattern that any competent judge would take seriously."

"But having the name would end it faster."

"Having the name would end everything faster. Including, potentially, the informant's life, depending on who wants the name and why."

I heard the warning in his voice. David was not a dramatic man—he dealt in understatement, in implication, in the quiet vocabulary of someone who has spent thirty years in rooms where saying too much can get people killed. When David said depending on who wants the name, he was telling me something: be careful about what you're looking for, because the people who want CI-7's identity may not be the people you think they are, and the consequences of finding it may not be the consequences you intend.

I filed this. Added it to the question I'd filed earlier—why the blackmail when there's a legal path?—and felt the two questions click together like adjacent pieces of a puzzle whose picture I couldn't yet see.

"David."

"Yeah."

"Thank you. I know this isn't easy."

"Nothing involving you has ever been easy. I mean that as a compliment."

I smiled. He couldn't see it, and I was glad, because the smile was the kind that reveals too much—not happiness but something more fragile, the involuntary softening that happens when someone who once held all of you holds just a piece and does it with such care that you remember why you loved them.

"There's one more thing," he said. His voice had changed. Slightly. The shift from professional to something else—not personal exactly, but adjacent. The David voice. The one that lived in the space between the deputy director and the man who used to bring me coffee at three in the morning when I couldn't sleep.

"While I was in the Bright Horizon files, I came across a reference. A cross-index. It linked to another operation—different theater, different agency, but the same network of informants. The reference was flagged but not explained. Just a file number and a notation that said 'see related.'"

"Related to what?"

"I don't know. The file number was a format I recognized from—

from our time. Agency format. Iraq-era. I didn't open it. I'm telling you because you should know it exists, but I want to be clear: I didn't open it, and I'm not going to."

Iraq-era. Agency format. A file cross-referenced with a DEA operation in Colombia that linked back to the intelligence community's operations in the Middle East a decade ago. The hairs on my arms rose. I didn't move. I didn't breathe differently. I gave no external signal that the words Iraq-era had detonated something in my chest that felt like a flashbang in a quiet room.

"Okay," I said. Neutral. Level. The voice of a woman who has been trained to receive devastating information without changing her breathing.

"Cat."

"I heard you."

"Are you okay?"

There it was again. The question he asked instead of how are you, because how are you is social and are you okay is a man who remembers finding his wife on the bathroom floor at three in the morning, staring at nothing, with the thousand-yard stare that the agency gives you for free and takes a lifetime to return.

"I'm fine," I said.

"You're not fine. But you're working, so I'll leave it. Be careful with whatever you're doing down there. Cartagena is not a forgiving city."

"I know what Cartagena is."

"I know you do. That's what worries me."

He hung up. Not abruptly—David never hangs up abruptly. He lets the conversation reach its natural end and then closes it with the care of a man who understands that the last words in any exchange are the ones that linger. I stood in my hotel room with the phone in my hand and the ghost of his voice in my ear and I thought: David, you impossible, careful, decent man. You are the best person I know, and I let you go, and some mistakes don't get fixed no matter how clearly you see them.

I put the phone down. I didn't think about the Iraq-era file. Not yet. That door was bolted and chained and I was not going to open it in Cartagena with four days left on a clock and a man named Andrés who had no last name and was taking me to dinner tonight and made me feel things I hadn't felt in years. One crisis at a time.

By late afternoon, I had the architecture of the solution.

Not the solution itself—that would take execution, leverage, and a conversation with Rafael Herrera that I hadn't yet figured out how to arrange. But the shape of it was clear, and the shape was this:

Miguel Herrera's conviction was built on CI-7's testimony. That testimony was compromised—two other convictions from the same operation had already been overturned on exactly these grounds. A third appeal was pending. The legal precedent existed. The Bogotá law firm was already working the case. What they lacked wasn't a legal argument. What they lacked was access—to the sealed files, to the internal DEA documentation that would confirm the pattern of compromised testimony across all fourteen Bright Horizon convictions.

I couldn't give them CI-7's name. David couldn't get it, and even if he could, revealing an informant's identity was a line I wouldn't cross—not for Rafael, not for Kessler, not for anyone. An informant's life was not a bargaining chip. That was one of the few bright lines I'd kept from the agency, and I intended to keep it until I died.

But I could give them the pattern. The documented inconsistencies. The internal DEA concern. The fact that the agency itself knew Bright Horizon was built on a cracked foundation and had been quietly letting convictions fall rather than acknowledge the scope of the problem. That information, delivered to the right lawyers, would be enough to accelerate Miguel's appeal from years to months. Maybe faster, if the DEA decided that a quiet settlement was preferable to a public unraveling.

The question was how to deliver it to Rafael in a way that made him stand down. He had photographs that could get the President's son killed. I needed him to destroy those photographs in exchange for something he valued more: a real, legitimate, permanent path to his brother's freedom. Not a pardon—justice. Not a political favor—a legal remedy that would survive any change of administration, any shift in political winds.

I could see it. The solution was there, floating just beyond my reach, waiting for me to close the gap between knowing what to do and figuring out how to do it.

I looked at the clock. Six-fifteen. Andrés had said eight.

I had an hour and forty-five minutes to be Cat Sloane, problem solver, before I had to become Catherine, the woman in the softer dress, the woman whose armor was developing cracks she didn't want to repair.

I picked up the phone and called Kessler. It was time to tell him what I'd found and what I needed next.

Four days left. The angle was there. The solution was forming. And somewhere in the back of my mind, in the room I wasn't entering, a file number in Iraq-era agency format sat waiting for a woman who wasn't ready to look at it.

I wasn't ready. I was beginning to suspect I might never be.

CHAPTER FOURTEEN

THE SECOND NIGHT – *Cartagena*

He called at seven.

Not texted. Called. His voice on the line, that London-accented English, and the sound of something behind him—traffic, a horn, the particular acoustics of a man standing on a Cartagena street in the early evening with his phone to his ear. He asked if I was still free for dinner. I said yes before I'd finished deciding, which told me everything I needed to know about where my judgment was on the subject of Andrés and how much of it I was willing to trust.

"I know a place in Getsemaní," he said. "Not the restaurants the hotels recommend. A place where the food is made by a woman who has been cooking the same twelve dishes for thirty years and has perfected every one of them and refuses to add a thirteenth because she says twelve is the number of the apostles and she's not going to improve on God's math."

"That," I said, "is either the best or the worst restaurant recommendation I've ever received."

"It's both. Eight o'clock. I'll pick you up."

He picked me up in a dark SUV driven by a man he didn't introduce, which I noted and filed. A driver meant either wealth or security or habit, and in Cartagena all three often lived in the same car. The driver dropped us at the edge of Getsemaní and Andrés told him something in rapid Spanish that I caught fragments of—later, not yet, I'll call—and then we were walking through the neighborhood that I'd read about but hadn't visited, and Getsemaní at night was a different city than the old city, a different frequency entirely.

Where the walled city was preservation and performance—every stone restored, every balcony photographed, every restaurant designed for people who wanted beauty with their dinner—Getsemaní was the thing itself. Raw. Alive. The buildings were painted in colors that no designer would have chosen and that worked anyway: turquoise beside orange beside a yellow so bright it looked like it was arguing with the sunset. Music came from everywhere—salsa from an open doorway, reggaeton from a passing car, a man playing a cajón on a corner with his eyes closed and his hands moving faster than I could follow. The streets smelled like frying plantain and cilantro and something sweet I couldn't identify. People sat on stoops and leaned from windows and lived their lives in the open air, and the neighborhood had the energy of a place that knew exactly what it was and didn't care whether you approved.

"This is my Cartagena," Andrés said. Not boasting. Stating. "The old city is beautiful, but it's a museum. Getsemaní is the city that's still alive."

The restaurant didn't have a sign. It was a ground-floor room in a building whose upper stories were residential—laundry on a line above our heads, a television flickering through a window—with six tables covered in plastic tablecloths and a kitchen that was visible through a serving window. A woman in her sixties stood at a stove that looked older than she was, stirring something in a pot large enough to bathe a child. She saw Andrés and her face changed—not the deference of a woman receiving a powerful customer, but the genuine warmth of a woman seeing someone she liked. She said something in Spanish that I didn't entirely catch but that included mijo, which is an endearment that means my son and is reserved for people who have earned it.

Andrés kissed her cheek. Introduced me as Catherine, his friend from New York. She looked at me with the frank assessment of a woman who has raised sons and knows what it means when they bring someone to her table. She approved, or at least she didn't disapprove, which in a Colombian mother figure amounts to the same thing. She brought us aguardiente without being asked, and rice, and a cazuela of fish in coconut sauce that was, without exaggeration, one of the best things I'd ever put in my mouth.

We ate. We drank. We talked.

Dinner conversations have a structure, even when they feel spontaneous. The first course is reconnaissance—light topics, shared references, the mutual calibration of two people establishing what kind of evening this is going to be. The second course is where the terrain deepens—personal history, carefully curated, the stories you tell to reveal exactly as much as you intend and no more. By dessert, if you're lucky, if the other person is worth it, the curation falls away and what's left is something closer to truth.

We were at the second course when Andrés told me about Buenaventura.

"Most Colombians don't talk about Buenaventura," he said. He was turning his glass slowly on the table—a gesture I'd noticed in him, the unconscious movement of a man thinking out loud. "It's on the Pacific coast. Colombia's largest port. Eighty percent of the country's maritime trade passes through it. And it's also one of the poorest, most violent cities in the Western Hemisphere. The wealth passes through but none of it stays. Like a river that gives nothing to its banks."

"You grew up there."

"I grew up in a neighborhood called Lleras, which is a word that sounds gentle and isn't. My mother cleaned houses in the neighborhoods where the port managers lived. My father left when I was four. The standard story—you've heard variations of it. What makes mine different is that I decided, at an age when most children are deciding what game to play, that I would leave Buenaventura and never be poor again, and I did both of those things with a determination that frightened everyone who knew me, including, eventually, myself."

He wasn't performing. I'd spent enough time reading people to know the difference between a man telling a story he's rehearsed and a man telling a story he's lived. The rehearsed version is polished—the beats land cleanly, the pauses are timed. The lived version has rough edges. It hesitates in places. It speeds up where the memory is painful and slows down where the memory is complicated. Andrés's story hesitated when he mentioned his father and slowed when he mentioned his mother, and both of those things were true.

"She read to me," he said. "Every night. García Márquez, Neruda, Borges. We didn't have books—she borrowed them from the houses she cleaned. The women she worked for never noticed, or they noticed and didn't care, which my mother preferred to interpret as generosity. She told me that words were the only thing in the world that couldn't be taken from you once you had them. She was wrong about many things, but she was right about that."

"Is she still alive?"

"No. She died when I was twenty-three. She saw me leave Buenaventura but not what I built after. I think about that sometimes—whether she would be proud or frightened. Both, probably. My mother had a talent for holding two contradictory feelings at the same time and refusing to let either one win."

"I know people like that," I said. I was thinking of myself.

He smiled. "I suspect you do."

My turn. He didn't ask—he waited, which is the same thing but better, because the space a person makes for your story matters more than the question they use to request it.

"I worked for the government," I said. "For a long time. The kind of work you can't talk about at dinner parties, which is both the appeal and the problem, because after enough years the secrecy becomes the architecture of your entire personality and you realize you don't know how to have a conversation that isn't built on omission."

"You left."

"I left. Or I was shaped into leaving—there was an incident, and after the incident there was a period where I was technically still employed but no longer the person I'd been when the work made sense, and eventually the gap between who I was and what the job required became too wide to bridge. I walked out. Started my own thing. Built something new."

"And you're good at it."

"I'm the best at it." No modesty. No qualification. The bald truth delivered in a voice that wasn't bragging but wasn't apologizing either, because I had learned—late, but I'd learned—that a woman who apologizes for her own competence is doing the world's work for free.

He looked at me across the table with the cazuela between us and the candle throwing shadows on his face and the sounds of Getsemaní drifting through the open doorway, and I saw something in his expression that I hadn't seen before: not attraction, which had been there since the party, but recognition. The look of a person seeing their own reflection in an unexpected place.

"We're the same," he said. Not as a pickup line. Not as flattery. As an observation, delivered with the quiet surprise of a man who had not expected to find himself at a plastic-tablecloth restaurant in Getsemaní looking at a woman from New York and seeing his own story.

We were the same. Built from nothing. Driven by a need that predated language. Lonely in the specific way that people who succeed alone are lonely—not for lack of company, but for lack of a mirror. And now, sitting across from each other in the candlelight, we'd each found one. The mirror was imperfect, distorted by the things we weren't telling each other—I didn't know what he'd omitted, what rooms he'd locked while showing me the rest of his house. I knew what I'd omitted. I'd given him an incident and a departure but not the forty-seven minutes, not Jimmy, not the specific weight of a dying man in my arms while someone on a radio told me to hold my position. I'd given him a career change but not the shrapnel, not the hospital in Germany, not the word never.

Neither of us was lying. We were both doing something more sophisticated than lying: we were telling the truth selectively, building portraits of ourselves that were accurate in every detail and incomplete in every way that mattered, and the space between what we said and what we didn't say was where the real intimacy lived. Because intimacy isn't the truth. Intimacy is the willingness to be in the room with someone while the truth sits in the corner, unnamed, and both of you know it's there.

The woman brought us dessert without asking—a cocada, sweet and dense and tasting of coconut and burned sugar. Andrés paid in cash, a quiet exchange with the woman that I didn't watch because watching a man pay is one of those acts that carries more social weight than it should, and I wasn't interested in performing gratitude for a dinner. We walked out into the Getsemaní night, which was louder now and warmer and smelled like everything all at once, and his hand found mine the way it had in the plaza, his fingers sliding between mine as if they'd always been there.

We went back to my hotel because his place was—he said—on the other side of the city, and mine was closer, and both of us understood that the reasons didn't matter because the destination had been decided somewhere between the aguardiente and the cocada, and probably before that, probably the moment he'd called at seven and I'd said yes before I'd finished deciding.

The room was dark. I didn't turn on the lights. The courtyard glow came through the French doors the way it had the night before—golden, warm, the light of a city that understood romance the way other cities understood commerce or culture, as an essential industry, a thing to be cultivated and protected and never allowed to dim.

He kissed me in the doorway. Slowly. His hands on my waist, pulling me close but not urgently—with the patience of a man who had all night and knew it and intended to use every minute of it. The first night had been hunger. This was something else. This was choice. Deliberate, unhurried, the conscious decision to take a woman apart slowly and watch what she became when the pieces rearranged.

We undressed each other. Not the efficient stripping of the first night—this was slower, more careful, each piece of clothing a negotiation. His jacket. My dress. His shirt, which I unbuttoned one button at a time while his eyes stayed on mine, and the restraint of not looking at what I was uncovering was its own kind of heat—the discipline of delayed gratification practiced by two people who were very good at discipline and wanted, for one night, to use it for something other than control.

He laid me on the bed. Not pushed, not pulled—laid, with his hand cradling the back of my head the way he had the first night, with that tenderness that kept ambushing me because I didn't know what to do with tenderness. I knew what to do with passion—I'd built an entire system for managing passion, for giving and receiving it without letting it reach the parts of me that were too damaged to survive being touched. But tenderness bypassed the system. Tenderness went straight to the locked rooms and tried the handles.

He moved down my body. His mouth on my collarbone. My sternum. The space between my breasts. Lower. And then he stopped.

His hand was on my left side. His fingers had found it before his eyes did—the ridge of scar tissue that ran from beneath my breast to the curve of my hip, four inches of raised, irregular skin that no amount of time or treatment would ever smooth. The evidence. The permanent record of a piece of metal that had entered my body in Fallujah and been removed in Germany and left behind a mark that told a story I had never once in my life told voluntarily.

He went still. His fingers rested on the scar the way you rest your hand on something unexpected—not recoiling, not pressing, just acknowledging. I felt his breath against my skin, warm and steady, and I waited for the question.

Everyone asks. That's the thing about scars—they're invitations that you didn't send, and people treat them as permission to inquire, as if the damage to your body is public property and the story behind it is something you owe to anyone who notices. Men, specifically, ask. In bed, in the vulnerability of skin against skin, when a man's hand finds a scar on a woman's body, he asks. He always asks. And then you have to choose: the truth, which is a grenade you're not willing to throw into a moment of intimacy, or a lie, which tastes like ash, or a deflection, which is what I usually choose, something vague about an accident, a long time ago, not a big deal. The deflection is its own kind of wound, because every time you minimize the thing that almost killed you, you're agreeing to be smaller than you are.

Andrés didn't ask.

He traced the scar with his fingertip. Slowly. From one end to the other, the way you'd trace a line on a map—not investigating, not probing, just following the path. His touch was light. Almost reverent. As if the scar were not damage but geography—a feature of the landscape of my body, as real and as permanent as a ridge on a hillside, and no more requiring explanation than any other part of the terrain.

Then he lowered his mouth and kissed it.

I want to tell you that I was fine. That I lay there with his lips on the worst thing that ever happened to me and I was composed, controlled, the woman who carries everything without breaking. But I wasn't. My hand went to his hair. My fingers tightened. My chest constricted in a way that had nothing to do with arousal and everything to do with the very simple, very devastating experience of being touched in a place that no one had ever touched with kindness.

David had seen the scar. David had loved me with the scar. But David knew the story, and the story was always in the room with us, and his tenderness toward the scar was inseparable from his tenderness toward the wound it represented—the loss, the guilt, the long years of trying to love a woman who was held together with scar tissue inside and out. David's touch said: I know what this cost you.

Andrés's touch said something different. It said: I don't know, and I don't need to. You are a woman with a scar, and the scar is part of you, and I am kissing you, all of you, including the parts that hurt.

I don't know how to explain what that did to me. I've spent fifteen years building a life around the principle that the scar—and everything it represents—is something to be managed, concealed, survived. To have a man find it in the dark and kiss it without asking why was an act of such simple, unearned grace that it dismantled something in me that I didn't know could be dismantled. Not the wall. Something behind the wall. Something older. The idea that the damaged parts of me needed to be explained before they could be accepted.

He didn't linger. He kissed the scar and then he continued—his mouth moving lower, his hands on my hips, his breath warm on my stomach. The tenderness didn't stop but it braided into something else now—desire, need, the specific hunger of a man who wanted a woman and was communicating that want with every part of his body. His mouth found me the way it had the night before, but slower this time, gentler, as if the scar had changed the register—as if having touched the place where I was most damaged, he now wanted to find the place where I was most alive.

I let him. I let go of the sheets I'd been gripping. I let go of the breath I'd been holding. I let my body do what my body wanted to do, which was rise toward him, open toward him, trust him with the specific vulnerability of a woman who is being seen in the dark by a man whose hands are telling her that she is not broken but whole.

I came slowly. Not the sharp, shocked orgasm of the first night but something that built in waves, each one deeper, each one closer to something I didn't have a name for—not just pleasure but its opposite, the relief that lives on the other side of holding everything together, the exhale after years of inhaling. I said his name. Not loudly. Almost a whisper. And his hand found mine and held it and I came with his fingers laced through mine and his mouth on me and tears on my face that I didn't realize were there until afterward.

Then he was above me. Inside me. And this time was different from the first time the way a conversation is different from a monologue—not just two bodies but two people, moving together with the particular synchronicity that comes from knowing each other's rhythms, from having learned in one night what some people never learn: how the other person breathes when they're close, where to press, where to slow, the specific calibration of pressure and patience that turns sex from an act into a language.

He was slow. I was slow. We were slow together, in the way that only happens when the urgency has been met and what's left is the luxury of time and the desire to make it last—not because the ending won't be good but because the middle is where the real intimacy lives, the sustained note between the opening and the resolution, the long middle passage where two bodies are joined and the world is reduced to breath and rhythm and the impossible, temporary miracle of not being alone.

When it ended—not abruptly but gradually, the way music fades rather than stops—we lay in the dark and I listened to his heartbeat and he traced absent circles on my shoulder and neither of us spoke for a long time. The courtyard was quiet. The ceiling fan turned. Somewhere in Getsemaní, very far away, someone was playing a guitar, and the melody drifted in through the open French doors like a visitor who knew it wasn't invited but came anyway.

I should tell you what I was thinking. I was thinking about the scar and how he'd kissed it. I was thinking about the tears, which had surprised me and which I hadn't explained and which he hadn't asked about, because he didn't ask. I was thinking about what he'd said at dinner—we're the same—and how true it felt and how terrifying that truth was, because the last time I'd felt this recognized by another person was David, and David and I had loved each other for twelve years and it hadn't been enough, and the arithmetic of that—love plus recognition still equaling failure—was the kind of math that makes you want to stop counting altogether.

I was thinking: this is the second night. And after the second night, there is a third or there isn't, and if there is, then this is something, and if there isn't, then this is a memory I'll carry in the same way I carry all the beautiful, unsustainable things—carefully, at a distance, in a drawer I open only when I'm strong enough to look at what's inside.

I was thinking: I don't know his last name.

And I was thinking—this is the part that matters, this is the part that will haunt me long after Cartagena is a city I used to visit and Andrés is a man I used to know—I was thinking: I don't want to leave this bed. Not tonight. Not tomorrow. Not ever. I want to stay in this room with this man and this gold light and this guitar that won't stop playing and I want to stop running and I want to stop performing and I want to stop being Cat Sloane, the woman who carries everything, and just be Catherine, the woman who is lying in the dark being held by someone who kissed her scar without asking why.

I didn't say any of this. I pressed my face into his chest and breathed him in—cedar, warmth, the salt of his skin—and I memorized it, the way I memorize everything I'm about to lose, because I am a woman who has learned that the things that matter most are always temporary and the only defense against their departure is to hold them so precisely in memory that their absence becomes a room you can visit instead of a void you fall into.

"Stay," I said. For the second time in two nights. The word becoming a ritual between us, a small ceremony of asking for the thing I didn't know how to ask for in any other language.

"I'm here," he said. And his arm tightened around me, and I closed my eyes, and I let the night hold both of us the way the sea holds a boat—gently, completely, with no promise about what comes with the morning.

In the morning he would be gone again. A note on the pillow. A few words in his handwriting. But tonight he was here, and his heart was beating beneath my cheek, and the guitar was playing, and I was the closest to happy I had been in longer than I could count, and I was so deep inside the lie that I couldn't feel its edges.

It wasn't his lie. Not yet. That would come later, and it would be devastating in ways I couldn't yet imagine.

The lie was mine. The lie I tell myself every time I let someone in: that this time will be different. That I'm capable of the thing I'm reaching for. That the woman who can't be still can learn to stay.

Three days left. And the crack had become a fissure, and the light was pouring through, and I had no idea—none—how much the light was going to cost me.

CHAPTER FIFTEEN

THE VILLA – *Cartagena*

The invitation came the next afternoon, delivered not by phone but in person—Andrés at my hotel, unannounced, standing in the lobby with the ease of a man who treated the Sofitel Legend Santa Clara like an extension of his living room. He was in linen today, pale blue, sleeves rolled to the forearm, and the sight of him in daylight—in the bright, unforgiving Cartagena afternoon rather than the merciful candlelight of evening—did nothing to diminish him. Some men are built for darkness. Andrés was built for any light you put him in.

"There's a gathering tonight," he said. "A friend's house outside the city. Beautiful place. Good people, mostly. Interesting people, definitely. I'd like you to come."

"Mostly good people," I said. "That's either an honest assessment or a warning."

"It's Cartagena. The distinction between good people and interesting people is a luxury that most of us gave up a long time ago."

I should have said no. I had three days left on the case, the CI-7 angle was developing but far from resolved, and I still hadn't arranged the meeting with Rafael that I needed. An evening at a private estate with a man whose last name I didn't know was not a productive use of time. But there was another calculation running alongside the professional one: Lucía had told me that the villa gatherings outside Cartagena were where the city's invisible economy socialized, where the cartel-adjacent and the cartel-proper drank champagne together on terraces overlooking the Caribbean and conducted the kind of business that never appeared on any ledger. If Andrés moved in these circles—and his invitation suggested he did—then the evening might give me something I needed: proximity to Rafael's world. A view of the ecosystem from the inside.

I told myself this was the reason I said yes. I was very convincing.

The villa was forty minutes south of the city, past Bocagrande and the airport and through a stretch of coastal road where the development thinned and the landscape opened up—mangroves, tidal flats, the Caribbean glittering beyond a fringe of palm. Andrés drove himself this time. No driver. A black Range Rover that he handled with the absent competence of a man who had been driving expensive vehicles on difficult roads his entire adult life. The road narrowed. A gate appeared—white stucco, security camera, a guard who waved us through without checking anything, which meant either lax security or a guest list confirmed in advance.

The house emerged from behind a stand of palms the way beautiful things in Colombia tend to emerge—suddenly, extravagantly, with no apology for the excess. White walls, terra-cotta roof, cascading terraces stepping down toward the sea. A pool that appeared to merge with the horizon. Gardens that had been designed to look wild but were maintained with the kind of precision that costs more than design. The architecture was modern but softened with colonial details—arched doorways, carved stone, the graceful iron railings that Cartagena exports along with its aesthetic DNA. It was the kind of house that appears in magazines with the caption private residence and the unspoken subtext: you will never be invited.

We were, apparently, invited.

Cars were parked along the drive—a Range Rover like Andrés's, a Porsche, two Mercedes, a Land Cruiser with tinted windows that I cataloged automatically because tinted windows in Colombia are either status or security and the distinction matters. Twenty cars, maybe twenty-five. A gathering, not a party—the difference being that parties are designed to be observed and gatherings are designed to be private.

Andrés put his hand on the small of my back as we walked toward the entrance. A possessive gesture, or a protective one, or simply the touch of a man who liked touching the woman beside him. I felt the warmth of his palm through the thin fabric of my dress—white tonight, linen, because the invitation had said casual, and in the language of Cartagena's upper reaches casual meant expensive but effortless—and I let myself lean into it for one step before correcting.

"Whose house is this?" I asked.

"A friend. Mauricio. He made his money in construction and shipping and now he collects art and throws evenings like these because he's bored and generous and likes being surrounded by people more interesting than himself. He's not as modest as he pretends, but the pretense is charming."

Construction and shipping. The two industries that Lucía had identified as primary laundering channels for the Cartagena corridor. I didn't react. I filed it. Added it to the architecture I was building in my head—the map of who was connected to whom, which legitimate businesses served as conduits, where the money moved when it moved through these circles.

We walked in.

The gathering was already underway, and it was beautiful in the specific way that events hosted by very wealthy people in tropical settings are beautiful—so effortlessly, so completely, that the beauty becomes its own atmosphere, a medium you move through the way you move through warm water. Lanterns hung from the palm trees. A bar had been set up on the lower terrace, backlit, the bottles glowing like amber and crystal in the dusk. Music—a DJ, not a band, playing something low and electronic that was more texture than melody, the kind of soundtrack that fills silence without demanding attention. The pool was lit from below, turning the water a luminous turquoise that reflected off the white walls and the underside of palm fronds and made everything look like a scene from a film about people whose problems are expensive and whose pleasures are exquisite.

The guests matched the setting. Thirty-five, maybe forty people, and the gender split was more even than Carmen's party—couples, mostly, but not exclusively, and the dynamic was different from the old city gathering. That had been social performance: see and be seen, network, calibrate your position in the hierarchy. This was something looser. More intimate. The champagne was flowing freely—Veuve Clicquot, served in real crystal, because even the casual gestures in this world were curated—and the conversations had the slightly liquid quality of people who had been drinking since sunset and had reached the hour where inhibitions soften and the boundaries between public and private begin to blur.

Andrés moved through the room the way he moved through every room—with the fluid confidence of a man who knew everyone and was known by everyone and managed both conditions without visible effort. He introduced me as Catherine, my friend from New York. Each introduction was calibrated: to some people he was warm, expansive, full of anecdotes and laughter. To others he was cordial but contained—a few words, a handshake, the minimum required by social obligation. I watched the calibration and admired it the way I admire any display of social intelligence—he was reading each person and giving them exactly the version of himself they expected, which is a skill I recognized because I practice it myself.

I met Mauricio. He was in his early sixties, barrel-chested, with a silver goatee and the deep tan of a man who spent his life outdoors or on boats or both. He shook my hand with genuine warmth and said, in English that was more Miami than London, "Any friend of Andrés is family in this house. Stay as long as you want. Drink whatever you find. And if anyone offers you aguardiente after midnight, say no—it's a trap."

I liked him. I cataloged him. Construction and shipping. Bored and generous and hosting thirty-five people at a villa with a security gate and a pool that merged with the Caribbean. These things were not contradictions. In Cartagena, Lucía had told me, the gradient between legal and illegal was not a line. Mauricio was somewhere on that gradient, and the exact location didn't matter tonight. What mattered was that I was inside the room, and the room was showing me things.

I saw money. Not the performed wealth of the old city—the actual thing, the weight of it, the way it shaped the space and the people and the air itself. A woman wearing a necklace that could have paid for a house in Getsemaní. A man checking his phone—three phones, actually, laid on the table beside his champagne glass like a display of connectivity that was also, I suspected, a display of operational compartmentalization. A conversation in the corner conducted in low voices with the body language of a negotiation: two men leaning in, one shaking his head, the other touching his arm in the particular way that says we're not done yet.

I saw the security, too. Less visible than at Carmen's party—no Grupo Escudo uniforms—but present. Two men on the perimeter who weren't drinking. A third near the gate. They moved with the economy of professionals, and their eyes never stopped scanning. Private security, not contracted—which meant Mauricio had his own people, which meant Mauricio had things worth protecting with dedicated personnel.

I filed everything. Smiled. Drank champagne. Played the role of a woman enjoying a beautiful evening at a beautiful house with a man she was falling for, which was not entirely a role, which was the problem.

The evening loosened as the hours passed. The music shifted—still ambient but warmer now, with a pulse underneath that suggested the night was moving toward something more deliberate. People drifted. The lower terrace became a dance floor, or the approximation of one—couples moving together in the lantern light with the particular fluidity that comes from good champagne and warm air and the permission that wealthy people grant themselves in private spaces to be less guarded than they are in public. The pool glowed. Someone had lit a fire pit near the garden wall, and the smoke mingled with the salt air and the jasmine.

Andrés was across the terrace, talking to Mauricio and another man I hadn't been introduced to. He caught my eye and smiled—a private smile, the one that was only for me, the one that made the crowded terrace feel like a room with two people in it. I smiled back and felt the specific warmth of being chosen by someone in a room full of options, which is a warmth that has nothing to do with temperature and everything to do with the primitive, unglamorous need to be preferred.

I was standing near the house, at the edge where the terrace met the interior, holding a glass I'd barely touched. The doors to the house were open—the villa was designed for the boundary between inside and outside to be theoretical rather than actual—and the breeze moved through the rooms carrying music and conversation and the occasional burst of laughter. I was half working, half drifting, my mind running the case in the background the way it always runs, cataloging and connecting, while the rest of me floated in the particular freedom of a night that was asking nothing of me except presence.

I turned to go back toward the bar. The hallway that led from the terrace into the house was softly lit—wall sconces, the kind that glow rather than illuminate, designed for ambiance rather than visibility. Doors lined the hall, most closed, leading to rooms I assumed were private. The hallway was empty. The party was behind me and below, on the terraces.

One door was ajar.

I didn't mean to look. That's the truth, though I'm aware of how unconvincing it sounds—a woman trained in surveillance claiming she accidentally looked through an open door. But there is a difference between operational observation and the involuntary glance that happens when movement catches the edge of your vision, and this was the second kind. A shift of light. A sound that was not the party, not the music, not the sea. A sound that was human and private and that my body recognized before my mind gave it a name.

Two people. In the room beyond the door. Visible through the gap—six inches of space between the door and the frame, enough to see without being seen, enough to frame what was happening inside like a painting in a vertical gallery.

A man and a woman. Not guests I recognized. He was leaning against a desk or a table—I could see his back, his white shirt untucked, his hands on her hips. She was facing him, close, her body pressed against his, and her head was tipped back, and his mouth was on her neck, and her hands were in his hair, and the sound I'd heard—the sound that had caught my attention—was her. A soft exhale. Not a moan—something before a moan, the breath that precedes the sound, the intake that says the body has received something it wanted and the mind hasn't caught up yet.

I should have looked away. I knew this in the way I knew my own name—immediately, certainly, without debate. This was private. These were strangers in a private room at a private gathering and I had no right to their moment and no reason to watch it and every reason to walk away.

I watched. One beat. Two. Three.

His hand moved from her hip to the small of her back, pulling her closer. Her spine arched. She said something I couldn't hear—his name, maybe, or a word that wasn't a name but served the same purpose, the particular vocabulary that exists only between two people in the dark. His other hand came up to her face. Cupped her jaw. Tilted her mouth to his. And the kiss was—

The kiss was unselfconscious. That's the word. Not passionate, though it was. Not tender, though it was that too. Unselfconscious. Two people who had forgotten that the world existed, who were operating in the total freedom of a closed room at a late hour after enough champagne to dissolve whatever distance they normally maintained, and the freedom was what caught in my throat and held me at the door for those three beats when I should have already been gone.

Because I wanted that. Not them—not the act, not the physical spectacle of two strangers pressing against each other in a lamplit room. I wanted the freedom. The unselfconsciousness. The ability to touch another person without calculating the angles, without reading the signals, without the constant low hum of observation that had been my companion for so long that I'd forgotten it was there until I saw its absence in someone else.

I thought about Andrés. Two nights. Two mornings of waking alone. Two evenings of conversation that felt like the realest thing in my life and was still, despite everything—despite the scar and the tears and the thing he'd said about building what you're capable of and calling it enough—still a performance. Still two people showing each other curated versions of themselves, still omitting the rooms that mattered most, still operating in the sophisticated space between truth and trust that people like me mistake for intimacy because we've never experienced the real thing.

The woman in that room was not performing. She was not calculating. She was not reading signals or filing observations or running a case in the background while her body occupied one space and her mind occupied another. She was entirely where she was, doing entirely what she was doing, and the purity of that—the simple, animal directness of a body responding to another body without the interference of a mind that won't stop working—was so far from my experience that watching it felt like looking at a country I'd never visit.

I felt the heat of it. In my chest. Lower. The specific arousal that comes not from what you're seeing but from what you're imagining—yourself in that room, yourself against that desk, yourself with your head tipped back and someone's mouth on your throat and the exquisite freedom of having forgotten, even for a moment, to be anyone other than what your body wants you to be.

I stepped back. Quietly. The door remained ajar. The sound continued—softer now, deeper, the rhythm changing as whatever was happening in that room moved past the prologue and into something I had no right to witness. I walked back down the hallway toward the terrace and the music and the lantern light and the world where I was Catherine, Andrés's friend from New York, a woman at a party, a woman with a glass of champagne and a cover story and a case that wasn't solving itself and a man somewhere on this terrace who made her feel things she couldn't afford to feel.

The night air hit me. Warm. Salt. Jasmine. I breathed it in and felt the arousal dissipate—not disappear, but recede, banking itself like coals that would glow for hours. The party moved around me. Someone laughed. The DJ played something with a bass line that I felt in my sternum.

Andrés found me. He always found me—it was one of his gifts, the ability to locate me in any room, in any crowd, as if I emitted a frequency only he could hear.

"You disappeared," he said.

"I went to find the bathroom."

"And did you?"

"I found something," I said, which was true and meaningless and he took it as a joke and smiled and put his arm around my waist and I leaned into him and felt his warmth and his solidity and thought about the woman in the room with her head tipped back and her hands in someone's hair and I thought: that is what it looks like to let go. I have never looked like that. I don't know if I can.

We stayed another hour. We danced on the lower terrace—slowly, his hand on the small of my back, my head against his shoulder. I let the music and the champagne and the warm air do their work, and for a few minutes I came close to the thing I'd seen through the doorway. Not the act. The freedom. My mind quieted. My body softened against his. The case receded. The performance dropped away, or almost dropped away—there was always a thread of it, always one layer still watching, still cataloging, but the thread was thinner tonight than it had ever been, and the woman underneath it was closer to the surface, and Andrés held that woman as if he knew she was fragile and temporary and would disappear the moment the music stopped.

The drive back to the city was quiet. His hand on my knee. The road unwinding in the headlights. The sea invisible but audible, breaking against the coast in the dark. I put my head against the window and watched the palms pass and didn't speak because speaking would have required choosing which woman to be, and I wasn't ready.

He dropped me at the hotel. Kissed me at the entrance—long, slow, his hand on the side of my face. Not coming up tonight. Not pushing. The kiss said: I'll be here. The restraint was, in its way, more intimate than anything that had happened in the bedroom.

"Goodnight, Catherine."

"Goodnight, Andrés."

I went upstairs alone. The room was dark. The courtyard was quiet. I stood at the French doors and looked out at the old city's sleeping rooftops and felt the coals still glowing—the banked heat from the hallway, from the doorway, from the glimpse of freedom I'd stolen and couldn't return—and I pressed my forehead against the cool glass and closed my eyes and let myself want without doing anything about it.

Wanting without acting. The particular torture of a woman who has taught herself that control is survival and who has just seen, in a lamplit room at a villa outside Cartagena, what survival costs.

Three days left. And the woman in the hallway—not the woman behind the door, but the woman standing outside it, watching, wanting, unable to cross the threshold—was, I was beginning to understand, the most honest portrait of myself I'd ever seen.

CHAPTER SIXTEEN

THE FIRST REVELATION – *Cartagena*

It arrived at ten in the morning. An encrypted file from Ezra, delivered to my laptop through the secure channel we use when the contents are too sensitive for a phone call. The subject line said: Rafael network — COMPLETE. Priority.

I was drinking coffee. I was thinking about Andrés. I was thinking about the villa, the dance on the terrace, the kiss at the hotel entrance, the way he'd said goodnight, Catherine with a tenderness that I was still carrying in my chest twelve hours later like a small, warm stone. I was thinking about whether to call him or wait for him to call me, which is the kind of calculation that a forty-seven-year-old woman should be too old and too experienced to make but isn't, because that particular mathematics never gets simpler no matter how many times you do it.

I opened the file.

Ezra had built what he called a network topology—a map of every person, entity, and communication pathway connected to Rafael Herrera, organized in concentric circles of proximity. Rafael at the center. His known contacts in the first ring. Their contacts in the second. Financial connections in the third. The map was dense, meticulous, the product of days of digital surveillance and financial tracing and the particular obsessive thoroughness that makes Ezra the best in the world at what he does.

I started at the center and worked outward. Rafael. Grupo Escudo. The Bogotá law firm. The VoIP relay through Panama. The Cayman Islands holding company. Names I recognized from Lucía's briefings, businesses I'd flagged, communication patterns I'd been tracking for days. The architecture was becoming clearer—a network of security, legal, and financial infrastructure that supported Rafael's operations and connected him to the broader ecosystem of Cartagena's invisible economy.

Then I reached the second ring.

Ezra had included photographs where available. Headshots pulled from corporate registries, social media, press archives. Most were low resolution, functional—the kind of images that exist in databases and tell you nothing about the person beyond the shape of their face. I was scrolling through them methodically, matching names to faces, filing each one, when my hand stopped on the trackpad.

The photograph was better quality than the others. A corporate headshot, formal, taken against a neutral background. The man in it was wearing a dark suit, no tie, white shirt open at the collar. His hair was dark, threaded with gray at the temples. His face was angular, lived-in, the kind of face that gets better with time because the bones were always the story. He was not smiling. His expression was neutral, composed, the face of a man sitting for a photograph he didn't want taken.

The name beneath the photograph was Andrés Salcedo.

I didn't move. I didn't breathe. I sat in my hotel room with the Caribbean light pouring through the French doors and the coffee going cold on the desk and I looked at the face of the man I'd been sleeping with for three nights and I understood.

Andrés. Andrés Salcedo. The head of the Salcedo cartel. The most powerful criminal in Cartagena. The man whose wife had slept with Cole Hartwell in St. Barts. The man whose wife's infidelity was the reason I was in this city. The man Lucía had described as the most polite man in Colombia who would also kill you without hesitation. The man who had kissed my scar in the dark and told me I was extraordinary and held my hand in the Plaza de Santo Domingo and said we're the same.

We're the same.

I closed the laptop. Slowly. The way you close a door on a room that's on fire—not because closing it will stop the fire but because you need one second, one single second, between seeing the flames and deciding what to do about them.

My training took over. Not immediately—there was a gap, maybe three seconds, maybe five, where I was not an operative and not a professional and not the best fixer in the world but just a woman sitting alone in a hotel room with the knowledge that she had been naked and vulnerable and honest with a man who was the center of the case she'd been sent to solve. Five seconds where I was just Catherine, and Catherine was falling.

Then Cat arrived. And Cat was ice.

I opened the laptop again. Read the full dossier. Andrés Salcedo. Born 1977, Buenaventura. That was true. His mother, the house cleaner who read poetry. That was true too. The London School of Economics—true. Four languages—true. The art collection, the literacy foundation, the dinners with the governor—all true. Everything he'd told me was true. Every word was accurate. The truths were so perfectly arranged that they formed a wall, and behind the wall was the thing he hadn't told me: an organization that moved more cocaine through the Caribbean corridor than any other operation in Colombia.

Investments. Logistics. I move things from places where they exist to places where they're wanted.

I remembered his voice saying that. The wry self-awareness. The charm. I remembered laughing. I remembered thinking: I like this man.

I went through the dossier line by line. His organization's estimated annual revenue. His known associates. His properties—four in Cartagena, two in Bogotá, one in Miami, one in Madrid. His wife.

His wife. Gabriela Montero. Thirty-two. The woman in the photographs with Cole Hartwell. The woman whose affair was the trigger for the crisis that had brought me to Cartagena. The wife of the man who had, four nights ago, traced a line on my shoulder in the dark and told me that words were the only thing that couldn't be taken from you.

He had a wife. He had a wife and he'd walked into a party and found me by the fountain and introduced himself as Andrés, just Andrés, and he'd taken me to dinner in Getsemaní and he'd kissed my scar and he'd said we're the same and none of it—none of it—had included the information that he was married to the woman at the center of my case.

The coffee was cold. The light was bright. The courtyard sounds drifted up—a bird, a fountain, the distant clatter of housekeeping. The ordinary world continuing while mine split down the middle.

I did not cry. I did not break anything. I did not call anyone. These are the things I did:

I read the entire dossier twice. I memorized the key details. I cross-referenced his known associates with the names I'd met at Carmen's party and at the villa. Mauricio—construction and shipping—was listed as a known business associate. Six other names from the villa appeared in the network map. The party where I'd met Andrés was a Salcedo social event. The villa was a Salcedo gathering. I had been moving through his world for days without knowing it.

Lucía had tried to point him out at Carmen's party. Tall. Navy suit. He was heading toward the back of the house. The rear courtyard. Where Andrés had gone to make a phone call.

The same man. The same man in the same suit walking through the same courtyard, and I hadn't seen it because I wasn't looking, because I was laughing, because a man I liked was standing in front of me and I'd decided he was safe.

I closed the laptop for the second time. I stood up. I walked to the bathroom. I turned on the shower. I stood under the water and I let it be as hot as I could bear and I stared at the tile and I didn't think about the scar or the kiss or the dance on the terrace or the way he'd said goodnight, Catherine. I didn't think about any of it. I put it in a box. I locked the box. I buried it.

When I got out of the shower, I was a different woman than the one who'd gone in. Not different—restored. The woman who'd been cracking open for days, who'd danced on a terrace and cried during sex and stood outside a doorway wanting a freedom she couldn't name—that woman was gone. In her place was the woman I'd been before Cartagena. Before the party. Before the balcony and the trumpet and the hand in the plaza.

Cat Sloane. Ice and angles and the particular clarity that comes from having your heart broken in a way that removes all ambiguity about what you're dealing with.

I got dressed. Dark clothes. Working clothes. No softness, no linen, nothing that the woman named Catherine would have chosen. I sat down at the desk and opened the laptop for the third time and I began to assess, with the cold precision of a woman who has been trained to turn devastation into data, exactly how compromised I was and what I was going to do about it.

Two days left. And the man I'd been falling for was the reason I was here.

CHAPTER SEVENTEEN

THE SECOND REVELATION – *Cartagena*

The first thing I did after I stopped shaking was call Ezra and tell him to look again.

Not the words I used. The words I used were precise, professional, stripped of everything that was happening inside me the way you strip a wire to get to the current underneath. I told him I needed a deeper analysis of the financial connections between Rafael Herrera's network and the Salcedo organization. I told him to trace every payment, every contract, every shell company that connected Grupo Escudo to any entity associated with Andrés Salcedo. I told him I needed it in hours, not days.

Ezra, to his credit, didn't ask why the urgency had changed. He heard something in my voice—I don't know what, because I was controlling it with the discipline of a woman who has been trained to lie under polygraph, but Ezra hears frequencies that machines miss—and he simply said, "On it. Give me four hours."

He delivered in three.

The financial architecture was elegant. That was the first thing I noticed, and I hated myself for noticing it, because elegant was the word I'd used in my head about Andrés's conversation and his suit and the way he moved through a room, and now I was using it about his money, and the consistency was making me sick.

Grupo Escudo—Rafael's security company—received its primary funding through a management company registered in Panama called Inversiones del Pacífico. Ezra had identified Inversiones del Pacífico three days ago as a node in the broader network, but he'd categorized it as a standard Cartagena holding structure—unremarkable, one of dozens. What he hadn't been able to see until I gave him the Salcedo connection to look for was what sat behind the Panamanian shell.

Inversiones del Pacífico was funded by a trust based in Liechtenstein. The trust was administered by a law firm in Zurich. The Zurich firm had exactly one other client in Latin America: a foundation called Fundación Horizonte, which funded literacy programs on the Pacific coast of Colombia. The foundation's board of directors included three names. One of them was Andrés Salcedo.

The literacy foundation. The one from the dossier. The one that made him look like a philanthropist, the one that journalists cited when they wrote careful profiles about the businessman from Buenaventura who had come so far and done so much for his community. The foundation was real. The literacy programs were real. And the same financial architecture that funded children learning to read also funded Rafael Herrera's security operation.

The money was clean by the time it reached Grupo Escudo—laundered through enough layers that any individual transaction looked legitimate. But the source was Salcedo. Follow the money far enough and every river led back to the same ocean.

Rafael didn't work for himself. Rafael worked for Andrés Salcedo.

The communication patterns confirmed it.

Ezra had cracked the VoIP relay through Panama two days ago but hadn't been able to identify the endpoint. Now, with the Salcedo organization as a reference frame, the data resolved. The relay routed to a communications hub that served multiple endpoints—one of which was a phone registered to a security consultant employed by a company that provided personal protection services to Andrés Salcedo's household.

Rafael's daily calls—the ones under ninety seconds, every evening between six and seven—weren't going to some anonymous handler. They were going to Salcedo's personal security apparatus. Rafael was checking in. Reporting. The way an employee reports to management, the way a soldier reports to command, the way a man who has been given a job confirms daily that the job is proceeding as planned.

The blackmail was not a desperate brother's gambit. The blackmail was an operation. Planned, funded, and directed by the same man who had looked at me across a candlelit courtyard and said, you're not from Cartagena.

I sat at the desk with Ezra's data on the screen and I let the full weight of it settle over me the way weather settles—slowly, completely, with the patient inevitability of something that was always coming and that I should have seen.

Andrés Salcedo had sent Rafael to St. Barts. Had put him on that hillside with a long lens. Had orchestrated the photographs of his own wife with Cole Hartwell. Had designed the blackmail to force the White House into a crisis that required exactly the kind of person the White House would send—someone smart, discreet, capable of investigating sealed federal files and navigating the space between legitimate and criminal.

Someone like me.

The question I'd filed in Chapter Thirteen—why the blackmail when there's a legal path?—now had an answer, and the answer was that the blackmail and the legal path were serving different masters. The lawyers in Bogotá were working Miguel Herrera's appeal because the appeal was real—Miguel's conviction was genuinely built on compromised testimony. That part of the story was true. But the blackmail wasn't about freeing Miguel. The blackmail was about something else entirely, something that required presidential-level attention and intelligence-community-level access, and I didn't yet know what that something was.

I could feel the shape of it. A third layer beneath the two I'd mapped. The surface: a desperate brother blackmails the President. The second layer: the blackmail is orchestrated by Salcedo. The third layer: Salcedo's actual objective, the real game, the thing the entire crisis was built to achieve.

I didn't have the third layer yet. But I could feel it the way you feel a room you haven't entered—the draft under the door, the sound of something moving behind the wall.

I should have called Kessler.

The professional calculation was straightforward: the case had fundamentally changed, the client needed to know, and withholding material information from the White House Chief of Staff was the kind of decision that ends careers and occasionally ends people. Kessler had hired me to neutralize a blackmail threat. The threat was not what he thought it was. He needed to know.

I didn't call him.

I should have called Sophie.

Sophie was my operational coordinator. She tracked every thread of every case. She maintained the files, managed the communications, anticipated what I needed before I knew I needed it. She was, in every way that mattered, my partner, and partners don't keep information from each other because information is oxygen and a partner who can't breathe is a partner who can't function.

I didn't call her.

I could tell you the reasons. I could explain that I needed to verify before I escalated, that incomplete intelligence is more dangerous than no intelligence, that the responsible course of action was to wait until I understood the full picture before I brought anyone else into it. These are the reasons a professional would give, and they are not wrong. They are also not the truth.

The truth is that I was ashamed.

Not of sleeping with Andrés. I'm a grown woman; I make my choices and I live with them. The shame was something more specific, more surgical: I had been fooled. I had looked at a man across a room and failed to see what he was. I, who read people for a living, who had spent twenty years in a profession where misreading someone could get you killed, who had built an entire post-agency career on the foundation of my ability to see through surfaces to the structure underneath—I had looked at Andrés Salcedo and seen a man who understood me. I had looked at the most polite man in Colombia who would also kill you without hesitation and I had seen a mirror.

The mirror was a lie. Or it wasn't—and that was worse, because if the recognition was real, if the connection was genuine even though the context was a deception, then I had experienced something true inside something false, and the task of separating the real from the manufactured was the kind of emotional archaeology that I was not equipped to perform, not now, not with two days left and a case that had just detonated in my hands.

So I carried it alone. The way I carried everything. The way I'd carried Fallujah, and the scar, and the word never, and the forty-seven minutes that lived in a locked room in my chest. I added Andrés Salcedo to the inventory of things I couldn't share and I closed the ledger and I went to work.

I spent the afternoon rebuilding the case from the ground up.

Everything I'd done in Cartagena needed to be reassessed through the lens of Salcedo's involvement. Every contact, every conversation, every piece of intelligence—tainted or not? Reliable or planted? The party at Carmen's mansion—had Andrés known who I was when he approached me at the fountain? Had the meeting been accidental or engineered? The villa—was I being shown something, or was I being monitored? Every memory had to be reopened, examined, and either verified or discarded.

This is the work that doesn't appear in the stories people tell about intelligence. Not the car chases, not the seductions, not the clever gambits in candlelit rooms. The real work is sitting alone at a desk, going through data, questioning everything you thought you knew, rebuilding the architecture of a case that someone has deliberately filled with mirrors. It is tedious and necessary and it is the difference between surviving and being played.

I started with what I could verify independently. Lucía. Was she compromised? Had she known who Andrés was when she'd pointed out the man in the navy suit at Carmen's party? I replayed the conversation. She'd said: I saw his face but not for long. She'd described him heading toward the back of the house. Had she been lying? Had she known I was standing with Salcedo and chosen not to tell me?

No. I ran the logic. Lucía had been across the room. She'd been trying to reach me. She'd seen a man matching Salcedo's general description moving through the crowd and then moving toward the rear courtyard. She had not seen me with him. She had not connected the man she'd glimpsed with the man I'd been talking to. Two women in a crowded room, each tracking a different thread, and the threads had been the same thread all along.

Lucía was clean. I was almost certain. I would verify further, but the logic held.

Ezra. Clean. He was in Lisbon, working from data, and his work had been the thing that revealed the truth. If he'd been compromised, the truth would never have surfaced.

David. Clean. The DEA files, the CI-7 investigation, the Iraq-era cross-reference—all genuine intelligence obtained through legitimate channels.

The only compromised element in my operation was me.

I had been inside Salcedo's house—literally, at the villa. I had been inside his social circle. I had been inside his bed. If he knew who I was —if he had known from the beginning that I was the fixer the White House had sent—then every moment we'd spent together was intelligence. He knew my face, my voice, my habits, my vulnerabilities. He knew I had a scar that I didn't talk about. He knew I cried during sex. He knew I said stay in the dark and meant it.

He had mapped my interior the way Ezra had mapped his financial network—carefully, thoroughly, with the patience of someone who understands that the most valuable intelligence is not the kind you steal but the kind that's given to you freely by someone who doesn't know they're giving it.

I felt something move in my chest. Not grief. Not heartbreak. Something colder. The specific, clean fury of a woman who has been used, and who knows exactly what it feels like because she has been used before—by institutions, by operations, by the machinery of a profession that treats people as instruments and calls it patriotism.

Fallujah was an institution using me as a tool and calling it duty. Andrés was a man using me as a tool and calling it intimacy.

Different mechanism. Same result. The expendable woman, asked to hold her position while something she can't see plays out around her.

The fury was useful. Fury, unlike grief, has a direction. It moves you forward. It sharpens the focus and narrows the field and turns the scattered energy of devastation into something pointed, something with an edge. Grief sits. Fury acts.

I chose fury.

At six in the evening—the hour when Rafael Herrera would be making his daily check-in call to Salcedo's security apparatus—I stood at the French doors and looked out at the city that had become, in the space of six hours, an entirely different landscape. The same rooftops. The same cathedral dome. The same wall tracing its line to the sea. But the city I'd been falling in love with was a stage set now, and the beautiful man who'd walked me through its streets at midnight was the director, and I had been performing a role I didn't know I'd been cast in.

My phone lit up on the desk. A text from a number I recognized. Andrés.

Tonight? I miss you.

Three words and a question mark. The same warmth. The same casual confidence. I miss you. As if missing were something he was entitled to do, as if the word carried no weight beyond its surface, as if a man could orchestrate a crisis and seduce the woman sent to solve it and then text her I miss you at sunset and mean it.

Did he mean it? That was the question I couldn't answer and couldn't afford to ask. Because the answer might be yes, and a yes would mean that something real had existed inside the deception, and the existence of something real would make everything infinitely more complicated than the clean narrative of a woman deceived by a monster.

I wanted him to be a monster. Monsters are simple. Monsters don't kiss your scar in the dark and tell you you're extraordinary. Monsters don't talk about their mothers.

I picked up the phone. I typed a response. Kept it short, warm, normal. The response of a woman who didn't know. Because I needed him to believe I didn't know. Because whatever the third layer was—whatever Salcedo was actually after—I couldn't reveal that I'd seen behind the curtain. Not yet. Not until I understood the full game.

Can't tonight. Early morning. Tomorrow?

I sent it. Set the phone down. Looked at the city. Breathed.

Two days left. The man I'd been falling for was the architect of the crisis I'd been sent to solve. The blackmail was orchestrated. Rafael was an employee. And somewhere beneath it all, a third layer waited—the real game, the actual objective, the thing that all of this theater had been built to achieve.

I was going to find it. And then I was going to dismantle it with the same precision that had built it, and when I was done, Andrés Salcedo was going to understand that the woman he'd underestimated was the most dangerous person he had ever invited into his life.

I am very good at what I do. And what I do, when someone uses me as a tool, is become the sharpest tool in the room and cut my way out.

CHAPTER EIGHTEEN

THE FULL PICTURE – *Cartagena*

It came together at three in the morning, the way the worst revelations always do—not in a flash but in a slow, nauseating click, like a bone settling into a socket that was never meant to hold it.

I was at the desk. I hadn't slept. The room was dark except for the laptop screen and the faint courtyard light through the French doors, and I'd been staring at Ezra's data for hours, running the same patterns, asking the same questions, and getting answers that I didn't want because the answers pointed to something so much larger than what I'd been hired to solve that the original case—the photographs, the blackmail, Cole Hartwell's safety—now looked like a movie set built to disguise the construction happening behind it.

The question I'd been circling was this: Why?

Salcedo had orchestrated the crisis. Sent Rafael to photograph his own wife with the President's son. Engineered the blackmail. Designed the threat to force the White House into action. But for what? What did Salcedo want that required this level of elaborate, expensive, dangerous theater?

Not Cole. Cole Hartwell was an insult—a man who'd slept with his wife—but Salcedo was not a man who built operations to address personal insults. He was a strategist. A businessman. Every action served an objective, and the objective was always structural, never emotional. The crisis wasn't about Cole.

Not leverage over the President. Blackmail against the White House was a high-risk, low-reward strategy for a man who already had political connections on three continents. Salcedo dined with the governor. He had relationships with officials in Bogotá, Washington, Madrid. He didn't need to manufacture leverage through photographs. He had subtler, safer instruments.

So what required this? What required a crisis severe enough to force the President's hand, urgent enough to demand the deployment of someone with intelligence community access, sensitive enough that the person deployed would need to dig into sealed federal files?

CI-7.

The word surfaced in my mind like a body rising from dark water.

I went back to the data. Operation Bright Horizon. Fourteen convictions. One informant underpinning all of them. Two convictions overturned because the informant was compromised. Miguel Herrera's thirty-year sentence built on the same testimony.

But CI-7 wasn't just a witness who testified against drug traffickers. CI-7 was an informant who had been inside or close to the Salcedo organization. The testimony that convicted Miguel Herrera included detailed knowledge of trafficking routes, logistics networks, distribution chains—the operational architecture of the Caribbean corridor. That level of detail didn't come from casual observation. It came from someone embedded in the system. Someone close to the center.

CI-7 was a mole in Salcedo's operation. And Salcedo had been hunting the mole for years.

The entire architecture of the crisis crystallized. Salcedo didn't care about the photographs. He didn't care about Cole Hartwell. He cared about CI-7. He needed the informant's identity, and the identity was sealed behind walls that he couldn't breach through his usual channels—no amount of money, no political connection, no legal maneuver could access a DEA compartmented file protected by real-time monitoring.

But the White House could. If the President's son was in mortal danger, the White House would send someone capable of accessing those files. And that someone would investigate Operation Bright Horizon because the blackmail pointed there—Rafael's brother, Miguel's conviction, the CI-7 testimony. The investigator would dig. The investigator would find the sealed files. The investigator would push for access, lean on contacts, use whatever clearance and connections they had to surface the informant's identity.

And then Salcedo would take it from them. Through negotiation, or leverage, or the simple fact that the investigator was now compromised—sleeping with the cartel boss, photographed in his company, embedded in his social circle, carrying intelligence that would be career-ending if it became public.

The entire crisis was a machine built to extract one piece of information: a name. CI-7's name. The identity of the person who had betrayed Andrés Salcedo from inside his own organization.

And I was the extraction tool.

I sat in the dark and I let it wash over me—the full scope, the complete architecture, the breathtaking sophistication of a plan that used a president's love for his son, a woman's desire for freedom, a brother's devotion, and a fixer's competence as interlocking gears in a machine designed to produce a single output.

I had been played. Not carelessly, not clumsily—played with the precision and patience of a man who understood systems the way I understood people. Salcedo had built a trap so elegant that the person inside it would do exactly what he needed without ever knowing they were trapped. Every step I'd taken in Cartagena—every call to David, every analysis of the DEA files, every push toward CI-7—had been the intended outcome. I wasn't solving a case. I was running an errand for the man who'd designed the case for me to run.

Fallujah. The word rose from the place I keep it and I couldn't push it back.

Hold your position, Sloane. We need you to hold.

A radio voice. A dying man beside me. The forty-seven minutes where I held my position because I was told to hold my position, while the operation I couldn't see played out around me, and the institution that had sent me there used my obedience and my competence and my love for the man bleeding on the floor beside me as instruments in a calculation I was never supposed to understand.

The same thing. The same thing dressed in a different suit, speaking a different language, kissing my scar instead of issuing orders. The expendable woman, positioned where she's useful, kept ignorant of the larger game, used until the using is done and then left to carry whatever damage the using inflicts.

I closed the laptop. I put on shoes. I picked up the car keys that Lucía had left for me—a rental, anonymous, parked in the hotel garage —and I walked out of the room because if I stayed in that room for one more minute I was going to break something, and I wasn't certain whether it would be the furniture or myself.

I drove. Not to anywhere—away from. Through the sleeping streets of the old city, out through the wall gate at the Torre del Reloj, along the bay road toward Bocagrande where the high-rises were dark except for the occasional lit window of someone else who couldn't sleep. The road was empty. The city was quiet. The Caribbean was invisible to my right, audible only as a low, constant susurration—the sound the world makes when it doesn't care what's happening to you.

I pulled over on a side street off the main road. A residential block. Dark houses, parked cars, a streetlamp at the far corner casting enough light to see by and not enough to be seen. I turned off the engine. The car ticked as it cooled. The air conditioning died and the Cartagena heat moved in immediately—thick, humid, the kind of warmth that presses against your skin like a hand.

I sat in the dark and I breathed and I tried to think and I couldn't think because my body was doing something my mind hadn't authorized.

The adrenaline had been building for hours. Since the revelation. Since the moment the full picture assembled itself and I understood what had been done to me and by whom. My body had been in crisis mode—elevated heart rate, shallow breathing, the low-grade tremor in my hands that I'd been hiding by keeping them flat on the desk or wrapped around a coffee mug. Survival chemistry. The ancient flood of cortisol and adrenaline that the body produces when it perceives a threat, designed to make you run or fight, useless when the threat is a man who isn't in the room and a realization that can't be outrun.

And now, in the parked car on the dark street, the chemistry was converting. This is the thing about adrenaline that nobody tells you, or that everyone knows and nobody says: the pathways are shared. Fear and arousal run on the same wiring. The same flood, the same heat, the same narrowing of focus to a single point. The body doesn't always know the difference. My body had never known the difference. The agency had taught me many things, but the thing my body had taught itself—without permission, without consultation, without my consent—was that when fear peaks, desire follows, because desire has a beginning and a middle and an end that resolves, and fear has no end, and the body, in its animal wisdom, will choose the sensation that offers closure over the one that doesn't.

I felt it building. The heat low in my belly that had nothing to do with the temperature and everything to do with the chemicals flooding my system, looking for an outlet, looking for a resolution the mind couldn't provide. I was furious and I was terrified and I was turned on, and the combination was so fundamentally inappropriate that a different woman might have been horrified.

I had been a different woman. Years ago. I had been horrified, and then ashamed, and then I'd spent a long time in a profession where your body is the only instrument you can trust when everything else is lying, and I had learned that when my body tells me something, the smartest thing I can do is listen.

I listened.

My hand moved without ceremony. Under the waistband of my trousers, past the elastic edge of cotton, to the slick heat that was already there—my body ahead of my decision, as always, the flesh committing before the mind agrees to follow. I was wet. The kind of wet that arrives without invitation and answers a question you didn't ask, and the first touch of my own fingers sent a shock through me that had nothing to do with pleasure and everything to do with relief—the relief of finally, finally doing something with the unbearable energy that had been building in me for hours.

I didn't close my eyes. I watched the dark street. The empty houses. The distant streetlamp. The windshield misted faintly from the heat of me in the cooling car, and the air smelled like the sea and the leather seats and sweat and the sharp, private scent of my own arousal, and I worked myself with the efficiency of a woman who knows exactly what she needs and is not performing for anyone—no tenderness, no seduction, no narrative of desire. Just pressure. Rhythm. The focused, deliberate pursuit of a single outcome.

My breath shortened. My left hand gripped the steering wheel. I thought about nothing—that was the point, that was the gift, the ten seconds where the mind stops its relentless grinding and there is nothing in the world except the body and what the body is feeling. Not Andrés. Not the case. Not Fallujah. Not the forty-seven minutes or the scar or the word never. Just the building wave, and my fingers, and the slickness, and the heat, and the knowledge that for these few seconds I was not a woman who had been used but a woman using herself, and the distinction was everything.

I came hard. Harder than I expected. A sound I didn't recognize—half gasp, half something rawer—and my body clenched around the absence of anyone and the presence of my own hand and the wave broke and I let it break and I rode it with my eyes open and my teeth clenched and the streetlamp blurring through the misted windshield. Thirty seconds. Maybe less.

The aftermath was immediate and physical. My heart hammering. My hand trembling against the damp cotton. The taste of adrenaline in the back of my throat—metallic, sharp. I withdrew my hand. Wiped it on my thigh. Breathed.

There are women who would be horrified by this. Who would see a problem to be solved, a dysfunction to be treated, a symptom of damage so fundamental that it requires professional intervention and a vocabulary of clinical terms. I used to be one of those women. Then I spent fifteen years in a profession where your body is the only thing you can trust when everything else is lying, and I learned that when my body finds a trapdoor, I'm not going to board it up just because the exit is undignified.

The truth is simpler than the psychology. The truth is that for ten seconds, I wasn't afraid. And fear is the thing I'm least willing to feel and most unable to escape, and if my body has found a way through it —brief, graceless, solitary, conducted in a parked car on a dark street in a city that has betrayed me—then I will take that way and I will not apologize and I will not explain it to anyone, including you.

I sat in the car for another minute. The windshield cleared. The night reassembled itself—the street, the houses, the distant sound of the sea. My heartbeat returned to something approaching normal. The tremor in my hands was gone. The fear was still there—the fear is always there—but it had been momentarily displaced, and in the space that the displacement created, something else moved in.

Clarity.

I started the car.

I drove back to the hotel with the windows down and the warm salt air moving through the car and I began to think—not with the frantic, circular thinking of the previous hours but with the clean, linear thinking of a woman who has discharged the static and can finally hear the signal.

Salcedo wanted CI-7's name. I didn't have it. David couldn't get it. The identity was compartmented behind walls that would require a sustained assault to breach, and any such assault would trigger alarms that would burn David and expose the operation. The CI-7 angle was a dead end—I couldn't deliver what Salcedo wanted, even if I'd been willing to, which I wasn't.

But Salcedo didn't know that.

Salcedo didn't know what I had and what I didn't have. He knew I'd been investigating Operation Bright Horizon. He knew I'd been in contact with the intelligence community. He knew, because his people had been monitoring me since I arrived, that I was pushing on the DEA files. What he didn't know was whether I'd succeeded. He was waiting for me to surface the name—waiting for the tool to deliver its output.

I could bluff. I had enough from the sealed files to be credible—the operation's details, the documented inconsistencies, the two overturned convictions, the internal DEA concern. I knew the shape of CI-7 even if I didn't know the face. In a negotiation, I could imply knowledge I didn't have. I could let Salcedo fill the gaps himself. I could play poker with an empty hand and a perfect face.

But a bluff only buys time. It doesn't solve the underlying problem. Even if I convinced Salcedo I had CI-7's name, the exchange has no enforcement mechanism. He gives me the photographs. I give him the name. He can always make copies of the photographs. I can only give the name once. The moment the trade is complete, his leverage regenerates and mine is spent.

I needed something better than a negotiated exchange. I needed leverage that didn't expire. I needed something that Salcedo couldn't replicate, couldn't copy, couldn't regenerate. Something he valued more than CI-7, or at least something whose loss would threaten him more than CI-7's continued anonymity.

I turned onto the bay road. The high-rises of Bocagrande to my left, the dark sea to my right. The first hint of dawn on the eastern horizon—not light yet, but the suggestion of light, the sky going from black to the deepest possible blue.

And then I saw it. The way you see anything important—not gradually, not through analysis, but all at once, the complete picture arriving in your mind like a photograph developing in a tray of chemicals, the image rising from nothing to everything in the space of a single breath.

Gabriela.

Gabriela Montero. Salcedo's wife. The woman in the photographs with Cole. The woman whose affair had been the trigger—or rather, the manufactured trigger—for the entire crisis. She'd been in Salcedo's house for six years. She'd seen the meetings. Heard the names. Watched the money move. Salcedo had treated his wife like furniture, and the thing about furniture is that furniture is always in the room.

If Gabriela was in Colombia, Salcedo controlled her. If Gabriela was outside Colombia—outside his reach, in the hands of someone who could protect her, with a deal and a debrief and a new identity—she was a nuclear weapon pointed at his entire operation. Everything she'd seen, everything she'd heard, everything she knew. Not a bluff. Not a trade that expires. A permanent deterrent, a structural stalemate, a Sword of Damocles that hangs as long as she draws breath.

I didn't need to give Salcedo what he wanted. I needed to take what he couldn't afford to lose.

I pulled into the hotel garage. Turned off the engine. Sat in the car as the dawn broke over Cartagena and the plan assembled itself in my mind with the precision and speed of something that had been waiting to be built—every piece clicking into place, every contingency accounted for, the entire architecture rising from the foundation of everything I'd learned in this city and everything I'd become in this profession and the specific, clarifying rage of a woman who has been played and intends to play back.

I needed Lucía. I needed Ezra. I needed Sophie—not in New York, in Cartagena. I needed David. I needed Kessler. I needed a yacht. And I needed Cole Hartwell.

I got out of the car. Walked to the elevator. Pressed the button for my floor. Looked at my reflection in the mirrored doors—dark clothes, no sleep, eyes that were red but clear, the face of a woman who has been through something and come out the other side not unscathed but sharper.

Two days. I had two days to build an extraction operation in a city controlled by the man who had engineered my presence here. Two days to move his wife out of Colombia, get her onto a boat in the Caribbean, reunite her with the man she'd reached for in St. Barts, and call Andrés Salcedo from international waters to tell him that the woman he'd underestimated had just dismantled the most important relationship in his life.

It was the most complicated thing I'd ever attempted. It was also, I realized with something between fury and satisfaction, the most Cat Sloane thing I'd ever done.

I went upstairs. I made coffee. I started making calls.

CHAPTER NINETEEN

THE MASK – *Cartagena*

He suggested coffee. I said yes. These are the words that do the work of arranging two people across a table from each other—simple, efficient, revealing nothing. He texted a café name and a time. I showed up four minutes late because punctuality is a tell and tells are things I could no longer afford.

The café was in the old city, a block from the cathedral, one of those small Colombian places where the coffee is exceptional and the pastries are afterthoughts and the tables are close enough together that you lower your voice without being asked. He was already there when I arrived. Corner table. Two coffees ordered. The chair angled so he could see the door, which I noticed because I would have done the same thing, which I noticed because I was now seeing everything about this man through a lens that stripped away charm and left only structure.

He stood when he saw me. Kissed my cheek. His lips warm against my skin. The scent of him—cedar, warmth, the particular smell of his neck that I had breathed in while falling asleep against his chest—hit me with a specificity that was almost violent, because the body doesn't know what the mind knows, and my body still responded to him the way it had before the photograph, before the dossier, before the parked car and the dawn and the architecture of what he'd done.

I sat down. I picked up the coffee. I smiled.

This is what it's like to perform for someone who is also performing: a hall of mirrors, every surface reflecting a surface, the real thing hidden behind iterations of the false thing so deep that you can't be sure the real thing still exists. I was pretending to be Catherine, the woman who didn't know. He was pretending to be Andrés, the man with no last name. And underneath both performances, the two actual people—the fixer and the cartel boss—sat across a table in a Cartagena café and played a game that would have been absurd if the stakes weren't lethal.

"You look tired," he said. Concern in his voice. Warmth in his eyes. The hand reaching across the table to touch mine—a gesture so natural, so unforced, that I felt my chest constrict with something that was either rage or longing and might have been both.

"Long night," I said. "The case."

"The case." He repeated it with a faint smile, the way he'd repeat anything I said that touched the edges of my professional life—interested, patient, careful not to push. I'd found this charming a week ago. I'd interpreted it as the respectful curiosity of a man who understood that my work was private and my privacy was sacred. Now I saw it for what it was: a door left open. An invitation to walk through it.

"Is it going well?" he asked.

"Complicated," I said. "More complicated than I expected."

"Cartagena has a way of complicating things. The city looks simple—beautiful weather, beautiful buildings, beautiful people. But underneath, every story has three layers, and the one you see first is almost never the one that matters."

Three layers. He'd said it without emphasis, casually, a man making conversation about his city. But the words landed in me like a knife because three layers was the exact architecture I'd mapped at three in the morning: the surface story, the orchestration, and CI-7. He was describing his own operation in the language of local wisdom, and the elegance of the misdirection—hiding the truth inside a truism—

was so characteristic of him that I wanted to laugh. Or scream. I did neither.

"Three layers," I said. "That sounds like experience talking."

"Business in Colombia is always three layers. The transaction. The relationship. And the thing nobody says out loud that determines whether the other two things are real." He sipped his coffee. His eyes steady on mine. "Your work must be similar. Consulting. Discretion. You must spend a great deal of time trying to determine what's real."

There it was. The opening. Gentle, almost imperceptible—the way a fisherman lets the line drift before he sets the hook. He was steering us toward my work. Toward the case. And the steering was so deft, so woven into the natural fabric of conversation, that a woman who didn't know what I knew would have walked straight through the door he'd opened and never noticed it was a door at all.

"I do," I said. "This case especially. There's a legal situation—I can't say much—that involves federal records. Sealed files. The kind of thing where the truth is locked behind doors that most people can't open, and the people who can open them aren't sure they want to."

I fed him this deliberately. Watched his face. A woman who didn't know would have offered it as a general complaint about the difficulty of her work—an intimate disclosure, the kind you make to someone you trust. I offered it as bait.

His expression didn't change. That was the tell. Because the appropriate response to a woman mentioning sealed federal files over coffee is mild interest at most—a polite question, a sympathetic murmur. What Andrés gave me was the precise absence of reaction that only a man who is controlling his response produces. The face didn't change because the face was being managed, and faces are only managed when the information being received matters enough to require management.

"Sealed files," he said. Neutral. Curious. The voice of a man who has no stake in the answer. "That sounds frustrating. What kind of case requires sealed federal files?"

"The kind where someone was convicted on testimony that might be compromised. An informant. The prosecution built its case on this person's word, and now there are questions about whether the word was reliable."

I watched him the way I'd been trained to watch—not his face, which he controlled beautifully, but the periphery. His hands. His posture. The microexpressions that live in the muscles around the eyes, the ones that fire before the conscious mind can intercept them. His right hand, the one with the scar between the thumb and forefinger—the scar I'd wanted to trace, the scar I now wondered had its own story that he'd never told me—his right hand tightened fractionally around the coffee cup. One degree of additional pressure. A fraction of a second. Then it relaxed.

He was interested. He was very, very interested. And he was working extremely hard not to show it.

"An informant," he said. "In Colombia, informants are—complicated. People inform for many reasons. Money. Protection. Revenge. And the people they inform on have long memories. If the testimony is compromised, the informant may be in as much danger as the person who was convicted."

This was not idle commentary. This was a man telling me, through the scrim of general observation, exactly why he wanted CI-7's name. Long memories. An informant inside his organization who had betrayed him, whose identity was sealed behind walls he couldn't reach, who was still out there, still a threat, still carrying knowledge that could bring down everything he'd built. He was telling me the stakes of his own hunt while pretending to make conversation.

"Have you been able to access the files?" he asked. Still casual. Still the tone of a man making polite inquiry into his lover's work. But the question itself was a surgical instrument—Have you been able to access the files?—and I felt it enter the conversation with the precision of a scalpel.

"Partially," I said. "I have a contact in Washington. Former government. He's been able to confirm that the informant existed and the testimony has problems. But the identity itself is behind a wall that's—difficult. Very classified. Very protected."

I gave him this because I wanted to see what he did with it. I was playing the conversation the way I'd play an interrogation—releasing information in controlled quantities, watching the response, calibrating the next release based on what the response revealed. The difference was that in an interrogation, the subject knows they're being interrogated. Andrés didn't know I was interrogating him. He thought he was interrogating me.

The layering made me dizzy if I thought about it too long. So I didn't think about it. I operated.

"Very protected," he repeated. And there—there—in the repetition, in the way he held the words, tasting them, a pause that lasted one beat too long before he set them down and moved on. The pause of a man calculating whether "very protected" meant inaccessible or merely difficult, and how much more pressure he would need to apply to move the needle from the second to the first.

"But not impossible," he said. Not a question. A statement. Testing the boundary.

"Nothing is impossible with enough time and the right leverage," I said. And I let the sentence sit there between us, weighted, ambiguous, a stone dropped into water whose ripples he would read however he chose.

He smiled. The warm smile. The one I'd fallen for on the balcony. The one that crinkled the skin at the corners of his eyes and made him look ten years younger and made me feel—even now, even knowing everything—made me feel seen. Which was the cruelest part of all this, the part that I would carry long after Cartagena: that the weapon he'd used against me was the thing I wanted most in the world, and the weapon still worked even when I could see it in his hand.

"You're remarkable, Catherine," he said. "The way you talk about your work—the precision, the determination. I don't think I've ever met anyone who approaches a problem the way you do."

Flattery. Validation. The specific kind of praise designed to make the recipient feel exceptional and therefore willing to continue performing the exceptional behavior being praised—in this case, digging into sealed DEA files and moving closer to CI-7's identity. He was reinforcing the behavior he wanted. The way you train an animal. The way you cultivate an asset.

I knew this. I knew exactly what he was doing. And the compliment still landed, still warmed something in me that I couldn't extinguish no matter how clearly I saw the mechanism. Because the mechanism and the sincerity might coexist—he might genuinely find me remarkable while simultaneously using that admiration as a tool—and the possibility of coexistence was the thing that made Andrés Salcedo the most dangerous man I'd ever sat across from.

"Thank you," I said. And meant it. And hated that I meant it.

The conversation drifted. He talked about a building he was restoring in the old city—a colonial house that had been a merchant's residence, then a school, then abandoned for twenty years. He described the process of restoration with the same attention to detail and the same love of structure that he brought to everything, and I listened and I watched and I thought: you are describing your own life. The restoration of a thing that was once valuable and fell into ruin and is being rebuilt by a man who understands that the bones are what matter, that the surface is decoration, that the real work happens in the structure nobody sees.

He was describing his cartel. He was describing the careful, patient, structural work of building an organization that moved cocaine through the Caribbean corridor with an efficiency that legitimate businesses would envy, and he was disguising it as architecture, and the disguise was so seamless that I almost admired it. Almost.

His hand was on mine. He'd moved it there during the conversation about the building—a natural escalation, the touch of a man who is comfortable with physical contact and uses it the way some people use punctuation, to emphasize, to connect, to close the distance between two sentences. His thumb traced the same pattern on my hand that it had traced in the plaza, the slow circular movement that I had once found soothing and now found unbearable, because his thumb on my skin was a lie and the lie felt exactly like the truth and I could not, in this café, at this table, with his eyes on me and his hand on mine, find the seam.

I didn't pull away.

I need you to understand why. Not because it felt good—though it did, and the feeling-good was its own kind of torment. I didn't pull away because pulling away would be a tell. A woman who has spent three nights with a man and is falling for him does not pull away when he touches her hand over coffee. A woman who has suddenly discovered that the man she's falling for is the head of a cartel might. The difference between those two women was the distance between my survival and my exposure, and I could not afford to close that distance by so much as the retraction of a hand.

So I let him touch me. I let his thumb move on my skin. I looked at his face—the face that was angular and lived-in and got better with time, the face I'd watched in profile on a balcony, the face I'd held between my hands while I kissed him in a dark street—and I performed the woman who didn't know with a discipline that would have made my instructors at the Farm proud and my therapist, if I'd had one, weep.

He asked if I was free tomorrow evening. He wanted to cook for me, he said. At his place. He'd never mentioned his place before—the geography of our relationship had been my hotel, neutral restaurants, other people's houses. His place was new territory. An escalation. In the language of the relationship we'd been building, it meant trust. In the language of the operation I now understood him to be running, it meant something else: moving me deeper into his world, increasing my dependence, making the eventual leverage stronger.

Or it meant he wanted to cook me dinner. That was the other possibility, the one I couldn't dismiss no matter how much I wanted to, because people are not chess pieces and motivations are rarely singular and the man sitting across from me might be simultaneously running an operation and falling in love, and the coexistence of those two things was the particular cruelty of this situation—that I would never know which was real, because the answer might be both, and both is worse than either.

"I'd like that," I said.

I wouldn't be there tomorrow evening. By tomorrow evening, if everything went the way I was planning, his wife would be on a boat in the Caribbean and his world would be on fire and the woman he'd been performing for would be the one holding the match.

But he didn't know that. He smiled. He squeezed my hand. He said, "It's a date," and the words hung in the air between us—ordinary, warm, the words of a man making plans with a woman he cared about—and I received them and held them and felt them cut.

We walked out of the café together. The old city was mid-morning bright, the sun already brutal, the streets filling with tourists and vendors and the daily commercial chaos of a neighborhood that has been selling its beauty to visitors for four hundred years. He kissed me at the corner. Not a long kiss—a goodbye kiss, the kiss of a man who has somewhere to be and will see you tomorrow. His mouth on mine. Brief. Warm. The taste of coffee.

I watched him walk away. Tall. Navy suit. Moving through the crowd with the ease of a man who owned the city—not metaphorically but actually, structurally, the way a landlord owns a building, the way a general owns a battlefield. I watched until he turned the corner and was gone.

Then I walked in the other direction, and as I walked I cataloged what I'd learned:

He was hunting CI-7. Confirmed. The conversation had been an extraction attempt—gentle, sophisticated, wrapped in intimacy, but an extraction attempt nonetheless. He wanted to know if I'd accessed the sealed files. He wanted to know if the identity was within reach. He wanted to know how much more time and leverage the tool required before it delivered its output.

He believed I didn't know who he was. Confirmed. Nothing in his behavior suggested he suspected my awareness. He was performing the same role he'd been performing since the fountain—the charming stranger, the man with no last name, the lover who asked about her work with just enough curiosity to seem invested without seeming intrusive. The performance was flawless. If I hadn't seen the photograph, I would still be inside it.

He was planning to bring me to his home. New. Significant. Either an escalation of the personal relationship or an escalation of the operation or both. The invitation to his place meant he was moving me closer to the center of his world, and the center of his world was where Gabriela lived.

Gabriela. The wife who had been in that house for six years. The wife who had seen the meetings, heard the names, watched the money move. The wife who was, at this moment, somewhere inside Andrés Salcedo's carefully constructed empire, and who would need to be outside it by tomorrow evening.

I walked through the old city streets with the sun on my face and the crowd pressing around me and the taste of his coffee still on my lips, and I thought: twenty-four hours. I have twenty-four hours to build an extraction operation, move a woman out of a cartel boss's compound, get her onto a yacht in the Caribbean, and end a game that was designed by one of the most sophisticated criminal minds in Colombia.

I had done harder things. Not many. But some.

I turned the corner onto my street and walked toward the Sofitel and didn't look back, because looking back is something you do when you're leaving and I wasn't leaving. Not yet. I was going to my hotel room to make phone calls and move pieces and build the thing I'd been building in my head since a parked car on a dark street at four in the morning.

Cat Sloane was going to work.

CHAPTER TWENTY

THE PLAN – *Cartagena*

I called Kessler at noon Washington time because noon is when Martin Kessler is at his most rational—after the morning briefings have burned off the day's first anxieties and before the afternoon's crises have generated new ones. There is a window, roughly forty-five minutes, where the White House Chief of Staff is capable of hearing something he doesn't want to hear without immediately converting it into a political calculation. I needed that window.

"Martin," I said. "The case is not what we thought it was. I need twenty minutes without interruption."

Silence. Not the silence of a man who hasn't heard you—the silence of a man clearing his deck. I heard a door close. The ambient noise of the White House—distant voices, the hum of a building that never sleeps—went quiet.

"Talk," he said.

I talked. I gave him everything, delivered in the compressed, precise language that Kessler requires—no narrative, no color, just architecture. The blackmail was orchestrated. Rafael Herrera works for Andrés Salcedo, head of the Salcedo cartel. Salcedo engineered the entire crisis—the affair, the photographs, the threat against Cole—to force the White House to deploy someone with intelligence community access. The objective was never a pardon for Miguel Herrera. The objective is CI-7: the identity of a sealed DEA informant whose testimony put multiple members of Salcedo's network in prison. CI-7 is a mole inside Salcedo's organization, and Salcedo has been hunting them for years. He built the crisis as an extraction mechanism—a machine designed to make us dig into the sealed files and surface the name for him.

I paused. Let it land.

"How certain are you?" Kessler asked. His voice had not changed. This is what makes Kessler good at his job—he receives catastrophic information the way a surgeon receives a patient: with a steady hand and no visible reaction until the assessment is complete.

"Certain enough to rebuild the case around it. The financial connections are documented—Salcedo funds Rafael's security company through a chain of shells that my tech specialist has traced. The communication patterns confirm Rafael reports to Salcedo's personal security apparatus daily. And I confirmed the CI-7 angle in a face-to-face conversation with Salcedo himself."

A beat. "A face-to-face conversation."

"He's been in contact with me since I arrived in Cartagena. Under his first name only. I didn't identify him until my team pulled his photograph from a corporate registry."

I gave Kessler this without elaboration. He could fill in whatever blanks he chose. The important thing was the operational reality, not the personal wreckage underneath it, and Kessler was a man who understood that distinction better than anyone I'd ever worked for.

"The CI-7 situation," he said. "Can we give him what he wants?"

"No. Three reasons. First, I don't have the identity. My contact at CIA was able to confirm CI-7 existed and the testimony is compromised, but the actual name is compartmented behind walls that can't be breached without triggering real-time monitoring. Second, even if we had the name, giving a cartel boss the identity of a federal informant is a death sentence for that informant. I won't do it, and you don't want the White House within a mile of it. Third, a negotiated exchange doesn't solve the underlying problem. Salcedo trades the photographs for the name. He can always have copies of the photographs. The moment the trade is complete, his leverage regenerates and ours is spent. We'd be buying time, not security."

"So the CI-7 angle is a dead end."

"As an exchange, yes. But I have something better."

I told him about Gabriela.

"Salcedo's wife has been in his house for six years. She has seen meetings, heard names, watched money move. She is the most comprehensive intelligence source on the Salcedo organization that has ever existed outside a federal database, and she's been sitting in his living room the entire time, treated like furniture. Furniture sees everything."

"You want to extract her."

"I want to extract her, get her out of Colombia, and put her somewhere Salcedo can't reach. Once she's outside his control and cooperating with American law enforcement—or even just credibly threatening to cooperate—she becomes a permanent deterrent. A nuclear weapon pointed at his entire operation. Not a trade that expires. A structural stalemate that holds as long as she's alive and free."

"And the photographs?"

"Become irrelevant. Once Gabriela is out, I call Salcedo and present the terms: leave the President alone, leave Cole alone, destroy everything connected to this operation. The alternative is that his wife, who has six years of firsthand intelligence on his organization, begins a formal debrief with federal prosecutors. The photographs become a minor embarrassment weighed against the dismantling of his entire enterprise. He's a businessman. He'll do the math."

Kessler was quiet. I counted the seconds—a habit from interrogation training, where silence is measured because silence is information. Five seconds. Seven. Ten.

"Does Gabriela want to leave?" he asked.

This was the right question. Not the political question, not the operational question—the human question. Does the woman at the center of this plan have agency in it? Kessler, for all his political calculation, had never lost the instinct to ask the question that mattered most.

"I believe so. She reached for Cole Hartwell in St. Barts. She chose that affair, or allowed it, which in the context of her marriage amounts to the same thing. A woman who risks everything to be with someone other than her husband is a woman who has already decided to leave. She just hasn't found the door yet. I'm going to build her one."

"You believe so. You don't know."

"I'll know within twelve hours. I have someone in Cartagena who can reach her."

Lucía. Who knew every door in this city and which ones could be opened quietly.

Kessler breathed. The sound of a man whose job is to protect the President being told that the protection requires an operation that, if it goes wrong, will create a crisis exponentially worse than the one it was designed to solve. The extraction of a cartel boss's wife from a compound in Colombia, orchestrated by a private consultant on an unofficial White House mandate, using CIA resources and a yacht in international waters. If it succeeds, it's a masterpiece. If it fails, it's an international incident.

"Walk me through the operation," he said.

I walked him through it. Five moving parts, coordinated across three countries, with a window of ninety minutes between Gabriela leaving the compound and Salcedo discovering she's gone.

"Part one: the misdirection. I request a meeting with Salcedo through intermediaries. Face-to-face. I present myself as having made progress on the CI-7 angle—I imply I'm close to the identity, that I need to negotiate terms for an exchange. This is the bluff. I have the shape of CI-7—enough operational detail to be credible—but not the name. I play poker with an empty hand and a perfect face. The meeting serves two purposes: it fixes Salcedo's attention on me, and it puts him in a location I control for the duration of the conversation."

"Part two: Sophie. My assistant flies to Cartagena tonight. Tomorrow, she checks into my hotel room. For the twelve hours before and during the extraction, Sophie performs Cat Sloane for Salcedo's surveillance. He has my room monitored—I'm certain of it. Sophie maintains the appearance that I'm at the hotel, working, while I'm actually running the extraction. She answers my phone, orders room service on my schedule, moves past the windows at the right intervals. She's twenty-four and she's been running my life for two years and she's smarter than anyone gives her credit for."

"Part three: Lucía. She's my local contact. Former journalist, current fixer, knows Cartagena's invisible infrastructure better than anyone. Lucía gets Gabriela out of the compound and to a rendezvous point at the marina. She has the access—she knows the staff networks, the delivery schedules, the gaps in Salcedo's domestic security. The compound is not a fortress. It's a home. And homes have vulnerabilities that fortresses don't."

"Part four: Ezra. My tech specialist in Lisbon. During the extraction window, Ezra provides digital cover. He generates false communications on my phone to reinforce Sophie's performance at the hotel. He loops or degrades the harbor security cameras for the departure window. He monitors Salcedo's communication channels in real time so we know the instant the operation is detected."

"Part five: the yacht. This is where I need you and David. I need a vessel in position in the waters off the Dutch Antilles—Curaçao or Bonaire, close enough to reach by rigid inflatable from Cartagena's harbor in a few hours. David arranges the receiving end: unofficial protection for Gabriela, a legal framework that keeps her out of Salcedo's reach, the beginning of a cooperation agreement with federal prosecutors. And I need Cole Hartwell on that yacht."

"Cole," Kessler said. The word carried the weight of the President's only son.

"Cole is the reason Gabriela will get on the boat. He's the reason she'll cooperate. He's the person she reached for when she was reaching for a way out, and if he's on that yacht when she arrives, she'll know this is real. Not a trick. Not another powerful man moving her from one cage to another. A choice. Her choice."

"You want me to put the President's son on a yacht in the

Caribbean while you extract a cartel boss's wife from a compound in Cartagena."

"Yes."

"And if it goes wrong?"

"If it goes wrong, I'm the one in Cartagena with Salcedo, not Cole. Cole is in international waters on a private vessel with no official connection to the United States government. He's a young man on a boat. The exposure is mine, not his, and not yours."

This was true. If the extraction failed, I would be the one facing Salcedo's fury in a city he controlled. The risk was mine. It had always been mine. That was the deal—the unwritten clause in every contract I'd ever taken: Cat Sloane absorbs the risk so the client doesn't have to.

Kessler's silence this time was longer. Fifteen seconds. I let it run.

"What do you need from me?" he said.

"Two things. Stay out of my way for the next twenty-four hours. And make sure the Department of Justice cooperates when this is over. Gabriela's protection needs to be real—not a promise, not a memo, but a formal agreement that survives any change in administration. If she's going to risk her life leaving that compound, she needs to know the door she's walking through doesn't close behind her."

"I'll make the calls," Kessler said. "David will have what he needs within the hour. Cole—" He paused. "I'll speak to the President."

"Martin."

"Yes."

"The President doesn't need to know the details. He needs to know his son is going to be on a boat and that the woman his son loves is going to be on it with him, and that both of them are going to be safe. That's all he needs."

"The President is not a man who accepts 'that's all he needs' from anyone."

"Then tell him Cat Sloane said so, and remind him that I'm the reason his son's photograph isn't on the front page of the Washington Post."

A sound that might have been a laugh. Kessler didn't laugh often, and when he did it was more exhalation than amusement, the release of tension rather than the expression of joy. "I'll call you back within the hour," he said, and hung up.

I made the calls.

Sophie first. I didn't explain everything—I gave her what she needed and nothing she didn't, because Sophie was twenty-four and brilliant and the daughter of a man who died because of an operation like this one, and I was not going to put her in danger without being precise about the scope. I told her I needed her in Cartagena by tomorrow morning. I told her she'd be performing as me for twelve hours—staying in my room, maintaining my patterns, keeping Salcedo's surveillance believing I was at the hotel while I was somewhere else. I told her there was risk.

"What kind of risk?" she asked. Her voice was level. She didn't sound scared. She sounded like her father.

"The man who's monitoring me is dangerous. He's not going to come to the room—he has no reason to suspect anything is wrong if you do this right. But if something goes sideways and he discovers the deception, you need to be out of that hotel in minutes. I'll give you an exit protocol. Lucía will have a car waiting."

"Cat."

"Yeah."

"I can do this."

I knew she could. That wasn't what worried me. What worried me was that she wanted to, with the same hungry competence her father had carried into every room he'd ever entered, the same need to prove herself by standing in the line of fire and not flinching. Jimmy had died with that need still burning. I was not going to let his daughter follow the same path.

"I know you can," I said. "Book the flight. Text me the confirmation. And Sophie—pack a bag you can run with."

Ezra next. I gave him the technical requirements: false communications to reinforce the hotel deception, harbor camera manipulation for a sixty-minute window, real-time monitoring of Salcedo's communication channels. He listened in the particular silence of a man who is already coding the solutions while you're still describing the problems.

"The harbor cameras are municipal," he said. "Municipal in Colombia means underfunded, which means outdated, which means the security patches they should have applied in 2019 are still sitting in someone's inbox. I can loop the feeds. Sixty minutes is generous—I can give you ninety."

"Sixty is what I need. Ninety is what I want. Build for ninety."

"Done. And Cat—the Salcedo communication channels. I've been monitoring his security team's encrypted line since yesterday. If anyone in his organization sends an alert, I'll see it within seconds. You'll know you've been made before he does."

"Ezra."

"Yeah."

"If this goes wrong, you're in Lisbon. You're clean. Don't do anything heroic from a distance."

"I never do anything heroic. Heroism requires leaving the apartment. I'll be brilliant from my desk instead."

David. This was the hardest call, not because of the operational content but because of everything underneath it. I told him what I needed: a legal framework for Gabriela's protection, a cooperation agreement that Justice would honor, and a vessel positioned in the waters off the Dutch Antilles.

"You're extracting Salcedo's wife," David said. Not a question. The voice of a man who had spent thirty years in intelligence and could see the shape of an operation from a single data point.

"Yes."

"From his compound."

"Yes."

"In a city he controls."

"David."

"I'm not trying to talk you out of it. I'm trying to understand the risk profile so I can build the receiving end accordingly. If you pull this off, Gabriela needs to land somewhere airtight—protection that Salcedo's lawyers can't challenge and his people can't circumvent. I need to know how much time I have to build it."

"Twenty-four hours."

A pause. The David pause. The one where he weighs the impossible against the necessary and decides which one matters more.

"I'll have it," he said. "The yacht is doable—I have a contact in Curaçao who owes me a favor from a previous life. The legal framework is harder, but Kessler's involvement changes the equation. If the White House is backing this, Justice will move. Not happily, but they'll move."

"Thank you."

"Cat."

"Yeah."

"Be careful. Please."

The please landed in me the way all of David's tenderness landed—softly, precisely, in a place I'd armored against exactly this kind of impact and that was apparently still vulnerable to a man who said please the way other people say I love you.

"I'm always careful," I said, which was a lie we both recognized and neither of us corrected.

Lucía. I told her I needed to get a woman out of a private residence in the Manga district and to the Cartagena marina within a ninety-minute window. I didn't name Salcedo. I didn't need to.

"The compound on Calle del Bouquet," she said. Not a question.

"You know it."

"I've been watching that house for three years, Cat. I know the staff rotation. I know the delivery schedules. I know that the eastern wall has a service entrance that's monitored by camera but not by personnel between the hours of two and four in the afternoon, because the guard assigned to that post takes his lunch at a cevichería on Avenida del Arsenal and has never once come back early."

Of course she knew. Lucía had been building the map of Cartagena's invisible economy for years, and the Salcedo compound was the center of that map. She'd been waiting for this. Maybe not this specifically—but for the moment when the information she'd been accumulating became operational, when the map became a plan.

"The woman in the house," I said. "Is she accessible? Can you reach her without going through Salcedo's people?"

"There's a woman on the household staff—the cook's assistant. She's from Buenaventura, like Salcedo, but her family was displaced by the same violence his organization profits from. She talks to me. Not about Salcedo directly—about the house. The routines. The mood. And she's mentioned the wife. Gabriela. She says Gabriela is—" Lucía chose her word carefully. "Ready."

"Ready for what?"

"Ready for a door. She just needs someone to open it."

The same image I'd used with Kessler. A door. The woman needed a door. And the woman standing in a hotel room making phone calls to four people across three countries was going to build one.

"Tomorrow afternoon," I said. "The two-to-four window. Can you get her out?"

"I can get her to the service entrance. From there to the marina is eleven minutes by car if traffic cooperates and fourteen if it doesn't. I'll need a vehicle that isn't registered to either of us."

"Ezra will arrange it."

"Then yes. I can get her out."

I stood in the hotel room with the phone in my hand and the plan assembled around me like a machine that had been waiting to be built. Five parts. Five people. One window. Ninety minutes between Gabriela leaving the compound and Salcedo discovering she's gone. In that ninety minutes, I needed to be sitting across from Salcedo in a face-to-face meeting, holding his attention with a CI-7 bluff while his wife was driven to the marina, put on a rigid inflatable boat, and motored out of Cartagena's harbor into the open Caribbean.

The last call was the one I hadn't made yet. The one that required a different kind of courage than the others, because the others were operational and this one was personal and the distance between those two categories had collapsed so completely that I could no longer tell where one ended and the other began.

I called Cole Hartwell.

He answered on the first ring, which told me he'd been waiting for this call, or a call like it, since the morning I'd sat across from him in St. Barts and he'd told me he loved her and asked if I could save her.

"Cole," I said. "Gabriela is in danger. I can get her out, but I need you to do something."

"Anything," he said. Without hesitation. Without asking what, without asking the risk, without the careful calculation that his father would have performed and that Kessler would have demanded. Just: anything. The voice of a twenty-six-year-old man who loved a woman and would walk into whatever was required to reach her.

I told him where to go and when to be there and what he would find when he arrived. I told him there would be a yacht and there would be a woman on it and the woman would need him to be steady and calm and present, and he said yes to all of it, and the simplicity of his yes—the purity of it, the absence of negotiation or condition—was the most moving thing I'd heard in a week of hearing things that broke me.

I hung up. Set the phone on the desk. Looked at the room—the desk covered in laptops and notes, the French doors open to the courtyard, the bed that had held me and Andrés and now held nothing but clean sheets and the ghost of something I was never going to have.

Tomorrow. Everything happens tomorrow.

I sat down. I opened the laptop. And I began to write the operational timeline—minute by minute, contingency by contingency, the architecture of an extraction that would either be the finest thing I'd ever done or the last thing I'd ever do.

I was not afraid. I was past fear. I was in the clear, cold space on the other side of fear where the only thing that exists is the work, and the work was the thing I was born for, and tomorrow I was going to prove it.

CHAPTER TWENTY-ONE

THE SETUP – *Cartagena*

Sophie arrived on a 7 a.m. flight from Miami, which meant she'd left New York at midnight, which meant she'd packed, closed the office, rerouted my communications, briefed my answering service, and made it to JFK in under four hours, which was exactly the kind of operational efficiency that made her indispensable and also made me want to tell her to get on the next flight home.

I met her at the airport. Not inside—I waited in Lucía's car in the pickup lane, sunglasses on, watching the terminal doors through the windshield. When Sophie came through the sliding glass, she was carrying one bag—a black duffel, the kind you can run with, exactly as I'd instructed—and she was wearing dark jeans and a white blouse and she looked like what she was: a twenty-four-year-old woman stepping off a plane in a city she'd never visited, squinting in the equatorial sun, looking for the person who'd asked her to come.

She saw the car. Walked toward it. Got in the back seat. Set the duffel on the floor. Looked at me.

"Hi," she said.

"Hi."

I looked at her and I saw Jimmy. I always see Jimmy—in the set of her jaw, in the particular directness of her gaze, in the way she held herself with the unconscious confidence of someone whose body has never let them down. Jimmy's eyes. Jimmy's hands. Jimmy's daughter, sitting in the back of a car in Cartagena because I'd asked her to come, and the weight of that—the weight of having summoned the only living piece of Jimmy Navarro into a city controlled by a man who would not hesitate to use her or harm her or both—settled on my chest like a stone.

I had done many difficult things in my career. Fallujah. The divorce. The seventeen-hour negotiation in Ankara that ended with a hostage walking free and my hands shaking so badly I couldn't hold a glass of water. But asking Sophie to fly to Cartagena was the hardest thing I had ever done, and the difficulty had nothing to do with the operation and everything to do with the twenty-four-year-old woman in my back seat who trusted me with the same completeness her father had trusted me, and look what that trust had cost him.

I didn't say any of this. I said: "Lucía, this is Sophie. Sophie, Lucía. She's going to drive us to a location where I'll brief you. Not the hotel—the hotel isn't clean."

"Bugged?" Sophie asked. No surprise. No drama. A professional question from a woman who had grown up adjacent to a world where rooms were bugged and the appropriate response was logistical, not emotional.

"Audio confirmed. Possible video on the hallway. Ezra will have the full map by noon."

Sophie nodded. Lucía pulled into traffic. The drive to the safe location—Lucía's apartment in Getsemaní, a third-floor walk-up that I'd vetted and Ezra had swept remotely—took twenty minutes, during which Sophie looked out the window at Cartagena with the frank curiosity of someone seeing a new city for the first time and the quiet alertness of someone who understood that the city was not what it appeared to be. Jimmy's daughter. My girl. The person I was most afraid of losing, sitting in a car I was driving toward danger because there was no version of this plan that worked without her.

The briefing took two hours.

Lucía's apartment was small, clean, filled with books and the residual scent of strong coffee. We sat at her kitchen table—the three of us, plus Ezra on a secure video call from Lisbon, his face green-lit by multiple monitors, a cup of something caffeinated permanently in his hand. I ran the operation from the top, the way I'd run any briefing: objective, timeline, individual assignments, contingencies.

"The objective is to extract Gabriela Salcedo from the compound in Manga and get her to a yacht in international waters. The operation has two phases. Phase one: I meet Salcedo face-to-face for the CI-7 negotiation. This fixes his attention on me and keeps him in a location I control. During this meeting, Lucía extracts Gabriela from the compound and brings her to the marina. Phase two: the switch. I leave the meeting, return to the hotel visibly—Salcedo's surveillance sees me entering the building. But I never go to my room. Sophie takes over as me inside the hotel while I exit through the service entrance, get to the marina, and run Gabriela out of the harbor on the RIB. By the time anyone realizes I'm not in my room, we're in international waters."

I looked at each of them. Lucía: composed, watchful, the face of a woman who had been building toward this for years. Ezra on the screen: focused, already running calculations behind his eyes. Sophie: still, alert, her hands flat on the table the way her father used to sit in briefings—grounded, ready, the body calm while the mind worked.

"The timing is everything," I said. "Phase one buys us the extraction window—while Salcedo is with me, his attention is off the compound and off the harbor. Lucía moves Gabriela during this window. But Salcedo's people will eventually discover she's gone, and when they do, the first thing they'll check is me. If I'm in my hotel room, acting normally, there's no reason to connect me to Gabriela's disappearance—at least not immediately. Sophie buys me the second window. The window where I get Gabriela from the marina to open water."

I turned to Sophie. "Your assignment."

Ezra pulled up his surveillance map on the shared screen. A floor plan of my hotel suite with every monitoring device marked in red.

"Two audio devices," Ezra said. "One in the main room—behind the headboard, built into the frame, professional installation. One in the bathroom, which is aggressive—someone wanted comprehensive coverage. No video inside the room, which is either restraint or a technical limitation. But there's a camera on the hallway—third-floor corridor, positioned to capture anyone entering or leaving the suite. The feed goes to Salcedo's security apparatus."

"Here's how it works," I said. "You go to the hotel this afternoon. You enter my room through the service stairwell—not the hallway, not the elevator. Ezra will confirm when the hallway camera has a gap in monitoring—he's found a six-second cycle in the camera's pan. You enter during the gap. Once you're in the room, you stay dark. Lights off. No sound. No movement. You sit and you wait. The audio bugs pick up an empty room, which is consistent with me being out for the afternoon—I'll be at the meeting with Salcedo."

Sophie was taking notes in the small, precise handwriting that I recognized because it was the same handwriting her father had used—another inheritance, another thing that made me want to lock her in a room and throw away the key and keep her safe forever, which was not a thing I was going to do because Sophie Navarro was not a woman who could be kept, and trying would be the fastest way to lose her.

"The switch happens when I leave the Salcedo meeting," I continued. "I drive back to the hotel. I walk through the lobby. Salcedo's people see me enter the building—this is visible and intentional. I get in the elevator. The moment I text you a single word—now—you open the suite door into the hallway. The hallway camera sees a woman stepping from the doorway. The surveillance team registers Cat Sloane returning to her room. Meanwhile, I ride the elevator back down to the basement level and exit through the service entrance to a car Lucía has parked on Calle del Torno."

"So the camera sees me opening the door, thinks it's you arriving," Sophie said.

"Exactly. From that moment, you're me. Lights on. Shower runs—eight minutes, that's my pattern. Room service call: café con leche, arepa with cheese. Phone call to New York—Ezra will feed you lines about the CI-7 investigation. The content is designed to suggest I'm still working the case. Walk past the window at regular intervals. Wear my clothes—the white linen shirt, dark trousers. They're listening for rhythm and tone, not content."

I pulled the performance script from my folder—the minute-by-minute schedule I'd written based on my actual patterns over the past week.

"You maintain this for as long as it takes me to get Gabriela from the marina to international waters. Ninety minutes to two hours. After that, Ezra will send you the all-clear and you leave through the service stairwell the same way you came in. Lucía picks you up. You go to the airport. You fly home."

"What if they realize it's not you before the all-clear?" Sophie asked.

I looked at her. This was the part I'd been dreading.

"If something goes wrong and they send someone to the room, you go out the bathroom window. It opens onto a service corridor that leads to the back stairwell. Lucía will have a second car on Calle del Torno as backup. You go down the stairs, out the service exit, into the car. You don't stop. You don't look back. You go directly to the airport and you get on the first flight to Miami and you do not come back to this city. Do you understand?"

"I understand," she said. Her voice was level. Her eyes were steady. She understood the contingency the way a soldier understands a retreat order—not as failure but as survival.

"Sophie."

"Yeah."

"If something goes wrong, you leave me. That's not a request. That's the only condition under which I will let you do this."

Something passed across her face. Fast, barely visible. An emotion she caught and controlled before it could settle. I knew what it was because I'd seen it in the mirror: the particular anguish of being told that the person you love most will sacrifice themselves for you and that your job is to let them.

"Okay," she said. Quiet. Final. The word of a woman who is agreeing to something she will honor even if it destroys her, because she was raised by a man who honored his word until his last breath, and the daughter of that man does not break promises.

I moved on. If I stayed in that moment any longer, I was going to lose the operational clarity I needed to run this briefing, and clarity was the only thing keeping the fear from eating me alive.

"Lucía. The extraction."

Lucía spread a hand-drawn map on the kitchen table—the Manga compound, sketched from three years of observation with the detail and care of a woman who understood that good intelligence is the difference between an operation and a disaster.

"The compound is a colonial house on Calle del Bouquet. Three stories. Walled garden. Main entrance on the street, service entrance on the eastern wall. Salcedo's personal security: four men in rotation, two on duty at any time. They cover the main entrance and the garden. The service entrance is monitored by camera only—no personnel between two and four p.m. The camera feed goes to a security room on the ground floor, but during the afternoon shift the guard monitoring screens is also managing deliveries at the main entrance. His attention is divided."

"Gabriela's routine?" I asked.

"Tuesday and Thursday afternoons she takes a yoga class in the garden—a private instructor who comes to the house. The class ends at two-thirty. After the class, the instructor leaves through the service entrance. Gabriela usually goes upstairs to shower."

"Tomorrow is Thursday," I said.

"Tomorrow is Thursday. The instructor leaves at two-thirty through the service entrance. If Gabriela comes down the back stairs instead of going up to shower, she can walk out the same door the instructor used. I'll be in a car on the street. Eleven minutes to the marina. I bring her to the RIB and stay with her until you arrive."

"And Gabriela knows?"

Lucía nodded. "I made contact yesterday through the cook's

assistant. The message was simple: a door is opening tomorrow. Be ready. She sent back one word."

"What word?"

"Finally."

The word sat in the room like a held breath. Finally. A woman who had spent six years in a beautiful house that was also a prison, who had reached for Cole Hartwell in St. Barts because reaching was the only freedom she had left, who had been waiting not for rescue but for a chance to rescue herself. Finally. The door was opening and she was going to walk through it, and the courage required to walk through a door when the man on the other side of it is Andrés Salcedo was a courage I recognized because it was the same courage—the decision to leave a life that is killing you, even when leaving might kill you faster.

"Ezra. Digital cover."

Ezra's face on the screen shifted from listening mode to operational mode—a straightening of posture, a focus in the eyes, the transformation of a man who spent ninety percent of his life in ironic detachment into the other ten percent, where he was one of the most capable technical operatives I'd ever worked with.

"Four layers," he said. "First: the hallway camera cycle. I've mapped the pan timing—there's a six-second blind spot every forty-three seconds when the camera sweeps past the suite door. Sophie enters and exits during those windows. Second: the phone clone. I'll route all of Cat's incoming communications to a device Sophie will carry. Outgoing calls will show Cat's number. Anyone monitoring Cat's phone traffic sees normal patterns originating from the hotel's cell tower. Third: harbor cameras. I've identified the municipal feeds covering the marina and the harbor exit. When Cat is on the water, I'll loop twelve minutes of pre-recorded footage on each camera. The loop is clean—same time window from last Thursday, same light conditions and boat traffic. Fourth: Salcedo's communications. I'm monitoring his security team's encrypted channel, his personal phone, and the VoIP relay through Panama. The moment anyone in his network sends an alert, I see it. Cat will have real-time updates through her earpiece throughout."

"How confident are you on the harbor cameras?" I asked.

"Nine out of ten. The system is running software from 2017 with patches last applied in 2020. The administrative credentials are—and I say this with genuine professional embarrassment on behalf of the city of Cartagena—the factory defaults. I could loop these cameras in my sleep. I have, actually, looped cameras in my sleep. Long story. Involves a ferry in Lisbon and a very poor decision regarding energy drinks."

"Save it," I said. But I almost smiled, and the almost-smile was a gift, because there had not been much to smile about in the last forty-eight hours and Ezra's particular brand of casual brilliance was the closest thing to levity this operation was going to get.

The yacht was already in position.

David had moved fast. Through his contact in Curaçao—a man whose name I didn't ask and didn't need—he'd chartered a sixty-foot motor yacht under one of Ezra's shell companies. The vessel was registered in the Cayman Islands, crewed by two men who asked no questions and spoke no English, and had arrived in Cartagena's harbor that morning under the cover of a corporate retreat booking. One of fifty charter vessels in the harbor. Anonymous. Unremarkable. Invisible.

Cole Hartwell had boarded the yacht at a marina in Bonaire twelve hours earlier, having flown commercial from Washington to Miami to Bonaire on a ticket booked under his own name—because Cole Hartwell traveling to the Dutch Antilles was a rich young man on vacation, which was exactly what it looked like and therefore the best possible cover. He was on the yacht now, waiting. David's people had briefed him on the timeline. He knew that tomorrow evening a rigid inflatable boat would pull alongside the yacht in international waters, and on that boat would be a woman he loved and a woman he'd trusted to save her.

I thought about Cole. Twenty-six years old. The President's son. A man who had walked into a suite in St. Barts and told me the truth about Gabriela with the raw, undefended honesty of someone who hadn't yet learned to protect himself from his own feelings. He was on a boat in the Caribbean because I'd asked him to be, and he'd said anything without knowing what the anything was, and the faith in that—the blind, beautiful, terrifying faith of a man in love—was either the bravest or the most reckless thing I'd encountered in this case, and I suspected it was both.

Everything was in position. Sophie in Cartagena. Ezra in Lisbon. Lucía with the route mapped. The yacht in the harbor. Cole on the yacht. David in Washington, holding the legal framework together with the institutional authority of a CIA Deputy Director and the personal commitment of a man who had never once, in thirty years, failed to deliver what he promised.

And me. In a third-floor apartment in Getsemaní, looking at a hand-drawn map on a kitchen table, running the timeline in my head for the twentieth time.

The plan had two phases, two windows, two chances for everything to go wrong. Phase one: the meeting with Salcedo and Lucía's extraction of Gabriela. If Gabriela didn't walk through the service entrance, or if Salcedo's people detected Lucía, the operation was over before phase two began. Phase two: the switch at the hotel and the run to international waters. If the hallway camera caught the wrong face, or if Sophie's performance failed, or if the harbor cameras weren't looped cleanly, Salcedo's people would know I was on the water and they would come after me.

Two phases. Two windows. Ninety minutes of margin between the moment Gabriela walked out of the compound and the moment I had her in international waters beyond anyone's jurisdiction.

Lucía made coffee. Sophie studied the performance script. Ezra tested the camera loops. The afternoon light went gold through the apartment windows, and Getsemaní hummed outside with its music and its chaos and its life, and I sat at the table with my team around me

—this improbable, brilliant, devoted team that I had assembled from the wreckage of my professional life and my personal failures and my stubborn, unkillable belief that the right people, properly deployed, can accomplish almost anything—and I felt something I hadn't felt since before the revelations.

Not confidence. Confidence is a performance. What I felt was readiness. The bone-deep, cellular readiness of a woman who has done the preparation and run the scenarios and accounted for the contingencies and is now standing at the edge of the thing itself, and the only thing left to do is jump.

Tomorrow. Everything happens tomorrow.

I looked at Sophie. She was reading the script, making notes in the margins. She felt me looking and glanced up. Our eyes met. She smiled—a small smile, private, the smile of two people who share a history they don't need to name.

"We've got this," she said.

We've got this. Four syllables. The casual confidence of youth, or the inherited certainty of a woman whose father had walked into worse with less and come out the other side. Until the one time he didn't.

"Yeah," I said. "We do."

And I believed it. Not because the plan was perfect—no plan is perfect, and the distance between a perfect plan and a successful operation is measured in improvisation and luck and the willingness to adapt when the thing you didn't anticipate becomes the thing that determines everything. I believed it because the people sitting around this table were the best at what they did, and because the woman at the center of the plan—Gabriela, who had sent back one word, finally—deserved a door, and because I was Cat Sloane, and building doors for people who need them is what I do.

I picked up my coffee. It was cold. I drank it anyway.

Tomorrow.

CHAPTER TWENTY-TWO

THE GOODBYE – *Cartagena*

He called at seven. The same hour. The same voice. The same low, unhurried cadence that had reached through the phone and into my chest on half a dozen evenings, and my body—the traitor, the collaborator, the part of me that refused to update its responses regardless of what my mind now knew—my body still responded. A quickening. A warmth. The involuntary softening of a woman who hears a voice she wants to hear, even when the voice belongs to a man she is about to betray.

Betray. I tested the word and found it inadequate. What I was about to do to Andrés Salcedo was not betrayal. Betrayal implies a broken promise, and I had never promised him anything except my presence, which I had given honestly and which he had used as a tool. What I was about to do was closer to justice, or self-defense, or the particular moral calculus of a woman who has been played and is playing back. But none of those words sat right either, because the truth—the miserable, complicated, unresolvable truth—was that the man calling me at seven o'clock on my last night in Cartagena was someone I had loved, or the beginning of loved, and nothing I'd learned about him had managed to kill it. Damage it. Wound it. But not kill it. The thing was still breathing, and I was going to have to sit across from it tonight and pretend it was healthy while I prepared to put a knife in its chest.

"Catherine." The way he said my name. The specific music of it in his mouth, the extra weight on the second syllable, the slight rasp that came from speaking English after a day of speaking Spanish. "I want to see you tonight. Before your case takes you away from me."

Before your case takes you away. He already knew. Not the specifics—not the yacht, not Gabriela, not the plan I'd spent the day assembling in Lucía's apartment. But he knew I was leaving. He could feel the departure the way you feel weather changing, the shift in atmospheric pressure that tells you something is coming even when the sky looks clear.

Or he was fishing. Testing whether I'd confirm a timeline. Either way, I needed to go.

"Where?" I said.

"My place. I promised to cook for you."

His place. The compound on Calle del Bouquet where Gabriela was, at this moment, going about her evening routine, unaware that the door she'd been promised would open in sixteen hours. The compound that Lucía had mapped in meticulous detail on a hand-drawn diagram that was now folded in my bag. I would be walking into the building from which, tomorrow afternoon, I was going to extract his wife.

The irony was so dense it had its own gravity.

"I'd love that," I said. And the ease with which the lie came out of my mouth—warm, natural, the voice of a woman accepting an invitation she wanted—was a measure of how completely I had returned to the person I was before Cartagena. The woman who could say anything to anyone and mean none of it and feel the absence of meaning like a phantom limb. I'd been that woman for fifteen years. I'd stopped being her for five days. Now I was her again, and the fit was perfect, and the perfection was the saddest thing about it.

He sent a car. The same driver as the Getsemaní evening—a silent man who navigated Cartagena's streets with the automatic competence of long practice. We crossed the old city, passed through the Manga bridge neighborhood, and arrived at a house that was, from the outside, exactly what Lucía's map had prepared me for: colonial, three stories, a walled garden visible above the stucco, the quiet, curated beauty of a man who had the resources to restore a piece of history and the taste to do it well.

I cataloged everything. The gate: electronic, camera-equipped. The garden wall: eight feet, climbable but not easily. The service entrance on the eastern side: closed now, but I could see the narrow alley that led to it, the alley that Lucía would use tomorrow. The guard near the front entrance: professional, discreet, one hand resting near his waist in the posture of a man who carries a weapon as a matter of routine. I counted windows. Measured sight lines. Noted the neighbor's roofline that would provide partial cover for the service alley approach.

I did this in the three seconds between getting out of the car and walking through the front door, because three seconds is what you have, and I have been doing this for twenty years, and the operational part of my brain does not stop just because the rest of me is dying.

Andrés met me at the door. Not in the foyer—at the door itself, as if he'd been waiting. He was in a white shirt, sleeves rolled, no jacket. Barefoot. The informality was either genuine or performed, and I was so deep in the hall of mirrors by now that I couldn't tell and had stopped trying.

He kissed me. Soft. His hand on my jaw, tilting my face up to his. I let him. I kissed him back. The taste of wine on his mouth—he'd been cooking, he'd been drinking while he cooked, and the domesticity of this nearly undid me, because I could see the version of this evening where I didn't know what I knew and I walked into this house and drank wine and ate whatever he'd made and stayed the night and woke in his bed and the life I'd been imagining was the life I got to live.

That version didn't exist. But I could see it, the way you see a road you didn't take from a hillside—the path curving away through a landscape you'll never walk, beautiful and gone.

The house was extraordinary. I need to say this because it's true and because the truth of it is part of what made the evening unbearable. High ceilings with original beams. Thick stone walls that kept the interior cool despite the Caribbean heat. Art everywhere—not the art of a collector performing taste, but the art of a man who actually saw things and responded to them. A painting by a Colombian artist I recognized—deep blues, a woman dissolving into water—hung in the hallway where the light from the courtyard caught it in the late afternoon and made it glow. Bookshelves lined the study: García Márquez, Borges, Neruda. His mother's poets. The books she'd borrowed from the houses she cleaned. He'd bought his own copies. First editions, some of them. The boy from Buenaventura who had owned nothing now owned the most beautiful versions of the things his mother had given him for free.

This was not the house of a man I could reduce to a villain. This was the house of a man who loved beauty and language and light and who had also, according to every piece of intelligence I possessed, built an organization that destroyed lives with the same precision with which it moved product. Both things lived in this house. Both things lived in him. And the coexistence of beauty and brutality was not a contradiction but a condition—the particular condition of a man who had come from nothing and built everything and had never once been required to choose between the two, because the world he operated in had never asked him to.

I was going to ask him to. Tomorrow. Whether he understood that yet or not.

He cooked. Fish in coconut milk, rice with coconut, patacones. The kitchen was large and modern and he moved through it with the ease of a man who cooked often, not as performance but as practice—the rhythmic, unselfconscious competence of someone doing a thing they know how to do. He poured me wine. He talked while he cooked—about the building he was restoring, about a trip to Buenos Aires he was planning, about a book he'd been reading on the history of the spice trade. His voice filled the kitchen the way music fills a room, and I stood at the counter and drank wine and watched him and carried, silently, the knowledge that this was the last time.

The last time I would see him like this. Unguarded. Barefoot. A man in his kitchen making dinner for a woman he—what? Loved? Used? Was in the process of manipulating? All three? The taxonomy didn't matter anymore. What mattered was that tomorrow afternoon I would sit across from this man in a different setting entirely—the formal, charged atmosphere of a negotiation between two people who finally see each other clearly—and the man in that room would not be the man in this kitchen.

We ate at a small table in the courtyard. The garden was walled, private, filled with the scent of jasmine and night-blooming cereus. Candles. The sound of a fountain. The stars above Cartagena, which are different from the stars above any other city I've been in—brighter, closer, as if the sky here has less patience for distance.

He talked. I listened. I asked questions that were not operational, that were simply the questions of a woman who wanted to know the man sitting across from her, because I did want to know him—I wanted to know him the way you want to know anything that has the power to destroy you, not to prevent the destruction but to understand its architecture.

He told me about Buenos Aires. A woman he'd known there, years ago—a tango dancer who taught him that the lead in a dance is not the person who moves first but the person who listens best. He told me about his first trip to London, at nineteen, when he'd stood in front of a Vermeer at the National Gallery and wept because he'd never seen light used that way and hadn't known it was possible. He told me about a building he'd lost in a negotiation early in his career—the one failure he couldn't let go of, the lesson that taught him never to want anything so visibly that the wanting could be used against you.

Never to want anything so visibly that the wanting could be used against you.

I held my wine glass and I looked at the candle flame and I thought: you are telling me the rules of your life, and I am the violation of those rules, and you don't know it yet.

Or you do. And this dinner is your way of saying goodbye to the violation before you close it down.

I couldn't tell. That was the cruelest part. I couldn't tell whether the evening was genuine or managed, and the inability to distinguish was its own kind of torture, because it meant that everything I was feeling —the tenderness, the grief, the desperate, stupid wish that this could be real—existed in a space where verification was impossible, and I would carry the ambiguity forever.

After dinner. The courtyard. He moved his chair closer to mine. Not touching me—close enough to touch, the distance between his body and mine reduced to inches, the space charged with the specific electricity of two people who have been intimate and are choosing, for the moment, not to be.

He reached for my hand. I gave it to him. His fingers closed around mine the way they always did—warm, certain, the grip of a man who holds what he wants and doesn't let go.

We sat in the garden with the stars and the jasmine and the sound of the fountain, and for a few minutes neither of us spoke, and the silence was the kind I'd felt only with him—alive, full, a silence that was not the absence of words but the presence of something that words would diminish.

Then he spoke. And what he said nearly destroyed me.

"I have not been honest with you, Catherine."

My heart stopped. Not metaphorically. I felt the muscle in my chest seize, a half-second arrhythmia that was pure autonomic response, the body reacting to a threat before the mind can assess whether the threat is real. I didn't move. I didn't change my breathing. I held his hand and waited.

"When we met," he said, "I told you I work in investments and logistics. That's true. But it's not the whole truth. The whole truth is more complicated than I can explain tonight, and some of it I may never be able to explain, because there are parts of my life that exist in a space where explanation is not possible without consequence. I have done things. Built things. Made choices that a man from Buenaventura makes when the options available to him are not the options available to other men. I am not—"

He stopped. Looked at the garden wall. The candle threw shadows on his face, and in the flickering light he looked older, the lines deeper, the mask thinner. Something underneath was showing—not a calculated vulnerability, not a performance of confession designed to create intimacy, but something rawer. Something that looked, to a woman who had spent her life reading faces, like pain.

"I am not the man you think I am," he said. "But I am the man who is sitting here with you tonight, and that man is real, and I need you to know that before—"

He stopped again. Before what? Before tomorrow? Before whatever he suspected was coming? Before the game changed and the masks came off and the two people sitting in this garden had to face each other across a different kind of table?

"Before you leave," he finished. Quietly. And the way he said leave —not as a fact but as a wound, the word carrying the weight of a man who has watched many people leave and has learned to hear the departure before it arrives—the way he said it broke something in me that I thought I'd already broken. A secondary fracture. The bone that breaks again along the same line, weaker the second time, more painful because the body remembers what it's like to be whole.

I should have said something honest. I should have said: I know. I know who you are. I know what you've done. I know about the photographs and the blackmail and CI-7 and the machine you built with me as its instrument. I know all of it, and I am sitting in your garden holding your hand because I am performing for you the way you've been performing for me, and the performance is perfect, and the perfection is the saddest thing either of us has ever done.

Instead I said: "Whatever you are, Andrés, I'm glad I met you."

And this was not a lie. This was the truest thing I said all evening, and the truth of it was what made it work as a performance, because the best lies are the ones that are also true, and I have known this since the first day of training and I have never hated knowing it more than I hated it in that garden.

He lifted my hand to his mouth. Kissed my knuckles. His lips warm against the ridges of bone. A gesture so old-fashioned, so tender, so out of character for a man who ran a cartel and orchestrated international crises—or so perfectly in character for a man who contained multitudes and refused to be reducible to any single one of them.

I wanted to stay. I wanted to stay in the garden and the jasmine and the candlelight and his hand around mine and I wanted to walk upstairs to whatever bedroom existed in this house and I wanted to lie down beside him and I wanted him to trace the scar the way he'd traced it in my hotel room and I wanted to cry the way I'd cried the second night and I wanted, with a desperation that felt like drowning, to be the woman who didn't know.

But I did know. And the woman who knows cannot stay.

"I should go," I said. "Early morning. The case."

He nodded. He didn't argue. He walked me to the door. He kissed me one more time—slow, deep, his hand on the side of my face, his thumb tracing my cheekbone the way his thumb had traced my palm in the plaza, the circular motion that was his signature, his fingerprint on my skin.

"Goodnight, Catherine."

"Goodnight, Andrés."

I walked to the car. I got in. The driver pulled away. I turned and looked through the rear window at the house on Calle del Bouquet—the gate closing, the garden wall, the upstairs window where a light was on, the silhouette of a man standing at the glass watching me leave.

I faced forward. I pressed my hands flat on my thighs. I breathed.

The hotel room was dark. Sophie was gone—she'd moved to Lucía's apartment for the night, out of the surveillance radius, and would return before dawn to begin the performance. The room was empty in the way that rooms are empty when they've been inhabited by someone you love and then vacated, the furniture maintaining its arrangement but the air depleted, the life drained out through the door.

I didn't turn on the lights. I walked to the bathroom. I turned on the shower. I took off my clothes and I stepped under the water and I sat down on the tile floor and I let the water fall on me.

Hot at first. Then warm. Then cool. Then cold. I didn't adjust the temperature. I sat on the shower floor with my knees drawn up and my arms around my shins and the water beating on my shoulders and my back and I let it go from hot to cold the way I was letting everything go from hot to cold—the man, the garden, the hand around mine, the confession that might have been real, the kiss at the door, the silhouette in the window.

I didn't cry. I was past crying. Crying is what happens when the body has an emotion it can process, and what I was feeling was not an emotion but a landscape—vast, featureless, the terrain of a woman who has been stripped of the thing she wanted by the truth about the person who gave it to her. You can't cry about a landscape. You can only sit in it and wait for it to become bearable.

The water went cold. The tile was hard under my body. My skin prickled with gooseflesh. I sat in the cold water and I felt the absence of him—not the intellectual absence, not the strategic removal of an asset from an operation, but the physical absence. The place where his hand had been on my face. The place where his mouth had been on my knuckles. The place where his body had been next to mine in a bed that was now made with clean sheets by a housekeeper who didn't know what those sheets had held.

I wanted him to touch me. That was the thing I couldn't outrun, the thing the cold water couldn't numb. I wanted his hands on me—not in the abstract, not as a concept, but specifically, precisely, the particular pressure of his thumb on my hip, the weight of his body, the warmth of his mouth on the scar he'd kissed without asking. I wanted to be touched by a man I could never let touch me again, and the wanting was so specific, so located in my body—in my skin, in the nerve endings that remembered him with an accuracy my mind couldn't override—that sitting in the cold water without his hands was its own kind of violence. The violence of absence. The specific cruelty of a body that remembers pleasure and can't have it and won't stop remembering.

I did not touch myself. This is important. In the car on the dark street, I had taken what I needed, because what I needed then was release from fear, and the body has mechanisms for release that can be accessed alone. What I needed now was not release. What I needed was him, and no amount of my own hands could approximate what I was missing, because what I was missing was not sensation but presence, not pleasure but the particular way another person's body says you are not alone, and you cannot give yourself the thing you are not.

So I sat in the cold water and I felt the absence and I didn't fill it and I didn't numb it and I didn't try to make it smaller or more manageable or less real. I let it be what it was: the full, devastating weight of wanting someone I couldn't have, someone who might not exist in the form I wanted him, someone who had kissed my knuckles in a garden and said I am not the man you think I am and might have meant it in a way I would never be able to verify.

The water was very cold. I was shaking. Not from the temperature —from something deeper, the tremor that lives beneath the surface of every controlled person, the one that emerges only when you are alone and the performance has stopped and there is no one watching and no reason to be steady.

I turned off the water. I stood up. I toweled off in the dark. I put on clean clothes—dark, operational, tomorrow's clothes. I didn't look in the mirror. I didn't want to see the woman who had sat on a shower floor until the water ran cold because a man had kissed her hand in a garden and she couldn't bear what she was about to do to him.

I set my alarm for five a.m. I lay on the bed. Not in it—on it. On top of the covers, fully dressed, the way soldiers sleep when they know they'll be called before dawn. The room was dark. The courtyard was quiet. Tomorrow was already forming in the darkness, the hours stacking up like cards in a hand I was about to play.

I closed my eyes. I thought about Gabriela, who had said finally and meant it. I thought about Cole, on a yacht in the dark. I thought about Sophie, in Lucía's apartment, practicing the script, learning my rhythms. I thought about David, building the legal architecture that would keep Gabriela safe. I thought about Ezra, testing camera loops in Lisbon at three in the morning because that's when Ezra is at his best and his best is better than anyone else's everything.

I thought about the man in the window, watching me leave.

Then I stopped thinking about him. I had to. Tomorrow I was going to sit across from that man and play the most important hand of my life, and the hand required a face that showed nothing, and nothing was what I was going to give him, and nothing was what I had left.

I slept. Not well. But I slept.

The alarm would ring in six hours. And then the doors would open, and the game would begin, and Catherine would disappear, and Cat Sloane would do what Cat Sloane does.

CHAPTER TWENTY-THREE

THE PLAY – *Cartagena*

Five a.m. The alarm. I was already awake.

I'd been awake since four, lying on top of the covers in yesterday's clothes, running the timeline in my head the way a musician runs a score before a performance—every note, every rest, every transition mapped and memorized until the execution becomes automatic and the mind is free to improvise when the thing you didn't plan for arrives. Because it always arrives. In twenty years of operations, the thing you didn't plan for has a perfect attendance record.

I got up. Showered. Dressed. Black trousers, black blouse, flat shoes I could run in. No jewelry. Hair pulled back. The uniform of a woman going to work, if the work involves sitting across from a cartel boss and lying to his face while his wife is escorted out of his house.

I picked up my phone. Sent the first text of the day: a single word to four numbers.

Go.

Sophie checked into my hotel suite at six-thirty a.m.

I wasn't there. I'd left through the service exit at five-fifteen, before the hallway camera could register my departure in morning clothes that didn't match my patterns. Sophie entered through the lobby, carrying a room service tray she'd ordered from the restaurant—café con leche, fruit, arepa with cheese. She was wearing my clothes: a white linen shirt, dark trousers, the silhouette close enough to mine that a camera in a hallway would register the right shape. From Lucía's apartment, Ezra confirmed the feed.

"She's in," Ezra's voice said through my earpiece. "Hallway camera shows a woman entering the suite at six-thirty-two. Room service call logged at six-twenty-eight. Audio bugs are picking up movement in the room. She's running the shower. Eight minutes. On script."

Sophie Navarro, performing Cat Sloane, in a hotel room wired by a cartel. The shower running for exactly eight minutes because that was my pattern and the pattern had to hold. I stood in Lucía's kitchen with my hands around a coffee mug and I breathed and I let the professional part of my brain take the wheel and I did not think about what would happen to Sophie if the performance failed.

"Lucía?" I said.

"In position. Parked on Avenida del Arsenal, two blocks from the compound. She'll move to Calle del Bouquet at one-forty-five for the two o'clock window. The yoga instructor is confirmed for two p.m."

"The yacht?"

"Moved to the rendezvous point at oh-four-hundred. Twelve nautical miles north-northwest of Cartagena, in international waters. Cole is aboard. The RIB is prepped and fueled at the marina, slip fourteen. Cat, everything is green."

Everything is green. The phrase from a world I used to live in, where green meant go and red meant abort and the space between them was measured in human lives. I set down the coffee. I checked the earpiece—a flesh-colored device so small it was invisible unless you knew to look, transmitting on an encrypted frequency that Ezra had set up through a relay that would take Salcedo's people hours to trace even if they detected it.

The morning passed. I waited. Waiting is the hardest part of any operation—harder than the action, harder than the improvisation, harder than the moment when everything goes wrong and you have to adapt in real time. Waiting is the space where fear lives, because fear requires emptiness and waiting is nothing but emptiness, and I sat in Lucía's apartment and I waited and I did not let the fear win.

At noon, Ezra reported: "Sophie ordered the ceviche. On script. Audio confirms typing at the desk. The three o'clock call is prepped—I'll feed her the CI-7 lines. Salcedo's monitoring team should hear exactly what they expect to hear."

At one-fifteen, I left the apartment. Lucía's second car—a nondescript Toyota registered to a name that didn't exist—was parked on the street. I drove to the location I'd arranged for the meeting with Salcedo: a private room at a restaurant in Bocagrande, neutral territory, the kind of place where Cartagena's business class conducts the conversations that don't happen on the record.

At one-forty-five, Ezra: "Lucía is moving to Calle del Bouquet."

At two-oh-three: "Yoga instructor has arrived at the compound. Confirmed by Lucía."

At two-fifteen, I walked into the restaurant. The private room was upstairs—a small, well-appointed space with a single table, two chairs, a window overlooking the bay. I'd arrived early. Deliberately. The person who arrives first chooses the chair, controls the sight lines, sets the temperature of the room. I chose the chair facing the door. I ordered water. I placed my hands flat on the table.

And I waited for Andrés Salcedo to walk through the door.

He arrived at two-thirty. Punctual. Of course he was punctual—a man who orchestrates international crises with the precision of a watchmaker does not arrive late to negotiations.

He was different today. I saw it immediately—the shift in register, the recalibration from the man in the garden to the man in the room. He wore a dark suit, no tie, the uniform I'd first seen at the party. His face was composed, careful, the expression of a man who knows that what happens in the next hour will determine something significant. He was flanked by two men who stayed outside the door—security, discreet, the same professional stillness I'd seen at the villa.

He walked in. Saw me. And his face did something I hadn't expected: it softened. For half a second, before the mask settled back into place, the man from the garden was there—the man who had kissed my hand and said I am not the man you think I am. Then he was gone, replaced by the man who sat down across from me with the controlled composure of someone who had been waiting for this conversation.

"Catherine," he said.

"Andrés."

And then, because the performance required it, because the script I was running demanded that the masks come off in a specific order and at a specific pace: "Or should I say Andrés Salcedo."

The air in the room changed. Not dramatically—the way air pressure changes before a storm, a shift you feel in your inner ear before you see it in the sky. His expression didn't change. His body didn't tense. He simply looked at me with the steady, evaluative gaze of a man who has just been told something he expected to hear eventually and is now calculating what it means.

"You know," he said. Not a question.

"I know."

"How long?"

"Long enough."

Silence. The room held it. The bay glittered outside the window. Somewhere below us, the restaurant carried on—dishes, conversation, the ordinary business of a Thursday afternoon in Bocagrande. And in this room, two people who had been naked together sat across a table and began the real conversation.

"I assume," he said, "that this meeting is not about dinner."

"This meeting is about CI-7."

There. The word between us. The reason for everything—the photographs, the blackmail, the crisis, the machine he'd built with me as its instrument. CI-7. I said it and watched his face the way a doctor watches a patient's face when delivering a diagnosis: for the involuntary flicker, the micro-expression, the truth that escapes before the will can contain it.

He gave me nothing. His face was stone. Beautiful stone—the

angular lines, the gray at the temples, the mouth I had kissed in the dark—but stone nonetheless.

"You built all of this for a name," I said. "The photographs. Rafael. The threat against Cole Hartwell. The crisis that brought me here. All of it—an elaborate, expensive, dangerous machine designed to produce one output: the identity of the DEA informant who testified against your network. CI-7. The mole you've been hunting for years."

He was very still. The stillness of a man who is being seen clearly for the first time by someone who has the training to see him and the proximity to make the seeing dangerous.

"And did the machine produce its output?" he asked. His voice was level. Almost conversational. The voice of a man conducting business, which is what this was, regardless of whatever else it had been in gardens and bedrooms and candlelit courtyards.

In my ear, Ezra: "Two-thirty-five. Yoga class ends in five minutes. Lucía is in position."

Five minutes. I needed to keep him here, keep him focused on the conversation in this room, keep his attention fixed on the thing he wanted most—the name—while the other thing he didn't know he was losing walked out of his house.

"The machine produced a great deal," I said. I reached into the folder I'd brought—a leather portfolio, slim, professional—and withdrew three sheets of paper. I placed them on the table, one at a time, with the deliberate pace of a woman who understands that information delivered slowly is more powerful than information delivered all at once.

"Operation Bright Horizon. Two-year DEA operation, 2016 through 2018. Fourteen convictions. CI-7's testimony underpinned all of them." I touched the first page. "Two convictions overturned on appeal. The courts found the informant's testimony was inconsistent with physical evidence in one case and financially motivated in the other. A third appeal is pending."

He looked at the pages. Didn't touch them. His eyes moved across the text with the rapid, focused scan of a man who reads intelligence the way I read intelligence—quickly, structurally, looking for the data that matters and discarding the rest.

"CI-7 testified to specific knowledge of trafficking routes, logistics, distribution chains," I continued. "The level of detail indicates someone with sustained access to your operational infrastructure. Not a peripheral source. Someone close to the center."

I was feeding him what I had. The shape. The architecture. Everything David had been able to confirm from the sealed files—the documented inconsistencies, the internal DEA concern, the pattern of compromised testimony. I delivered it with the confidence of a woman who knows more than she's saying, which is the foundational posture of every successful bluff: let the audience fill the gaps with their own assumptions.

In my ear, Ezra: "Two-forty-one. Yoga instructor leaving through the service entrance. Lucía confirms."

The instructor was leaving. In minutes, Gabriela would either walk downstairs toward the service entrance or go upstairs to shower. Everything depended on a woman I'd never met making a choice I couldn't influence from a restaurant in Bocagrande.

"The identity," Salcedo said. His voice had changed. Subtly. The conversational tone was gone, replaced by something harder, more direct. The voice of a man who was done with preamble and wanted the thing he had built a crisis to obtain. "Do you have it?"

The question I'd been waiting for. The fulcrum on which the entire bluff balanced.

"I have access to it," I said. Which was a lie. A perfect, credible, carefully constructed lie built on a foundation of enough truth to bear its weight. I had access to the sealed files. I had a contact in the CIA who had confirmed the informant's existence. I had the operational details, the testimony patterns, the documented flaws. What I did not have was the name, and what Salcedo could not know—must not know—was that the name was behind a wall that neither I nor David nor anyone short of the DEA Director could breach.

"Access," he repeated. Tasting the word. Measuring it. "Access is not the same as possession."

"In my world, they're closer than you think. The question isn't whether I can get the name. The question is what you're offering in return."

I leaned back in my chair. Controlled. Relaxed. The body language of a woman who holds the stronger hand, which I did not, and who knows it, which I performed so completely that the performance became, for the duration of this conversation, indistinguishable from reality. This is what I do. This is the thing I was trained for and the thing I am best at: sitting across from the most dangerous person in the room and making them believe I am more dangerous.

"The photographs," he said. "Rafael's operation. Everything connected to Cole Hartwell. Destroyed. Permanently. You have my word."

"Your word," I said. And I let the two words carry just enough skepticism to make him work for it, just enough to suggest that the woman across from him was not easily bought and would require more than a promise from a man who had been lying to her for a week.

In my ear: "Two-forty-seven. Cat—Gabriela is moving. Lucía has visual. She's coming down the back stairs."

My heart rate spiked. I didn't show it. Twenty years of training, twenty years of sitting in rooms where a visible reaction could get you killed, held my face in place while my pulse accelerated and my hands stayed flat on the table and the voice in my ear told me that a woman I'd never met was walking toward freedom on legs that I could only hope were steady.

Keep him talking. Keep his eyes on you.

"The photographs are the beginning," I said. "But they're not the end. If I deliver CI-7, I need guarantees that extend beyond the immediate situation. Cole Hartwell's safety. Permanent. Not a promise—a structural guarantee. I need to know that the operation is over, completely and permanently, and that no element of your organization will ever approach Cole Hartwell, his family, or anyone connected to this matter again."

I was negotiating in slow motion. Drawing out each point, requiring elaboration, asking for specifics I didn't need because every minute I kept him in this room was another minute Gabriela moved closer to the car on Calle del Bouquet.

Salcedo engaged. He was meticulous—every guarantee examined, every term negotiated with the precision of a man who had spent his life making deals and understood that the details were where the traps lived. He was enjoying this, I realized. The negotiation itself was pleasurable for him—the intellectual exercise, the chess game, the encounter with an opponent who was playing at his level. I saw it in the slight animation of his eyes, the way his hands moved when he made a point, the almost-smile that appeared when I pushed back on a term he'd offered.

He was enjoying me. Still. Even now, across this table, in this formal and lethal conversation, he was enjoying the mind he'd encountered at the party and the challenge it presented. The recognition was still there. We're the same.

I used it. I used his admiration the way I used every tool available to me—without sentiment, without hesitation, with the cold efficiency of a woman who has been trained to turn human connection into operational advantage. I hated it. I did it anyway.

In my ear, Ezra: "Two-fifty-three. Gabriela is in the car. Lucía is driving. Eleven minutes to the rendezvous point."

Gabriela was out. She'd walked through the service entrance and gotten into a car and was now being driven through Cartagena's streets toward the rendezvous point in Getsemaní where I would pick her up. The first phase was working. But I needed more time in this room—time for Lucía to deliver Gabriela, time for me to leave the meeting cleanly, time for the switch at the hotel before I could get behind the wheel and drive Gabriela to the marina myself.

"Let's discuss the verification mechanism," I said. "How do I confirm that the photographs have been destroyed? I'll need access to Rafael's archives. Physical and digital. Supervised destruction with documentation."

Salcedo raised an eyebrow. "You're thorough."

"I'm the best."

He looked at me. A long look. The kind that held things that didn't belong in a negotiation—memory, desire, the ghost of a conversation in a garden about honesty and wanting and the gap between the thing you built and the thing you actually wanted.

"Yes," he said. "You are."

Ezra in my ear: "Three-oh-one. Lucía has Gabriela at the rendezvous point. Getsemaní. They're waiting for you."

I continued negotiating. Term by term, clause by clause. Each requirement consumed time. But I could feel the clock pressing now—Gabriela waiting on a street in Getsemaní, exposed, every minute increasing the risk. I needed to close this meeting.

"Andrés," I said. "I think we have the framework for an agreement. I need to make some calls—my contact in Washington, the person who controls access to the files. I'll need a few hours to confirm the delivery timeline."

He studied me. The evaluative gaze. Looking for the note out of tune.

"A few hours," he said.

"I'll call you this evening. We can finalize."

He nodded. Not happily—but the promise of CI-7 was close enough to taste, and a man who has been hunting a mole for years can endure a few more hours.

I stood. He stood. We faced each other across the table—the papers between us, the bay behind me, the weight of everything we'd been and everything we'd never be.

He reached for my hand. I let him take it. His hand around mine, warm, the grip I knew from the plaza and the garden and the dark.

"Catherine," he said. The name carrying everything it had always carried.

"I'll call you," I said. And walked out of the room and down the stairs and through the restaurant and into the Cartagena afternoon, where the sun was brutal and the traffic was loud and the world was exactly as indifferent as it had always been.

The switch.

I drove to the hotel at normal speed, taking the same route I'd taken every other day. Salcedo's people were behind me—Ezra confirmed a silver sedan, two cars back, standard tail. They would see me enter the hotel. That was the point. Every step I took from this moment had to look exactly like a woman returning to her room after an afternoon meeting, because the moment it looked like anything else, the surveillance team would alert Salcedo, and the hours I'd just bought would evaporate.

I pulled into the hotel's main entrance. Handed the keys to the valet. Walked through the lobby—unhurried, deliberate, the specific pace of a woman who has been in this hotel for a week and knows where she's going. Past the concierge desk, where I nodded at the woman who had booked my restaurant reservations. Past the bar, where two businessmen were drinking gin and tonics at three in the afternoon the way businessmen drink gin and tonics at three in the afternoon in every hotel in the world. Past the potted palms and the tile floor and the colonial archways that made this place beautiful and also made it a box with cameras and someone else's eyes.

The elevator bank. I pressed the button. Waited. The doors opened. I stepped in. Pressed three.

The elevator rose. I took out my phone.

One word: Now.

Sent to Sophie.

Third floor. The doors opened onto the hallway—the same hallway I'd walked every day, the same carpet, the same sconces, the same camera mounted at the far end with its forty-three-second pan cycle that Ezra had mapped to the millisecond.

I did not step out.

I stood in the elevator with my hand on the door-hold button and I counted. One. Two. Three. Four. Five. Six. Seven. Eight. Eight seconds for Sophie to receive the text, rise from the chair where she'd been sitting in the dark for hours, cross the room, and reach the suite door.

In my ear, Ezra, barely breathing: "Sophie's moving. She's at the door. Opening—now."

The hallway camera's field of view included my suite door and the elevator bank. In this moment—this precise, choreographed, unrepeatable moment—the camera would see two things simultaneously: the elevator doors open on the third floor, and a woman at the suite door, stepping back inside as if she'd opened it to glance down the hall. One woman arriving, one woman at the door. The surveillance team would register a single continuous action: Cat Sloane exits elevator, enters room. The fact that these were two different women standing thirty feet apart would be invisible, because the camera saw silhouettes and shapes and patterns, and both women were wearing the same clothes and moving with the same unhurried confidence, and the human eye sees what it expects to see.

"Clean," Ezra said. "Camera has her at the door. She's stepping back in. It reads."

I released the door-hold button. The elevator doors closed. I pressed B for basement.

The descent. Third floor to basement. Twelve seconds that felt like twelve minutes, the mechanical hum of the elevator the only sound, the mirrored walls showing me a woman in black with no jewelry and flat shoes and the face of someone who is exactly halfway through the most dangerous thing she has ever done. I looked at my reflection and I thought: the next time anyone in this hotel sees me on a security camera, I will either be a woman who pulled off the most elegant extraction of her career, or I will be a woman whose photograph is circulated to Salcedo's people with instructions I don't want to imagine. There is no middle ground.

Basement. The doors opened onto the service corridor—concrete floors, fluorescent tubes buzzing overhead, the smell of industrial laundry detergent and overworked air conditioning. A housekeeper pushed a linen cart past the elevator without looking up. I turned left. Past the laundry room where commercial machines churned behind a closed door. Past the maintenance office where a radio played vallenato and someone laughed. Past the storage cages and the electrical panels and the fire exit signs in Spanish that led to the service door on Calle del Torno.

I walked quickly but I did not run. Running in a hotel basement attracts exactly the kind of attention that gets you remembered, and I needed to be forgotten. I needed to be no one—a woman in dark clothes walking through a service corridor, unremarkable, invisible, already gone by the time anyone thought to look.

The service door. A push bar, no alarm. I'd checked it two days ago during a reconnaissance walk that I'd disguised as a wrong turn from the spa. The door opened onto a narrow alley that smelled like garbage bins and exhaust, and at the end of the alley, on Calle del Torno, a gray Toyota idled at the curb with a driver I didn't know behind the wheel.

I got in the back seat and closed the door and said, "Getsemaní. Calle de la Sierpe. Three minutes."

The driver pulled into traffic. Cartagena's afternoon swallowed us —the honking, the buses belching diesel, a fruit vendor's cart blocking an intersection, the productive chaos of a city that had no idea what was happening inside it. I was one car among thousands. Anonymous. Invisible.

In my ear, Ezra: "Sophie is on script. Shower running. Eight minutes. Audio bugs are picking up normal patterns. Salcedo's monitoring team has no reason to look for you anywhere but that room."

I exhaled. Not fully—I wouldn't fully exhale until I was in international waters with Gabriela on a yacht—but enough. The switch had worked. As far as Salcedo's surveillance was concerned, Cat Sloane had returned to her hotel room after the meeting and was doing exactly what Cat Sloane always did: working, thinking, preparing for the call she'd promised to make this evening.

Three minutes to Getsemaní. To Lucía and Gabriela, waiting for me on a side street near the wall. Then I would get behind the wheel and drive Gabriela to the marina, and put her on a boat, and take her out of this city.

The driver turned onto the road that skirted the old city wall. Through the windshield I could see the stone ramparts and the cathedral dome and the rooftops I'd looked at from hotel balconies and restaurant terraces and the arms of a man who had built this city into a trap with me at its center.

Two minutes to the rendezvous point. Everything was green. The machine was running.

And then Ezra's voice in my ear again. And this time the voice was different—the ironic detachment stripped away, replaced by something flat and urgent, the tone of a man delivering information he doesn't want to deliver.

"Cat. We have a problem."

CHAPTER TWENTY-FOUR

THE CHASE – *Cartagena*

"The compound security just made a call," Ezra said. "The yoga instructor was stopped at the main gate on her way out. Routine—the guards check everyone leaving. She mentioned that Señora Salcedo didn't come back for the cool-down. Said she assumed Gabriela went upstairs. The guard logged it and called the house. No one can find her."

I looked at my watch. Three-oh-seven. Gabriela had left the compound at two-fifty. Seventeen minutes. We'd planned for a minimum of thirty before anyone noticed. The yoga instructor's idle comment had cut our window nearly in half.

"How long before it reaches Salcedo?"

"They're still at the inquiry stage. Two guards searching the house. But the head of security just pulled his phone—I'm watching the encrypted channel. If he doesn't find her in the next five minutes, he'll escalate. Once it escalates, it goes to Salcedo, and Salcedo was just in a meeting with you about CI-7, and he is not a stupid man. He will connect the dots."

Five minutes. I was two minutes from the rendezvous point in Getsemaní. Three minutes to get Gabriela into my car. Then eleven minutes to the marina by the route we'd planned—the straight route, the fast route, the route that went along the bay road through Bocagrande.

The route that Salcedo's people would check first.

"Ezra. If they lock down, what do they cover?"

"The bay road. The airport road. And the marina—it's the obvious exit. If Salcedo's security is competent, and they are, they'll have someone at the Club Náutico within fifteen minutes of the alarm going up. Maybe sooner. He keeps people in Bocagrande."

Fifteen minutes. The arithmetic was brutal. Five minutes before the alarm. Fifteen minutes before the marina was watched. I needed twenty-two minutes on the planned route. I was going to arrive at a marina that was already locked down.

"Find me another way," I said.

Calle de la Sierpe. A narrow street in Getsemaní, painted buildings pressing close on either side, a fruit stall at the corner, two men playing dominoes on a plastic table. Lucía's car—a dark blue Chevrolet, anonymous—was parked halfway down the block. The engine was off. Lucía stood beside the driver's door, arms crossed, watching the street with the particular alertness of a woman who had spent three years watching this city and knew exactly what wrong looked like.

Gabriela was in the back seat.

I got out of the Toyota. Walked to Lucía. Our eyes met. She read my face in a second.

"How bad?" she said.

"The window is closing. They noticed sooner than we planned. I need to move now."

Lucía didn't waste time on the information she couldn't change. She handed me the car keys. "The Chevrolet is clean. Registered to a construction company in Turbaco. Full tank. There's a bag in the trunk with water, a phone, cash, and a change of clothes for her."

I looked past her into the back seat. Gabriela was sitting very still, her hands in her lap, a small bag pressed against her side. She was wearing dark clothes—jeans, a blouse, flat shoes, the outfit of a woman who had been told to dress for leaving and had chosen things she could move in. Her face was pale beneath olive skin. Her eyes were enormous. She looked like what she was: a thirty-two-year-old woman who had walked out of the only life she'd known for six years and was now sitting in a stranger's car on a street in Getsemaní, waiting to find out if the door she'd walked through led somewhere safe or somewhere worse.

I opened the driver's door. Got in. Adjusted the mirrors. Turned around to face her.

"Gabriela. I'm Cat. I'm going to get you out of here. I need you to stay low, stay quiet, and trust me. Can you do that?"

She nodded. Her hands were shaking but her eyes were steady—the eyes of a woman who has made a decision and is holding on to it with everything she has.

"Okay," I said. I turned back to the wheel. Started the engine. Pulled into the street.

In the side mirror I saw Lucía watching us go. She raised one hand—not a wave, exactly. An acknowledgment. The gesture of a woman releasing something she'd been carrying for three years.

Ezra in my ear: "Three-eleven. The head of compound security just called Salcedo's personal phone. Cat, the alarm is going up."

The alarm was going up. Right now. Salcedo was receiving a phone call telling him that his wife was not in the house, and in the next thirty seconds the most organized criminal mind in Cartagena was going to connect a missing wife to a meeting with a woman who had just demonstrated detailed knowledge of his organization, and the city was going to close around us like a fist.

I drove.

The planned route was dead. Ezra confirmed it within a minute: "Salcedo's security is mobilizing. Two vehicles leaving the compound now. One heading for the bay road, one heading for Bocagrande. He's got people at the Club Náutico in eight minutes, Cat. Eight. The marina is gone."

The marina was gone. The straight route was gone. The plan, as designed, was gone.

This is the moment that separates the people who survive from the people who don't: the moment when the plan fails and you have to build a new one from whatever is available, in real time, while driving a car through a city that is actively trying to trap you. I have been in this moment before. In Ankara, when the extraction route was blocked and I had to improvise a path through a market district with a hostage who couldn't walk. In Beirut, when the boat didn't show and I spent four hours in a parking garage with a diplomat who was having a panic attack, waiting for a second extraction that my handler wasn't sure was coming.

You don't panic. You assess. You adapt. You move.

"Ezra. The Club Náutico is the main marina. Is there another way to reach the RIB?"

Silence. Two seconds. Three. The silence of a man running scenarios at the speed of a processor that had probably cost more than my car.

"The RIB is at slip fourteen at the Club Náutico. If Salcedo's people are covering the main entrance, you can't walk in the front. But the marina has a service dock on the southern side—commercial, fishing boats, fuel deliveries. It's not gated. It's separated from the main slips by a fuel dock and a repair yard. If you can get to the service dock, you can access the main slips from the water side—walk along the pier, past the fuel dock, to slip fourteen. It's exposed but it's the back door."

"How do I get to the service dock?"

"Not through Bocagrande. That's where they're heading. Come through the old city instead. There's a road that runs along the inside of the wall—Calle del Colegio to Calle de la Universidad, through the Santo Domingo gate, then south along the outer wall to the Muelle de los Pegasos. From there it's a five-minute walk along the waterfront to the service dock. It's the long way around, but it keeps you inside the old city walls for most of it, and Salcedo's people aren't going to be looking for you inside the walled city. They're going to be watching the exits."

"Inside the walls," I said. "Through the old city."

"Through the old city," Ezra confirmed. "In a car. On streets that were built for horses in the seventeenth century. Cat, some of those streets are six feet wide."

"I know," I said. And turned the wheel hard left, away from the bay road, away from the planned route, and into the narrow mouth of a cobblestone alley that led into the heart of the walled city.

The old city was not designed for cars. This is a fact that every tourist discovers on their first afternoon and every driver discovers in their first five minutes, but it takes on a different dimension entirely when you are driving a Chevrolet sedan through streets that were laid out by Spanish colonial engineers who imagined mules and carriages, not automobiles, and certainly not an automobile driven at speed by a woman with a cartel boss's wife in her back seat.

Calle del Colegio. Narrow. Cobblestone. Buildings rising three stories on either side, their balconies reaching toward each other across the gap like hands that almost touch. Pedestrians—tourists with cameras, a man pushing a cart of coconuts, two teenagers on a scooter that squeezed past my side mirror with an inch to spare. I drove at the speed of the street, which was too slow, which was the only speed available because the street would not permit anything faster and forcing it would attract the attention I could not afford.

Gabriela was silent in the back seat. I glanced in the rearview. She was hunched low, the bag in her lap, her face turned toward the window but not seeing the buildings or the tourists or the balconies. She was somewhere inside herself, in the place you go when the fear is too big for the body and the mind retreats to the only room it can still control.

"Gabriela," I said. "Stay with me."

Her eyes met mine in the mirror. She nodded.

Ezra: "Three-fifteen. Salcedo's second vehicle is heading south on the bay road toward the Club Náutico. First vehicle is moving toward the old city—Cat, they're going to check the wall gates. If they post someone at Santo Domingo, you're boxed in."

The wall gates. The old city had a limited number of exits through the colonial wall—Torre del Reloj, Santo Domingo, a few smaller passages. If Salcedo's people covered them, every car leaving the walled city would be visible. I was driving into a box.

"How long before they reach Santo Domingo?"

"Seven minutes. Maybe six. The vehicle is on Avenida Venezuela, moving fast."

Six minutes. I was four minutes from the Santo Domingo gate if the streets cooperated. Two-minute margin. Not enough. One blocked street, one wrong turn, one delivery truck parked where it shouldn't be, and the margin disappeared.

I pressed the accelerator. The Chevrolet bounced over cobblestones. A woman with shopping bags pressed herself against a wall as I passed. The side mirror clipped a wooden shutter that jutted from a ground-floor window—the crack was sharp, a sound that would linger in someone's memory if anyone was paying attention, and I could only pray that no one was.

Left onto Calle de la Universidad. Slightly wider. A restaurant had put tables into the street—white tablecloths, candles, diners looking up as I threaded the car through a gap between a table and a parked motorcycle that was so tight I felt the breath of the diners on my arm through the open window. A waiter shouted something. I didn't hear it. I was already past.

Ezra: "Three-seventeen. Cat, I'm picking up chatter on Salcedo's security channel. They know she's not in the house. They're searching the neighborhood around the compound and they've issued a description to all units. Dark hair, medium height, may be in a vehicle. They don't mention you. Not yet. They think she left on her own."

They didn't know I had her. Not yet. They thought Gabriela had bolted—a wife who'd run, not a wife who'd been extracted. That was good. That bought time. The moment they connected Gabriela's disappearance to Cat Sloane, the search would change—from a runaway wife to an operation, from local security to the full weight of Salcedo's network, and the difference between those two searches was the difference between a net with holes and a net without them.

Right onto a street so narrow that both mirrors scraped the walls simultaneously. The sound of metal on stone was horrible—a grinding shriek that echoed between the buildings and made Gabriela flinch in the back seat. I didn't slow down. Couldn't. The street was a canyon of peeling paint and wrought-iron balconies and exposed electrical wiring, and at the end of it I could see the brightness of a wider street, and beyond that, the honey-colored stone of the city wall.

The Santo Domingo gate.

Ezra: "Three-nineteen. Vehicle approaching the gate from the outside. Two minutes."

Two minutes. I was one minute from the gate. I could see it now—the arched opening in the wall, the traffic beyond, the glimpse of sky and sea that meant the outside. One minute of cobblestone and tourists and a car that was too wide for the street it was on, and then the gate, and then the wall road, and then the waterfront.

I came out of the alley onto the small plaza in front of the gate at a speed that startled a dog and two pigeons and a man selling empanadas from a cart. The gate was open—it was always open, a breach in the wall that had been open for a hundred years, wide enough for two cars to pass though only one ever did because the angle was wrong and you had to commit to the turn with the faith of someone who believes in geometry more than their own eyes.

I committed. The Chevrolet slid through the gate with the passenger-side mirror folded flat against the door and the driver's side mirror catching the stone archway with a crack that shattered the glass and sent fragments scattering across the cobblestones behind us. I didn't stop. I was through the wall. Outside. The road opened ahead of me—not wide but wider, the wall curving to my left, the bay visible ahead, the air suddenly saltier and the light suddenly brighter because the claustrophobic compression of the old city was behind us and the sky was enormous and the sea was right there.

Ezra: "You're through. The vehicle reached the gate fifteen seconds after you. They're not following—they're posting at the gate. They didn't see you."

Fifteen seconds. We'd cleared the gate by fifteen seconds. The margin between escape and capture was the time it takes to tie a shoe.

Then Ezra said the thing I'd been dreading since I'd put Sophie in that room.

"Cat. Someone is approaching the third floor at the hotel. Elevator, coming up from the lobby. Salcedo's people."

The world contracted. The road ahead, the steering wheel under my hands, the bay to my right—all of it receded to the edges of my awareness and the center was occupied entirely by a twenty-four-year-old woman in a hotel room who was about to have company she wasn't expecting.

"How many?"

"One. Male. He came through the lobby two minutes ago and went straight for the elevator. He's not hotel security—wrong shoes, wrong posture. He's checking on you. On whoever he thinks is in that room."

Sophie. Alone. In a bugged room with one exit and a man coming up the elevator who worked for a cartel boss whose wife had just disappeared. Sophie, who was twenty-four and brave and had Jimmy Navarro's steady hands and who was in that room because I had asked her to be there, because I had needed a decoy, because the plan required a body and a performance and I had used the closest thing I had to a daughter as the instrument.

Fallujah. The word detonated in my chest.

Hold your position, Sloane. We need you to hold.

I was in a car on a road in Cartagena and Sophie was in a hotel room three miles away and I could not reach her. I could not help her. I could not do anything except drive and listen and pray to whatever gods oversee the particular category of operations where people you love are in danger because of decisions you made, and the only thing you can do about it is keep moving because the mission requires you to keep moving and the mission has always, always, always come first.

The same calculus. The same impossible, inhuman calculus that I'd faced in a burning building in Fallujah with Jimmy bleeding beside me and a voice on the radio telling me to hold my position. Someone I was responsible for, in danger, and I couldn't reach them. Couldn't help. Could only hold and hope and hate myself for the holding.

"Ezra," I said. My voice was steady. I don't know how. "What is Sophie doing?"

"She's moving. She heard the elevator—the audio bugs picked up the chime. She's in the bathroom. Cat, she's following the protocol."

The protocol. The bathroom window. The service corridor. The back stairs. The car on Calle del Torno. The exit plan I'd drilled into her with the intensity of a woman who knew that this moment was possible and had prepared for it the way you prepare for anything you're terrified of: obsessively, repeatedly, until the response is automatic and the body moves before the mind has time to be afraid.

"The man is in the hallway," Ezra said. "Walking toward your suite. He's trying the door. Cat—he's knocking."

Knocking. Not entering. Knocking meant he didn't have a key. Knocking meant he was checking, not assaulting. Knocking was better than the alternative, but knocking also meant that if no one answered, he would escalate—try the door handle, call for backup, return with a hotel master key.

Silence in my ear. Three seconds. Five. The longest five seconds since Fallujah.

"Sophie is in the service corridor," Ezra said. "Bathroom window. She's out of the room. She's on the stairs."

I breathed.

"The man is still at the door. Knocking again. No answer. He's on his phone—calling it in. He's leaving. Walking back toward the elevator."

He was leaving. He'd knocked, gotten no answer, and was reporting back. The room was empty. But the room was supposed to have someone in it, and the absence would generate questions, and the questions would eventually generate the realization that the woman they thought was Cat Sloane was not in the hotel, which meant the hotel ruse was burned, which meant the clock had just accelerated again.

But Sophie was out.

"Ezra. Sophie."

"She's in the stairwell. Ground floor. Moving to the service exit. Cat, she's fast—she's very fast."

Jimmy's daughter. Moving through a hotel stairwell at speed because a man had knocked on a door and she'd done exactly what I'd told her to do: window, corridor, stairs, car, airport, gone. No hesitation. No second-guessing. The clean, decisive action of a woman who had been prepared for this moment and who executed the preparation without flinching.

"She's out," Ezra said. "Service exit. She's in the car. The driver is moving. Cat—Sophie is clear."

Sophie was clear.

I was driving with tears on my face. I didn't realize it until I felt them on my jaw—two tears, maybe three, the involuntary response of a body that had been holding everything since five a.m. and had just received the one piece of information it could not absorb without breaking. Sophie was safe. The relief was so enormous it had physical weight—I felt it in my shoulders, in my spine, in the grip of my hands on the steering wheel. I wiped my face with the back of my hand and kept driving.

The waterfront road. Muelle de los Pegasos to the south, the bay stretching silver and flat under the afternoon sun. I could see the marina complex ahead—the Club Náutico's main building, the forest of masts and radar antennae, the breakwater that curved around the harbor entrance.

"Ezra. The service dock."

"Left turn in two hundred meters. There's a gravel road that leads to the commercial pier—fish market, fuel depot, repair yard. No gate. The road isn't on most maps. You'll see a blue warehouse with a corrugated roof and a chain-link fence with a gap where the fence meets the seawall. Through the gap, along the pier, past the fuel dock, and you're at the main slips. Slip fourteen is the fourth from the end."

"Salcedo's people at the Club Náutico?"

"Two men at the main entrance. One in the parking lot. They're watching the front. The service dock is three hundred meters south. They can't see it from where they are unless they walk the waterfront, and right now they're stationary."

Stationary. For now. But the man at the hotel had found an empty room, and that information was moving through Salcedo's network right now, and when it reached the people at the marina the search would expand and the service dock would be checked and the three-hundred-meter gap that was currently saving my life would disappear.

I turned left onto the gravel road. The Chevrolet bounced over potholes and broken concrete. The blue warehouse appeared—rusted corrugated roof, the smell of fish and diesel, a pickup truck parked at an angle with its bed full of nets. The chain-link fence ran along the waterfront, and there—where the fence met the seawall—a gap. Not a gate. A gap where the salt air had corroded the fence posts and someone had bent the chain link back far enough for a person to pass through.

I parked the car behind the warehouse, out of sight from the road. Turned off the engine. Turned to Gabriela.

"We have to walk from here. Fast. Stay behind me. If I tell you to run, you run. If I tell you to stop, you stop. Don't look back. Don't look at the marina entrance. Just follow me."

Gabriela clutched her bag. Her face was white. But she nodded, and when I opened the door she opened hers, and when I moved she moved behind me, and the two of us crossed the gravel yard and squeezed through the gap in the chain-link fence and stepped onto the commercial pier.

The pier was concrete, cracked, stained with fish oil and diesel. Fishing boats tied up on our left—small wooden pangas with outboards, a larger trawler being repainted by a man who didn't look up. The fuel dock ahead—pumps, hoses, a corrugated shed with COMBUSTIBLE painted on the side in faded red letters. Beyond the fuel dock, the main marina's slips began—cleaner, newer, the boats getting larger and more expensive as the pier extended north toward the Club Náutico.

I walked fast. Not running—two women running on a pier would be visible from a hundred meters. Walking with purpose. The gait of people who belong here, who are heading to a boat, who have every right to be on this pier at this time. Gabriela matched my pace. She was shorter than me and her stride was half a step behind mine, but she kept up, and the bag was against her chest, and she was breathing in short, controlled pulls that told me she was managing her fear the way I'd told her to—staying with me, staying present, not letting the fear eat the focus.

Past the fuel dock. The repair yard—a boat on blocks, its hull scraped and sanded, a worker crouched under the keel with a grinder that threw sparks across the concrete. Past the repair yard, the pier widened and the slips appeared—numbered, organized, boats rocking gently in their berths. Charter yachts. Sailboats. A catamaran with a Swedish flag.

Slip fourteen. Fourth from the end.

I saw the RIB before I saw the crew. Twenty-two feet, matte black hull, twin Yamaha outboards cocked up on their tilts. It sat low in the water, muscular and anonymous—a boat built for moving fast and not being noticed. The two crew members were on deck, one checking the engines, the other coiling a line. They looked up when they saw me.

"Vamonos," I said. Let's go.

The crew didn't ask questions. They'd been briefed. They lowered the outboards. One of them offered a hand to Gabriela, who took it and stepped down into the RIB with the uncertain balance of a woman who has not been on a boat in a long time and is doing it anyway because there is nowhere left to go but forward.

I stepped aboard. Moved to the helm. The controls were familiar—throttle, wheel, GPS, trim tabs. I'd driven boats like this before. Off the Lebanese coast in 2014, a night extraction that I'd never told anyone about and that had given me a permanent respect for rigid inflatables and a permanent distaste for Mediterranean chop. The memory arrived and departed in the space of a second—my hands already on the throttle, my body already remembering how a boat like this responds, the muscle memory of a skill I'd learned in darkness and fear and was now deploying in darkness and fear.

The crew cast off. I turned the key. The twin Yamahas caught and roared, a sound so loud in the quiet marina that every head within a hundred meters would turn toward it.

Let them turn. By the time anyone understood what they were looking at, we would be gone.

I pushed the throttle forward. The RIB surged away from the slip, the bow lifting, the hull biting into the flat water of the marina basin. Past the other slips—the charter yachts and the sailboats and the catamaran with the Swedish flag. Past the breakwater. Past the fishing boats and the fuel dock and the crumbling seawall where we'd squeezed through a gap in a chain-link fence three minutes ago.

In my ear, Ezra: "Harbor cameras are looped. You're invisible on the municipal feeds. But Salcedo's people at the main entrance just heard the engines. They're moving. They're running along the waterfront toward the slips."

I opened the throttle. The RIB climbed onto plane and the speed went from fast to violent—thirty knots, thirty-five, the hull slamming over the small chop of the harbor basin, the spray soaking the bow where Gabriela gripped the gunwale with both hands, her hair streaming behind her, her face turned forward into the wind and the salt.

The harbor mouth. The old fort on the left, its stone walls golden in the late afternoon light. The seawall on the right. The gap between them—the passage from harbor to open sea, the threshold between a city that held us and an ocean that didn't.

I aimed for it. The Yamahas screamed. The RIB shot through the harbor mouth and out—out into the Caribbean, out into dark blue water that stretched to every horizon, out into the vast indifferent ocean where no one controlled the roads and no one watched the gates and the only law was physics and the only direction was away.

Behind us, Cartagena. The wall. The cathedral dome. The high-rises of Bocagrande. Getting smaller. Getting gone.

Gabriela looked back at the city. Just once. Then she turned forward again and didn't look back.

I held the throttle wide open and drove us north.

CHAPTER TWENTY-FIVE

THE WATER – *Caribbean Sea*

Open water. The Caribbean was dark blue and enormous and did not care that we were on it.

The RIB pounded north-northwest at thirty-five knots, the twin Yamahas driving us over a low swell that lifted the hull and dropped it with a rhythm that was almost peaceful if you ignored the fact that we were fleeing a cartel in a twenty-two-foot inflatable with no lights, no navigation markers, and no certainty about what was waiting at the other end of the GPS coordinates blinking on the screen in front of me.

Cartagena was gone. I'd watched it disappear—the cathedral dome, the high-rises of Bocagrande, the wall that had contained me for a week—shrinking to a line of shapes, then a smudge, then a suggestion of something on the southern horizon, then nothing. The ocean filled the space where the city had been and kept filling it until there was nothing in any direction except water and sky and the thin bright line where they met.

Gabriela sat in the bow. She hadn't spoken since the marina. Her bag was in her lap, her hands wrapped around it, her body braced against the RIB's motion with the rigid posture of someone who is holding herself together by force of will and knows that any relaxation, any softening, will open a crack that lets everything in. I recognized the posture. I'd been sitting in it for a week.

The crew sat amidships—two men, silent, professional, their faces turned away from the wind. They asked nothing. They had been hired to drive a boat and they were letting me drive it instead, and the particular discipline of men who accept unusual circumstances without questions is the discipline of men who have done this kind of work before.

In my ear, Ezra: "Cat. Salcedo has connected you to Gabriela. His security team pulled the hotel surveillance. The man who went to your room reported no one there. Salcedo called your phone—it rang in the empty room. He knows the hotel was a decoy. He knows you have her."

There it was. The last wall down. Salcedo knew everything now—that the meeting was a stall, that the hotel was a performance, that the woman he'd been negotiating with over CI-7 had been extracting his wife while he sat across from her discussing verification protocols. He knew, and knowing meant that the full resources of his organization were now pointed at the Caribbean, at the water, at a twenty-two-foot RIB heading north-northwest toward a rendezvous point he didn't yet know the location of.

"What can he do?" I asked.

"From Cartagena? He has contacts at the harbor authority. He could request a coast guard intercept—but that takes time and official channels, and the coast guard doesn't scramble on the word of a private citizen, even a citizen with Salcedo's connections. More likely he'll send his own people. He has boats. The security team maintains a fast tender at the Club Náutico—I've seen it in the marina records. Thirty-foot center console, triple outboards. It's fast, Cat. Faster than you."

Faster than me. The words settled in my chest like ballast.

"How long before they launch?"

"They need to get to the marina, prep the boat, figure out which direction you went. The harbor cameras are looped—they won't see your departure on the municipal feeds. But they heard the engines and they know you launched from the marina area. They'll assume north.

Everyone runs north. I'd estimate twenty to thirty minutes before they're on the water."

Twenty to thirty minutes. I was twelve nautical miles from the rendezvous point at thirty-five knots. That was twenty minutes. If Salcedo's boat launched in twenty minutes and ran at fifty knots—which a triple-outboard center console could easily do—they would reach the rendezvous point thirty minutes after I did. Thirty-minute margin. Enough time to board the yacht and get moving. Maybe. If the yacht was where it was supposed to be. If the sea stayed calm. If nothing else went wrong.

If.

I drove. The GPS blinked. The ocean stretched ahead, featureless, the late afternoon sun dropping toward the western horizon and painting the water in shades of gold and copper that would have been beautiful under any other circumstances and were, even now, even in this, beautiful in a way that I resented because beauty should not exist in the same moment as fear and yet it always does, and the coexistence is the thing that makes both of them unbearable.

Twenty minutes on the open sea.

Twenty minutes is not a long time. It is the length of a commute, or a lunch break, or the silence between two people who are trying to decide whether to say the thing that will change everything. In a restaurant, in a car, in a bed, twenty minutes passes without notice.

On open water, in a boat with no lights, running from a man who has the resources to chase you across an ocean, twenty minutes is a lifetime. Every second is a decision to keep going. Every wave that lifts the hull is a question—is the yacht still there? Did the coordinates change? Did David's contact in Curaçao honor the arrangement, or did the money or the danger or the complexity of harboring a cartel boss's wife prove to be more than a favor from a previous life could cover?

The GPS showed twelve nautical miles. Then ten. Then eight. The numbers counted down with the mechanical indifference of a system that measures distance without understanding what the distance means, and I watched them and I drove and I tried not to think about the things that could go wrong because the list was so long that starting it would be the same as giving up.

Gabriela spoke. The first words since the marina.

"Is he going to find us?"

She was looking at me from the bow. The wind had pulled her hair loose from whatever she'd done with it and it was streaming around her face and she was squinting against the spray and the salt and her expression was not afraid, exactly—it was the expression of a woman who has been afraid for so long that fear has become a baseline, a constant, the air she breathes, and what she's asking is not will I be afraid but will the fear be justified.

"No," I said. And I said it with the authority of a woman who was not certain but who understood that certainty was not what Gabriela needed. What Gabriela needed was someone who would say no and mean it, and mean it not because the outcome was guaranteed but because the woman saying it had decided that the outcome was unacceptable and would act accordingly.

Gabriela looked at me for a long moment. Then she nodded. Turned forward. Held the gunwale.

I drove.

Six nautical miles. The sun was lower now, the light going from gold to amber. The sea had changed color—darker, deeper, the Caribbean blue that photographs can't capture because the color exists in three dimensions and photographs only have two. The swell was picking up. Not dangerously—a gentle increase in the rhythm, the ocean's breathing getting deeper as the afternoon moved toward evening.

In my ear, Ezra, quiet now: "Salcedo's boat is launching. They're at the Club Náutico. Triple outboards. Heading north."

They were coming. Behind us, invisible, getting closer with every minute because their boat was faster and the ocean offered no cover and the only advantage I had was time—the twenty minutes of head start that was the entire margin between Gabriela's freedom and Gabriela's capture.

Four nautical miles. The GPS blinked.

The sun dropped below a bank of clouds on the western horizon, and the light changed—suddenly, completely, the gold and amber replaced by a diffuse gray that flattened the sea and made the distance harder to judge. The horizon blurred. The water and the sky merged at the edges, and for a terrible moment I couldn't tell where the ocean ended and the air began, and the world felt infinite and empty and I was a woman in a small boat in the middle of it with nothing but a GPS coordinate and a belief that the coordinate meant something.

This was the despair moment. I know this because I've felt it before —in Fallujah, in the seventeenth hour of the Ankara negotiation, in the years after David when I lived alone in an apartment that felt like a country I'd been exiled to. The moment when the machinery of competence and will and forward motion falters, and what's underneath it is revealed, and what's underneath it is a woman who is very tired and very frightened and who has been running on adrenaline and fury and professional pride for so long that she can't remember what it feels like to stop.

I was forty-seven years old. I was driving a boat through the Caribbean with a stranger in the bow and a cartel behind me and a team scattered across three countries who had risked their careers and their safety because I'd asked them to, and the GPS said two nautical miles but the sea said nothing because the sea doesn't speak, and the horizon was empty, and the yacht was not there.

The yacht was not there.

I looked at the GPS. Two nautical miles to the coordinates. I looked at the horizon. Gray water. Gray sky. The merging of the two in a line that held nothing—no white hull, no mast, no navigation lights, no shape that suggested a sixty-foot motor yacht was sitting in international waters waiting for us.

The coordinates could be wrong. The yacht could have moved. David's contact could have spooked and relocated to a different position. The crew could have decided that the risk of sitting stationary in international waters waiting for a boat that might never arrive was greater than the risk of leaving. There were a dozen reasons the yacht might not be where it was supposed to be, and every one of them ended the same way: with me and Gabriela in a twenty-two-foot RIB in the open Caribbean, out of fuel eventually, nowhere to go, and Salcedo's boat getting closer with every minute.

One nautical mile. The GPS blinked.

I stared at the horizon. Willed something to appear. Felt the engine vibrating through the hull and the wheel and my hands, the mechanical heartbeat of a boat that was doing exactly what I asked and could not do the one thing I needed, which was to make the empty ocean produce a yacht.

Gabriela was watching me. I could feel her eyes on the side of my face. She had turned from the bow and was looking at me, and her expression was the expression of a woman who has trusted a stranger with her life and is now watching the stranger's face for the answer to the question she is afraid to ask.

I kept my face steady. I kept my hands on the wheel. I kept driving toward coordinates that pointed at empty water.

Half a nautical mile.

Ezra, in my ear: "Cat. Salcedo's boat is six miles south and closing. Fifty knots. You have maybe eight minutes."

Eight minutes. And the horizon was empty.

I thought: this is how it ends. Not with a confrontation or a negotiation or a clever play, but with an empty ocean and a miscalculation and a woman in a boat who ran out of road. I thought about Sophie, safe on a plane to Miami. I thought about David, building a legal framework for a woman who might never arrive to use it. I thought about Ezra, watching from Lisbon, running his monitors, unable to do anything except narrate the ending. I thought about Kessler, who had trusted me, and Cole, who was supposed to be on a yacht that wasn't here.

I thought about Andrés. In the garden. His hand around mine. I am not the man you think I am.

No. You're not. And I am not the woman who fails. Not today.

I looked at the GPS. Three hundred meters to the coordinates. I looked at the horizon.

And I saw it.

Not where I expected. A quarter mile west of the coordinates—the yacht had drifted on the current, or the crew had repositioned for the swell, or David's contact had adjusted the anchorage for reasons I would never know and didn't need to. What mattered was the shape on the water: white hull, low profile, the silhouette of a sixty-foot motor yacht sitting still on the Caribbean swell with its navigation lights off and its deck lights dimmed to the minimum and a single figure standing at the stern rail, looking south.

Looking for us.

"Ezra," I said. "I have the yacht. Quarter mile west of coordinates. Moving to intercept."

"Thank God," Ezra said. And the fact that Ezra—who cultivated ironic detachment the way other people cultivated gardens—said thank God told me exactly how close he'd been to believing we were lost.

I turned the wheel. The RIB banked hard, spray arcing over the gunwale, the hull slapping the swell as we cut across it at an angle. Gabriela grabbed the rail. The crew adjusted their weight. The yacht grew larger with every second—from a shape to a vessel, from a vessel to a thing with detail, the white hull resolving into fiberglass and chrome, the stern platform coming into view, the figure at the rail becoming a person.

Becoming Cole.

He was standing at the stern rail in a dark jacket, his hands gripping the chrome, his body leaning forward the way you lean forward when you're looking for something in the distance and you can't see it yet but you believe it's coming because someone you trust told you it would come. He was twenty-six years old and he was standing on a yacht in the Caribbean because a woman he'd met once in St. Barts had called him and said Gabriela is in danger and I need you to do something, and he had said anything, and here he was, doing the anything. Waiting.

Gabriela saw him.

I heard the sound she made—not his name, not a word, something more fundamental than language, the sound a body makes when it recognizes another body across a distance that has been too long and too dangerous and is suddenly, impossibly, closing. She stood up in the bow. One hand on the rail, the other pressed against her mouth, and her eyes were fixed on the figure at the stern and her whole body was leaning toward him the way a compass needle leans toward north—not choosing, not deciding, just obeying the pull of the thing it was made to find.

I brought the RIB alongside the yacht's stern platform. The crew secured the lines. The yacht rocked gently in the swell. Cole was above us, on the platform, his face—I could see his face now, and it held everything. Fear and hope and love so raw it was almost indecent, the unguarded emotion of a man who has not yet learned to hide what he feels because he has not yet been punished enough for feeling it.

Gabriela climbed the stern ladder. Her hands were shaking. She was crying—silently, the tears running down her face and disappearing into the salt spray that covered everything, and she reached the platform and Cole reached for her and their hands found each other and then their arms and then he was holding her, holding her the way you hold something you were told you'd lost, the fierce completeness of a grip that has no intention of letting go, and she was pressed against his chest and her face was in his neck and his mouth was in her hair and they were two people standing on a yacht in the Caribbean holding each other as if the ocean might take one of them back if they loosened their arms by a fraction of an inch.

I watched.

From the RIB, ten feet below, looking up at the stern platform where two people who had been pawns in someone else's game had found each other. I had planned this. I had built the door and opened it and driven the boat and navigated the streets and bluffed the man and deployed the team and absorbed the risk and carried the fear, and this—this moment, these two people, this holding—was the output. The thing the machine produced. The reason for all of it.

Cole looked down at me over Gabriela's shoulder. His eyes were wet. He mouthed two words: thank you.

I nodded. Didn't trust my voice. Climbed the ladder.

Ezra in my ear: "Salcedo's boat is three miles south. You need to move. Now."

"Captain," I called to the bridge. "North. Full speed. Now."

The yacht's engines rumbled to life. The crew on the RIB cast off and fell back, their job done. The yacht began to move—slowly at first, the bow swinging north, the stern wash spreading white across the darkening water. Then faster. The engines deepened. The hull climbed. And we were moving north through the Caribbean, the yacht cutting the swell with the steady determination of a vessel designed for open water, and behind us the empty ocean held nothing but the fading light and the distant shape of a fast boat that was three miles away and no longer closing because we were moving and the yacht was not a RIB but a sixty-foot motor yacht with twin diesels and a hull speed that could maintain twenty-two knots for as long as the fuel held.

They couldn't catch us. Not now. Not at this distance, with this heading, with the darkness coming on and the open ocean offering no chokepoints and no way to force a vessel to stop short of a navy warship, which Salcedo did not have.

Ezra confirmed it: "They're falling back. They've turned. They're heading back to Cartagena. Cat—it's over. You're clear."

Clear.

I stood on the stern deck and watched Salcedo's boat disappear into the southern darkness. The Caribbean was enormous around us—water and sky and the first stars appearing in the east, the universe reassembling itself the way it does every evening, indifferent to everything that happens beneath it. The yacht moved north. Cole and Gabriela were somewhere forward, together, beginning the first conversation of a life that Cat Sloane had made possible.

I went below.

The cabin was small. A bunk, a table bolted to the wall, a porthole that showed nothing but dark water and the reflection of a woman who looked like she'd been in a war. I sat on the bunk. Set my hands on my knees. Stared at the wall.

The adrenaline was leaving. I could feel it draining out of me the way water drains from a tub—slowly, completely, taking with it the tension and the focus and the superhuman clarity that had kept me upright and functional since five a.m., and what was left in its absence was a woman sitting on a bunk in a cabin on a yacht in the Caribbean, alone, in the dark, with the sound of the engines below and the sound of the sea outside and the sound of nothing inside because the inside was empty.

I was very good at what I did. I was the best in the world at what I did. I had just built the most elaborate door of my career and opened it and walked a woman through it and reunited her with the man she loved and outplayed the most dangerous criminal I'd ever faced and I had done it with a team of four people across three countries and a bluff and a rigid inflatable boat and a ninety-minute window and flat shoes I could run in.

And I would trade all of it—every bit of skill, every year of training, every operation, every door I've ever built—for what was happening on that deck right now.

Two people holding each other. That's all it was. The simplest thing in the world. A man and a woman, arms around each other, the ordinary miracle of two people choosing each other in a world that makes choosing difficult and staying harder and the having almost impossible. I could build it for others. I could see the architecture of it, plan the logistics, execute the extraction. I could deliver people to the threshold of the thing they wanted most and watch them walk through the door.

I could not walk through it myself.

The scar. The word never. The forty-seven minutes. The man who died beside me because I held my position. The husband who left because loving and living with someone are different skills. The man who kissed my scar in the dark and turned out to be the reason I was in the dark in the first place. The pattern—the long, merciless pattern of a woman who is good at everything except the one thing that matters, and who knows it, and who keeps going anyway because the alternative is stopping and stopping is the thing she fears more than failure.

I sat on the bunk and I stared at the wall and I felt the yacht moving through the water and I let the emptiness be what it was. I didn't cry. I didn't rage. I didn't reach for the fury that had carried me through the last three days. I just sat with it—the loneliness, the wanting, the knowledge that I was forty-seven years old and brilliant and brave and broken in a place that no amount of brilliance or bravery could reach.

Ten minutes. Maybe fifteen. The time it takes to feel something completely before the machinery starts up again and the woman who feels things is replaced by the woman who does things.

I stood up. I washed my face in the small sink. I looked at myself in the mirror above it—the face that Andrés had called extraordinary, the gray eyes that were my father's and that had never lied as well as they lied today, the fine lines that mapped every year of a life spent in rooms where the stakes were other people's futures.

I looked like myself. I looked like Cat Sloane.

That would have to be enough.

I went back up to the deck. The Caribbean night had settled—stars everywhere, the Milky Way visible the way it's visible only at sea, the universe showing you exactly how small you are in case you'd forgotten. The yacht hummed beneath my feet. The wake spread white behind us, a line drawn across the dark water that would disappear in minutes, the way all lines disappear, the way all evidence of passage is eventually erased by the medium it was drawn in.

Cole and Gabriela were on the foredeck, sitting together, her head on his shoulder, his arm around her. They looked up when I appeared. Cole's face was calm now—the raw emotion from the stern platform settled into something steadier, the beginning of relief, the first tentative belief that this was real.

"We're clear," I told them. "Salcedo's people have turned back. We're in international waters heading north. David has a team waiting in Aruba to receive Gabriela and begin the legal framework. You'll be safe."

Gabriela looked at me. The first time she'd really looked at me—not with fear or hope or the desperate assessment of a woman evaluating the stranger who held her life, but with something simpler. Recognition. The recognition of one woman by another, across the distance of their different lives, of the thing they had in common: the experience of being inside a structure built by a powerful man and choosing to walk out.

"Thank you," she said. Her voice was hoarse. Two words. But they were the right two words, and she said them looking at me with eyes that understood what the thank you was for—not just the boat and the plan and the escape, but the door. The fact that someone had seen her inside the beautiful prison and built a way out.

"You're welcome," I said. And meant it. And went to the satellite phone mounted on the bridge to make the call that would end this.

CHAPTER TWENTY-SIX

THE CALL – *Caribbean Sea*

The satellite phone was mounted on the bridge console, a bulky handset that belonged to a previous decade of maritime communication. I picked it up. The plastic was cold from the night air. I dialed the number I'd memorized from Ezra's surveillance logs—Andrés Salcedo's personal mobile, the one that routed through a VoIP relay in Panama before connecting to a device registered to a consulting firm that didn't exist.

He answered on the first ring.

Not because he was waiting for my call. Because he'd been waiting for any call—any piece of information, any thread he could pull to understand what had happened to his world in the last three hours. A man like Salcedo does not sit quietly when the architecture he's built starts collapsing. He works the phones. He mobilizes. He calculates. And when his phone rings from a number he doesn't recognize, he answers it, because the unknown number might be the piece that makes the picture whole.

"Andrés," I said.

Silence. One second. Two. The silence of a man who recognizes a voice and is recalibrating everything he thought he knew about the person it belongs to. When he spoke, his voice was controlled with a precision that was itself a form of violence—every syllable measured, every inflection managed, the vocal equivalent of a man holding a weapon very still.

"Catherine."

Catherine. Not Cat. He used the name he'd always used, the name from the dinners and the balconies and the bed, and the use of it was deliberate—a reminder, a claim, a way of saying I knew you before you became the person who did this to me. Or maybe not. Maybe it was simply the name he'd learned and the name he used and the interpretation was mine and the interpretation was wrong. I would never know. The ambiguity was permanent, and I was going to have to live inside it.

"I'm going to tell you what I know," I said. "And then I'm going to tell you what happens next. You can listen, or you can hang up, but if you hang up, the next call I make is to the Department of Justice, and that call will be less pleasant for you than this one."

He didn't hang up.

I told him.

I told him everything. Not as an accusation—as an architecture. The way you describe a building you've walked through and examined and understood, from the foundation to the roof. I spoke with the clinical precision of a woman presenting a case, because that's what this was—a case, built from evidence, and the evidence was comprehensive and the architecture was airtight and the man on the other end of the phone knew it because he was the one who'd built it.

"The blackmail of Cole Hartwell was designed and funded by you. Rafael Herrera works for you—his operation is funded through Inversiones del Pacífico, which routes through a Liechtenstein trust to a Zurich law firm to Fundación Horizonte, which is your literacy foundation. The same pipeline that funds children learning to read in Buenaventura funds the man who photographed your wife with the President's son. You built that, Andrés. You built all of it."

I could hear him breathing. Controlled. Even. The breathing of a man who is listening with his entire body and giving away nothing.

"The photographs of Gabriela and Cole in St. Barts were not an accident you discovered. They were an operation you commissioned. You allowed your wife's affair—or encouraged it, or engineered the circumstances under which it would happen—because the affair was the weapon and the photographs were the ammunition and the target was never Cole Hartwell. The target was the White House. You needed a crisis severe enough to force the President to deploy someone with intelligence community access. Someone who would dig into the sealed federal files connected to Miguel Herrera's conviction. Someone who would push on Operation Bright Horizon and surface the identity of CI-7."

Silence. The satellite connection crackled faintly—the sound of a signal bouncing off a satellite in orbit, traveling through space, connecting a woman on a yacht to a man in a city she'd just escaped from. The distance between us was measured in miles now, not inches, and the distance was a relief so profound it felt like a physical sensation.

"You built a machine," I said. "An elaborate, expensive, patient machine. And I was the tool. You brought me to Cartagena to do exactly what I did—dig into the files, push on the sealed records, use my contacts to get close to CI-7's identity. And while I was doing that, you were in my bed learning what I knew and how close I was getting. Every conversation. Every dinner. Every night. All of it—intelligence collection dressed up as intimacy."

I heard something on the line. A sound. Not a word—something shorter, something involuntary. It might have been a breath. It might have been the beginning of a denial he decided not to make. It might have been the sound a man makes when the person who understood him most completely describes the thing he did with an accuracy that leaves no room for the version of himself he preferred.

"You have been thorough," he said. His voice was quiet. Not defeated—Andrés Salcedo would not sound defeated if you dismantled his entire operation in front of him, because defeat is a posture and posture is a choice and he would choose to sound like exactly what he was: a man who is calculating his next move. But quiet. The volume of a man who is measuring every word because the wrong one could cost him something he hasn't yet finished assessing.

"I am thorough," I said. "It's the thing you liked about me. Among other things."

A pause. And then—impossible, infuriating, heartbreaking—a sound that might have been a laugh. Low, brief, the ghost of the laugh I'd heard over wine and candles, the laugh of a man who appreciated a well-constructed sentence and couldn't help responding to one even in the wreckage of his own design.

"Among other things," he said. "Yes."

The subtext ran beneath the conversation like a river under ice. Every word had two meanings. Every pause held a room we'd been in together. He said thorough and I heard his hand on my hip. I said among other things and I heard his voice in the dark saying extraordinary. The professional conversation and the personal history were braided together so tightly that pulling them apart would have required destroying both, and neither of us was willing to do that, because the braid was the only honest thing left between us.

"Gabriela is safe," I said. "She's with me. She's beyond your reach, and she's going to stay beyond your reach. I'm telling you this not as a threat but as a fact, because you are a man who respects facts and I am a woman who deals in them."

"Gabriela is my wife."

"Gabriela is a human being who spent six years in a house she couldn't leave, married to a man who used her body as a weapon in an operation she didn't know existed. You put her in a room with Cole Hartwell and then photographed what happened. You weaponized her loneliness. You turned her need for connection into ammunition, and you did it with the same precision you bring to everything, and the fact that you're calling her my wife right now—as if ownership is the relevant concept—tells me everything about why she walked out of your house today and didn't look back."

The silence that followed was different from the others. Heavier. The silence of a man who has been told something that lands not in the strategic part of his mind but somewhere deeper, somewhere he's built walls against, and the walls hold but the impact registers.

When he spoke again, his voice was harder. The calculating quiet replaced by something with an edge.

"You are in a difficult position, Catherine. You have taken my wife from my home. You have disrupted an operation that involves significant resources and significant people. The consequences of this—"

"The consequences of this are mine to manage," I said. "And I'm going to tell you exactly how I'm going to manage them, and you're going to listen, because the alternative is that I stop managing them and let them fall where they fall, and where they fall is on you."

I stood on the bridge of a yacht in the Caribbean, under stars I couldn't name, holding a satellite phone connected to a man who had kissed my scar and built a crisis around my competence and who was, right now, sitting in a city I'd just escaped from, calculating whether the woman on the phone was bluffing or whether she held what she claimed to hold.

I held enough. I held Gabriela.

"Here are the terms," I said. "They are not negotiable. They are not the beginning of a conversation. They are the end of one."

I could hear him breathing. Waiting. The discipline of a man who knows when to listen.

"First. The photographs of Cole Hartwell and Gabriela are destroyed. Every copy, every backup, every digital file. Rafael's operation is shut down completely and permanently. This is verified—I will have independent confirmation that the material no longer exists in any form. If a single photograph surfaces, anywhere, at any time, the arrangement is void and everything else I'm about to describe goes into effect immediately."

"Second. You leave the President alone. You leave Cole Hartwell alone. You leave their families alone. No contact, no leverage, no operations directed at or involving any member of the Hartwell family or the current administration. This is permanent. Not for a year. Not for a term. Permanent."

"Third. You leave me alone. You leave my team alone. You leave everyone who participated in this operation alone. No retaliation. No surveillance. No contact of any kind. I walk away from this, and I stay walked away, and so do you."

"Fourth. Gabriela lives a peaceful life in a location you will never know, under protection you cannot breach. She is cooperating with federal authorities—not yet, but she will be, under a formal agreement that the Department of Justice is preparing as I speak. The things she knows—the meetings, the names, the money, the logistics she observed during six years in your house—stay in a file. The file does not get opened unless you force my hand. She is a nuclear weapon pointed at your operation, Andrés, and the only thing keeping her from detonating is your compliance with these terms."

I paused. Let the terms sit. Let him hear the architecture of his own containment—the walls I'd built around him in the space of a single afternoon, using his wife and his secrets and the machinery of American federal law as the building materials.

"And CI-7," he said. His voice was careful now. The edge still there but controlled, directed, the voice of a man who is circling back to the thing he'd wanted from the beginning. "You said you had access to the identity. That access—does it remain part of this arrangement?"

CI-7. Even now. Even after everything—the extraction, the pursuit, the loss of his wife, the terms I'd just delivered—even now, the mole was the thing that pulled at him. The informant inside his organization, the person who had betrayed him from close range, the name he'd built an international crisis to obtain. The not-knowing was a wound that my terms hadn't addressed, and he was probing it the way you probe a wound—carefully, precisely, looking for the depth.

"CI-7 stays where it is," I said. "In a sealed file, behind a wall you cannot breach. I have the access. I have the ability to surface that name at any time. If you violate any element of these terms—if a photograph appears, if Cole Hartwell is approached, if anyone on my team is harmed—the name goes to the DEA, and the DEA goes to the informant, and the informant goes into witness protection, and the testimony gets rehabilitated, and your entire network comes under a level of federal scrutiny that will make Operation Bright Horizon look like a traffic stop."

The bluff. The beautiful, necessary, permanent bluff. I didn't have the name. I would never have the name. But Salcedo believed I had access to it, because I'd sat across from him in a restaurant and fed him enough detail from the sealed files to establish credibility, and the credibility held because the details were real even if the conclusion was a lie. He would spend the rest of his life believing that Cat Sloane could surface CI-7's identity, and that belief was the final lock on the cage I'd built around him.

Permanent stalemate. Gabriela as leverage. CI-7 as deterrent. Two weapons, one real and one imagined, holding a man in place for as long as both of us were alive.

"You have thought this through," he said.

"I have."

"You have thought it through with the kind of care and precision that I recognize because it is the way I think. The architecture. The layering. The redundancy of leverage—multiple pressure points, any one of which is sufficient, all of which together are insurmountable. You built this the way I would have built it."

"Yes," I said. "I did."

A long silence. The satellite connection hummed. I could hear the Caribbean around me—the slap of water against the hull, the low vibration of the engines, the wind crossing the open bridge. And through the phone, I could hear Cartagena—or I imagined I could. The distant noise of a city at night, the life continuing in a place I'd left behind, the world as indifferent to the conversation happening on this phone line as it was to everything else.

"You outplayed me," he said. Quietly. Not with anger—with something closer to wonder, or the particular recognition that arrives when you encounter someone who operates at your level and discover that they operate at a level beyond it. The chess player studying the board after the match, seeing the move he missed, understanding the architecture of his own defeat.

"I did what I had to do," I said. The same words I'd said in the restaurant. What I had to. The phrase that contained everything and explained nothing, because the truth was more complicated than any phrase could hold—the truth was that I had done what I had to do, and I had hated doing it, and I would do it again, and the doing of it had cost me something I hadn't finished paying for.

"Catherine."

"Andrés."

A pause. And then he said something that I did not expect, that I could not have predicted, that arrived through the satellite phone from a city two hundred miles south and landed in my chest with the force of a thing I would carry for a very long time.

"The garden was real."

Three words. The garden was real. He meant the evening before the operation—the courtyard, the jasmine, the stars, the dinner he'd cooked, the confession that might have been performance or might have been the one genuine thing he'd offered in a week of performances. I am not the man you think I am. He was telling me now, across two hundred miles of Caribbean darkness, that the man in the garden was not a performance. That the man who had held my hand and kissed my knuckles and said before you leave with the weight of a wound—that man was real.

Or he was performing still. One final manipulation—the parting gift of a man who understood that the most effective weapon in his arsenal had always been the possibility that what happened between us was genuine, and who was deploying that weapon one last time to ensure that the woman who had outplayed him would spend the rest of her life wondering whether she'd destroyed something real.

I would never know. That was the cruelty of it and the design of it and the thing I was going to have to live with. The ambiguity was not a flaw in his architecture. It was the architecture.

"Goodbye, Andrés," I said.

I didn't say the garden was real for me too, which would have been true. I didn't say I know, which would have been a lie. I didn't say anything about the scar or the dark or the way his hand felt on my hip or the second night when I cried and he stayed. I said goodbye, because goodbye was the only word that was both honest and safe, and I had learned—was still learning, would never stop learning—that honest and safe are rarely the same thing, and when they are, you should take it.

"Goodbye, Catherine," he said.

I hung up. Set the handset back in its cradle. Stood on the bridge in the dark.

The yacht moved north through the Caribbean night. The engines hummed. The wake spread white behind us, a temporary mark on dark water that the ocean erased as fast as we could draw it. The stars were impossibly bright—the dense, close stars of the tropics, the ones that make you feel both infinitely small and strangely accompanied, as if the universe is watching and doesn't care but is watching anyway.

I stood on the bridge and I felt the phone call settling into the place where I keep the things that have shaped me. Fallujah. Jimmy. David. The Intelligence Star I don't deserve. And now Andrés Salcedo, and a garden, and three words on a satellite phone that I would turn over in my mind for years, examining them from every angle, never arriving at a conclusion, because the man who spoke them had made certainty impossible and had done it on purpose or had done it by accident and the difference between those two things was the entire question and the question had no answer.

The garden was real.

Maybe. I would give him that. Maybe the garden was real. Maybe the man who cooked dinner barefoot and told me about a Vermeer that made him weep and said never want anything so visibly that the wanting can be used against you—maybe that man existed alongside the man who orchestrated crises and weaponized intimacy and built machines out of human beings. Maybe both men were real and the coexistence was not a contradiction but a condition, the same condition I'd recognized in his house: beauty and brutality, sharing the same rooms, refusing to resolve into something simple.

I would not resolve him into something simple. I would carry the complexity, because the complexity was the truth, and the truth was the only thing I'd ever been able to hold on to.

Somewhere forward, Cole and Gabriela were sleeping, or holding each other, or lying awake in the dark the way you lie awake when the world has changed and you haven't caught up to the change yet. They were safe. They were together. They were the output of an operation that had cost me more than any operation I'd ever run, and the cost was not measured in money or risk but in the specific currency of a woman who had opened herself to someone for the first time in years and discovered that the opening was the plan.

The yacht sailed north. The Caribbean held us. The night was vast and dark and indifferent to everything that had happened on its surface today—the chase, the extraction, the phone call, the three words, the silence after the three words. The ocean didn't care. The stars didn't care. The world kept turning at its usual speed, and the wake behind us disappeared, and the only evidence that any of it had happened was the fact that a woman was standing on a bridge in the dark, alone, holding a complexity she would never put down.

I stood there for a long time. Then I went below to sleep. Tomorrow there would be Aruba, and handoffs, and the beginning of Gabriela's new life, and the phone calls to Kessler and David, and the logistics of unwinding an operation and returning to a world that didn't know what I'd done and never would.

Tomorrow I would be Cat Sloane again. The fixer. The woman who builds doors.

Tonight I was just a woman on a boat, heading north, carrying everything.

CHAPTER 27
THE END

HOME – *New York*

The jet was a Cessna Citation, chartered out of Aruba, six seats and a cabin that smelled like leather and recycled air and the particular emptiness of a plane with one passenger. I'd booked it myself—one of the luxuries I allow after a case, the private flight home, the hours of solitude at altitude where no one can reach me and no one expects anything and I can sit in a cream-colored seat and stare out a window at clouds and let the machinery of my professional self wind down at whatever pace it needs.

It is an extravagance. I know this. A woman who flies private when she could fly commercial is a woman who has made a choice about how she spends money, and the choice says something about priorities, and the priority is this: after ten days of being watched and listening and performing and running and driving a boat through dark water with a stranger's life in my hands, I need to be alone. Not the alone of a hotel room with audio bugs. Not the alone of a yacht cabin after a phone call that will live in my chest for years. The actual alone—the kind you pay for, the kind that comes with a closed door and thirty-seven thousand feet of vertical distance between you and everything you're trying to leave behind.

The plane climbed out of Aruba and turned north. Below, the

Caribbean slid past—the same water I'd crossed in a RIB twelve hours ago, the same blue that had held us while we ran. From this altitude it looked harmless. Flat. Pretty. The kind of water you see in advertisements for resorts, not the kind you navigate in the dark with a cartel's wife in the bow and a GPS coordinate that points at empty ocean.

I had a glass of water. I had my phone, turned off. I had my bag, packed in Aruba at a hotel I'd checked into at two a.m. and checked out of at six. I had the clothes I was wearing—clean, dark, unremarkable—and a body that felt like it had been disassembled and put back together slightly wrong, the way you feel after sustained adrenaline when the chemistry finally wears off and what remains is the awareness of every muscle and joint and the specific fatigue of a nervous system that has been running at maximum capacity for too long.

I should have slept. The seat reclined. The cabin was quiet. Instead I sat with my forehead against the window and watched the water pass beneath me and I felt the particular emptiness that follows a completed case—the hollowed-out sensation of a woman who has poured everything into a vessel and the vessel is full and the woman is empty, and the emptiness is not peaceful but desolate, the landscape I'd sat in on a shower floor two nights ago, the terrain of a woman stripped of purpose who hasn't yet found the next purpose to replace it.

This emptiness was worse than usual. Every case leaves a residue, but Cartagena had left something heavier—not a residue but a presence, an inhabited space inside me that was full of things I couldn't put down. The man I'd slept with and the man he actually was. The woman I'd saved and the way she'd looked at me on the yacht—recognition, gratitude, the silent communication between two women who understood what it meant to walk out of a structure built by a powerful man. The team I'd trusted—Sophie in a hotel room, Ezra at his monitors, Lucía on a street corner, David building legal architecture from Washington. The fairy tale I'd assembled from intelligence and bluffs and a rigid inflatable boat—Cole and Gabriela on a yacht deck, holding each other, beginning a life I'd made possible and would never share.

The garden was real.

I closed my eyes. Opened them. The Caribbean was behind us now, replaced by the gray-green water of the Atlantic, and the clouds had thickened, and the altitude made everything look small and distant and manageable, which was a lie that altitude tells and I was grateful for it.

Three hours to Teterboro. I sat in the cream-colored seat and I carried everything and I watched the world get smaller from a very great height.

Sophie was waiting at Teterboro.

Not inside the terminal—outside, leaning against the black sedan she used for airport pickups, arms crossed, sunglasses on despite the overcast January afternoon. She was wearing a dark coat and jeans and she looked like what she was: a twenty-four-year-old New Yorker waiting for someone at a private airport in New Jersey, unremarkable, professional, the kind of woman you'd walk past without noticing unless you knew to look for the steadiness in her posture and the particular way she scanned the tarmac, watching for one person among the mechanics and the ground crew.

I came down the jet's stairs with my bag over my shoulder. The January air hit me—cold, sharp, the brutal clarity of a New York winter after the Caribbean's damp heat. The temperature difference was physical, a slap, and I welcomed it because the cold was honest and specific and it replaced the diffuse ache of the flight with something I could identify and address.

Sophie saw me. Pushed off the car. Walked toward me. And I saw something in her face that I hadn't seen before Cartagena—or maybe I had seen it and hadn't recognized it because I hadn't been looking. A knowingness. The particular expression of a woman who has done a hard thing and come through it and is now standing on the other side with the knowledge of what she's capable of, and the knowledge has changed her, and the change is permanent.

She took my bag. I let her, because letting Sophie take my bag was a small act of surrender that I could afford, and the small surrenders are the ones that keep you from collapsing under the weight of the large ones.

"Hi," she said.

"Hi."

We got in the car. Sophie drove. The route from Teterboro to Manhattan was automatic for her—through the industrial sprawl of northern New Jersey, across the George Washington Bridge, down the Henry Hudson. She drove the way she did everything: competently, without drama, with the quiet confidence of someone who doesn't need to prove she can do the thing she's doing.

For ten minutes, neither of us spoke. The bridge. The river. The skyline assembling itself through the windshield—the buildings I'd looked at from the window of my apartment for twelve years, the city I'd chosen after the divorce because it was the opposite of Washington in every way that mattered: anonymous, indifferent, a place where a woman could be alone without anyone asking why.

Then Sophie said, "Do you want to hear about the hotel?"

I did and I didn't. The professional part of me needed the debrief—the details, the timeline, the moment-by-moment account of how she'd handled the approach. The other part of me—the part that had listened through an earpiece while a man knocked on a door behind which her life depended on a bathroom window—that part wanted to never hear about the hotel again.

"Tell me," I said.

She told me. Matter-of-fact. The way I would have told it—chronological, detailed, emotionally compressed, the voice of a professional recounting an operational sequence.

The shower had run for eight minutes. She'd ordered the room service. She'd made the phone call to Ezra at three, delivering the CI-7 lines he fed her, her voice pitched to match my cadence—lower than her natural register, slower, the slight rasp I develop after a long day. She'd walked past the window at the right intervals. She'd typed at the desk. She'd maintained the pattern.

Then the elevator chime. The knock. The man's voice through the door—not speaking to her, speaking on a phone, confirming he was at the room, confirming no one was answering.

"I was already in the bathroom by the time he knocked," Sophie said. "The window was open. I had my bag. I went through the window into the service corridor and down the stairs. I didn't stop. I didn't look back." She glanced at me. "Just like you told me."

Just like I told her. The protocol, executed without improvisation, without panic, without the hesitation that kills people in situations where hesitation is a luxury the situation doesn't offer. She had done exactly what I'd trained her to do, and the training had worked, and the working was the thing that saved her.

I heard my own voice in this twenty-four-year-old woman—the compressed delivery, the operational precision, the instinct to lead with what she did right and bury what she felt underneath. I heard my own voice, and I felt two things simultaneously: pride so fierce it was almost physical, a heat in my chest that I recognized as the specific pride of a woman who has poured her competence into another person and watched that person become capable. And terror. Because the competence that had saved Sophie's life was the same competence that had put her in the room, and the person who had poured it into her was the same person who had asked her to use it in a situation where failure meant something I could not survive.

We were on the Henry Hudson now. The river on our left, gray and flat. The apartment buildings of Riverside Drive passing on our right.

"Sophie."

"Yeah."

"You did good."

She didn't look at me. Kept her eyes on the road. But something in her jaw shifted—a tightening, a control, the muscle memory of a woman holding an emotion in place.

"I know," she said.

Two words. I know. Not thank you, not I was scared, not the performative modesty that people offer when they're told they've done well and want to appear humble. I know. The clean, undecorated acknowledgment of a woman who understands what she did and doesn't need anyone else to validate it. Jimmy's daughter. My girl. The woman who was going to be extraordinary if the world didn't break her first, and whose primary risk of breaking came from the fact that she worked for me.

Silence. A mile. Two miles. The exit for the West Side approaching.

Then Sophie let one crack show.

"The knock," she said. Quietly. Not looking at me. Her hands steady on the wheel but her voice carrying something underneath the steadiness—a tremor, not of weakness but of honesty, the particular frequency of a person admitting a thing they'd kept hidden because keeping it hidden was how they'd survived. "When he knocked. The sound. I was already in the bathroom, I was already moving, but the sound—" She paused. "I didn't expect how loud it would be. How close. The door was right there. He was right there. And for about two seconds I couldn't move. My hand was on the window and I just—I couldn't move."

Two seconds. The frozen moment. The instant when the body's fear response overrides the training and the will and the preparation, and the person inside the operative is revealed—the twenty-four-year-old woman who was alone in a room in a foreign city with a man on the other side of the door who worked for people who would hurt her. Two seconds of paralysis. Two seconds of being human before the training took over and she moved.

I recognized it. Not from observation but from experience. The frozen moment was my oldest companion—Fallujah, when the radio said hold and my body held even though Jimmy was dying, the two seconds before I started trying to save him that I'd spent not moving because the sound of the order was louder than the sound of his breathing, and the two seconds had cost him everything and cost me everything and I had carried those two seconds for fifteen years.

"Two seconds is nothing," I said. "Two seconds is your body doing what bodies do. You moved. That's what matters. You moved."

Sophie nodded. Swallowed. Said nothing else about it. The crack sealed. The professional surface reassembled itself. But I had seen it—the fault line, the place where the competence rested on something vulnerable, the human underneath the operative—and I would not forget it, because forgetting it was how you lost people. Forgetting the vulnerability was how you kept asking them to do things that the vulnerable part couldn't sustain, and one day the thing you asked would be the thing that broke them, and you wouldn't see it coming because you'd stopped looking.

I was not going to stop looking. Not with Sophie. Not with Jimmy's daughter.

She took the exit. Turned onto my street. Pulled up in front of my building—a prewar six-story on the Upper West Side, the kind of building where the doorman knows your name and your schedule and notices when you've been away for ten days but doesn't ask where you went.

I reached for my bag in the back seat. Sophie was looking at me. Not at the road, not at the building, at me. Really looking—the way she did sometimes when the professional deference dropped and the person underneath emerged, the person who had known me since she was fourteen and who had watched me at her father's funeral and who understood things about me that I had never told her because she had inherited Jimmy's ability to see people clearly without requiring them to explain themselves.

"Are you okay?" she asked.

The question. The same question David would ask, and Kessler would not ask, and Ezra would ask sideways through a joke about energy drinks. Are you okay. The simplest question in the language and the hardest to answer honestly, because okay is a word that covers everything from fine to destroyed, and the distance between those two poles is the distance I lived in, and the honest answer would have required me to stand in that distance and describe the view.

I almost said something real. I felt it forming—the truth, or a piece of it, rising through the layers of control and professional composure and trained response toward the surface where it would become words, and the words would be something like: no, I'm not okay, I fell in love with a man who was using me and I don't know if any of it was real and I built a fairy tale for two people and I can't build one for myself and I am so tired, Sophie, I am so tired of being the one who carries everything and never puts it down.

I didn't say it. Not yet. The words reached the surface and I felt them there, pressing against the inside of my throat, and I swallowed them back down, because the car was not the place and the moment was not the moment and I was not yet the woman who could say those things out loud without the saying of them undoing the structure that held me together.

But I didn't say fine either. I didn't give her the automatic response, the deflection, the closed door. I gave her something in between—a pause. A look. A half-second of unguarded eye contact in which she could see, if she was looking—and she was looking, she was always looking—that the answer was complicated, and the complication was not a dismissal but an invitation, deferred.

"I will be," I said.

Sophie held my gaze for a moment. Nodded. Didn't push. The grace of a woman who understands that some doors open slowly, and the pushing closes them.

"See you Monday," she said.

"See you Monday."

I got out of the car. Walked into my building. The doorman said welcome home and I said thank you and the elevator took me to the fourth floor and I unlocked my apartment and walked into the silence of a place that had been empty for ten days and smelled like dust and the ghost of the coffee I'd made the morning I'd left for St. Barts, which felt like a year ago and felt like yesterday and felt like a life that belonged to a different woman, which it did.

I unpacked. The methodical ritual of a woman returning from a trip—clothes in the hamper, toiletries in the bathroom, shoes by the closet door. The physical acts of restoration, the body's way of reasserting the ordinary after the extraordinary, the small domestic gestures that say: you are home, this is your life, these are your things, you are still the person who lives here.

I was emptying the inside pocket of my bag when I found it.

A cocktail napkin. Cream-colored, thick stock, the kind that expensive parties use because the weight of the paper communicates something about the cost of the evening. It was creased from being folded and carried and pressed against other things in a pocket for ten days, and on it, in handwriting I recognized—precise, European-inflected, the handwriting of a man who had been educated in schools where penmanship mattered—were two words and a phone number.

Andrés. And his number.

He'd written it at the party. The villa in the hills above Cartagena, the night we met, the evening of the green dress and the balcony and the first conversation that had felt like recognition. He'd pressed the napkin into my hand when we said goodnight, and I'd put it in my bag, and the bag had traveled with me through St. Barts and back to Cartagena and through the old city streets and across the Caribbean and here, to this apartment, this moment, this silent room where a woman stood holding a cocktail napkin and trying to decide what to do with it.

I should throw it away. The operational logic was clear: the napkin was an artifact of a relationship that had been a cover for an intelligence operation, and the man who'd written his number on it had used me as a tool, and the tool was no longer in service, and the artifact had no value. Throw it away. Put it in the kitchen trash with the expired milk and the week-old takeout containers and the other debris of a life interrupted. Close the bag. Move on.

I didn't throw it away.

I stood in my apartment in the January dark—the lamps off, the city glow coming through the windows, the specific blue-gray light of a New York winter evening—and I held the napkin and I looked at his handwriting and I felt the thing I'd been carrying since the phone call on the yacht, the thing that three words on a satellite connection had planted in me and that no amount of professional analysis or operational logic could uproot.

The garden was real.

Maybe it was. Maybe the man who'd written his number on a cocktail napkin at a party in the hills above Cartagena was, in that moment, not performing. Maybe the hand that pressed the napkin into mine was the hand of a man who had looked at a woman across a room and felt what I'd felt—the shock of recognition, the gravitational pull, the instant and irrational certainty that the person across from you sees the world the way you see it and will therefore understand the parts of you that no one else has managed to reach.

Or maybe the napkin was the first move in a game I'd spent ten days losing. Maybe the number was bait. Maybe the handwriting was calculated, the press of the napkin rehearsed, the entire gesture—its intimacy, its old-fashionedness, its suggestion of a man who preferred paper to phones—was designed to create exactly the impression it had created: that I was being chosen by someone who chose carefully.

I would never know. The ambiguity was the architecture, and the architecture was permanent, and I was going to live inside it for a long time.

I opened the drawer of the small table by the front door—the drawer where I kept keys and stamps and the accumulated small objects of a life lived alone—and I put the napkin inside. Closed the drawer.

The reader—if there were a reader, if this were a story someone was telling—would understand why. Not because the napkin had operational value. Not because I was sentimental, which I am not, or nostalgic, which I can't afford to be. But because some part of what happened on those balconies was real—the conversations, the way he listened, the way he made me feel seen in a way I hadn't felt seen in years—and I was not ready to let that go. I was not ready to reduce ten days to a con, or a man to a villain, or myself to a mark. The truth was more complicated than any of those words, and the napkin was the complication, and the complication was the only honest thing left, and I kept it because I am a woman who keeps honest things, even when the honesty hurts, even when the honesty might be a lie.

That is either the bravest or the most broken thing about me. I have never been able to tell the difference.

I turned on the kitchen light. Made coffee. Stood at the counter and drank it and looked out the window at the city—the buildings, the traffic, the lives being lived in every window, the ordinary miracle of a million people doing a million things at once and none of them knowing or caring what a woman on the Upper West Side had done this week.

Tomorrow I would call Kessler and deliver the final debrief. Tomorrow I would call David and confirm that the legal framework was in place and Gabriela was safe. Tomorrow I would open my laptop and begin the documentation—the meticulous, comprehensive record of everything I'd done and why, the paper trail that would protect the people who'd helped me if the protection was ever needed. Tomorrow I would be Cat Sloane, the fixer, the woman who builds doors, the best in the world at what she does.

Tonight I was a woman in her apartment, drinking coffee, looking at a city, carrying a complexity she would never put down and a cocktail napkin she should have thrown away and hadn't and wouldn't because the not-throwing-away was the most honest thing she'd done all day.

The coffee was good. The apartment was quiet. The crack was widening—the one Sophie had seen, the one David would see, the one that let the light in or let the structure out, depending on whether you believed that cracks were openings or failures, and I had spent forty-seven years believing they were failures and was beginning, slowly, painfully, in the specific silence of a January evening in New York, to consider the possibility that they were something else.

I finished the coffee. I washed the mug. I set it in the rack to dry.

And then, because I am Cat Sloane and because Cat Sloane does not stop, I sat down at my desk and opened my laptop and began working on the next thing. Whatever the next thing would be. Whatever door needed building. Whatever impossible situation required a woman who was very good at impossible situations and very bad at sitting still.

The city hummed outside. The apartment held me. The drawer by the front door held a napkin with a man's handwriting on it, and the handwriting held a number I would never call, and the number held a voice I would hear in my sleep for longer than I wanted to admit.

Cartagena was over. The case was closed. The fairy tale was built.

And the crack was widening.

• • •

Cascais, Portugal — Three Weeks Later

The terrace faced the sea.

It was a small terrace—tiled in blue and white, the old Portuguese pattern, azulejos worn smooth by salt air and decades of morning coffee. A wrought-iron table. Two chairs. A clay pot of geraniums that someone had placed at the corner where the railing met the wall, the red blossoms catching the light the way red things do in southern countries, vivid and unapologetic.

Gabriela Montero sat in the chair closest to the railing. She wore a white cotton dress. No shoes. Her hair was down, loose around her shoulders, still damp from the shower. She held a cup of coffee in both hands, the way you hold something warm when the morning air is cool, and she was looking at the Atlantic—not the Caribbean, not the water she'd crossed in a boat with a stranger at the helm, but the other ocean, the one on the far side of the world from the life she'd left.

The coffee was strong. Portuguese coffee, dark and slightly bitter, served in a cup so small it seemed designed for a different species. She was learning to like it. She was learning to like a great many things—the bread from the padaria on the corner, the sound of Portuguese spoken quickly in the street below, the particular quality of January light on the Tagus estuary, which was softer than Caribbean light and arrived at a lower angle and made everything look like a painting that hadn't quite dried.

Cole Hartwell sat in the other chair. He had a cup of the same coffee, untouched, cooling on the table beside a newspaper he wasn't reading. He was watching Gabriela. Not with the careful, guarded attention of a man who is performing interest, but with the open, undefended gaze of a man who has been given something he didn't believe he'd get to keep and is still adjusting to the having of it.

She felt him watching. Turned from the sea. Their eyes met.

She put her hand on the table. He put his hand over hers. His thumb traced her knuckles—the slow, circular motion of a man who touches the same person every morning and hasn't stopped being amazed by the permission.

They didn't speak. They didn't need to. The morning held everything the morning needed to hold: the coffee, the terrace, the sea, the two of them. The ordinary miracle of two people who had chosen each other across a distance that should have made choosing impossible, and who were now sitting at a table in a small town on the Portuguese coast, not hiding, not running, not performing for anyone's surveillance or anyone's camera. Just living. The first morning of many mornings, each one a little less astonishing than the last, until the astonishment became the baseline, became the normal, became the life.

That was the goal. Not happiness, exactly—happiness was a word for greeting cards and people who hadn't learned yet that the thing you want and the thing you get are rarely the same shape. The goal was simpler: a morning. A table. A hand on a hand. The sea doing what the sea does. The ordinary accumulation of days that, taken together, constitute a life, and the life constituting something that neither of them had dared to name yet but that both of them recognized, the way you recognize a place you've never been but have been traveling toward for a long time.

Cole's phone buzzed on the table.

He glanced at it. An unknown number. A text message—two words on the screen, no signature, no context, the kind of message that most people would find cryptic and that Cole Hartwell understood immediately, the way you understand a language you didn't know you spoke.

You good?

He smiled. Not a large smile—a small one, private, the smile of a man remembering a woman who had sat across from him in a suite in St. Barts and listened to him tell the truth about the most reckless and important thing he'd ever done, and who had not judged him, and who had then spent ten days dismantling an international crisis and extracting the woman he loved from a compound in a city she controlled with a bluff and a boat and a team of four people, and who had delivered Gabriela to him on a yacht in the dark Caribbean and then gone below deck because the reunion was not hers and she knew it.

He didn't answer the text. The answer was obvious—it was sitting across from him in a white dress, holding coffee, with the Atlantic behind her and the morning light in her hair. And the woman who had sent it would hate the sentimentality. She would read a long reply and feel the discomfort of someone who has been thanked too much for something she considers her job, and the discomfort would come out as a dry remark, and the dry remark would be her way of saying you're welcome without saying you're welcome, because Cat Sloane did not traffic in sentiment and would not start now.

He set the phone face-down on the table. Picked up his coffee. Drank it. Looked at the woman across from him and felt the specific gravity of a life that had started three weeks ago on the deck of a yacht and was still starting, every morning, at this table, with this coffee, with this view.

Gabriela raised an eyebrow. "Who was that?"

"A friend," Cole said.

Gabriela smiled. She knew which friend. She knew because there was only one person in the world who would send a two-word text from an unknown number to check on the welfare of two people she'd saved and then expect no reply, because the absence of a reply was itself the answer—silence meaning safety, meaning peace, meaning the door she'd built was still open and the people she'd pushed through it were still standing on the other side.

The sun climbed. The sea did what the sea does—moved and glittered and stretched to the horizon, patient and indifferent and beautiful in the way that large things are beautiful, the way that things which will outlast you are beautiful, the beauty of the permanent in the presence of the temporary.

Somewhere far away—five thousand miles, a different ocean, a different winter—a woman in a New York apartment was already working the next case. Already moving. Already running from the stillness that would force her to feel what she'd built for these two people and could not build for herself. She was drinking coffee at a desk covered in files. She was returning calls. She was deploying the machinery of her competence against whatever problem had arrived next, because problems always arrived next, and the arriving was the thing that kept her going, and the going was the thing that kept her from stopping, and the stopping was the thing she feared most because the stopping would require her to sit in the silence and the silence would ask her questions she was not yet ready to answer.

She'd get there. Not today. Not tomorrow. But the crack was widening—the one her assistant had seen, the one her ex-husband would see, the one that a man in Cartagena had opened with a confession in a garden that may or may not have been real. The crack was widening, and the light was getting in, and the light was doing what light does to dark places: making them visible, making them navigable, making them—slowly, painfully, with the particular stubbornness of illumination—less dark.

That was enough. For now, that was enough.

On a terrace in Cascais, a man and a woman finished their coffee. The geraniums were red. The tiles were blue and white. The sea was the sea.

He reached for her hand again. She let him take it.

A NOTE FROM KIRA

Hi — thank you for reading. Seriously. There are approximately fourteen million books published every year and you just spent some of your very limited time on this one, and I don't take that lightly.

If you enjoyed The Cartagena Affair, the single most helpful thing you can do — more helpful than telling your friends, more helpful than posting about it, more helpful than anything — is leave a short review on Amazon. It doesn't have to be long. A sentence is enough. Something like "stayed up until 2 a.m., missed my alarm, regret nothing" counts. Amazon's algorithm uses reviews to decide which books to recommend to other readers, and for an independent author, those recommendations are everything. Every review, even a few words, helps Cat Sloane find the readers she was written for.

You can leave a review here: [Amazon link]

If, on the other hand, this book wasn't for you — if the pacing felt off, or Cat drove you crazy, or you thought the ending was too clever for its own good — I genuinely want to hear about it. I'd rather get that feedback directly than through a review, because it makes me a better writer and because honest criticism from a reader who cared enough to finish the book is worth more to me than you know. You can reach me at kira@kiralennox.com. I read every email. I may not respond instantly (I'm probably in a fictional country getting a fictional woman out of fictional trouble), but I read them all.

The next Cat Sloane novel is already in progress. If you want to know when it's out, sign up for my newsletter at kiralennox.com — I email rarely, I never spam, and I occasionally say something funny. That's the best deal in publishing.

Thank you for being here. Cat and I are glad you came along.

— Kira

ACKNOWLEDGMENTS

Every book is a lie that takes a village to make convincing.

To my editor, who saw what this book was trying to be before I did, and who had the patience to say "almost" forty-seven times before saying "yes" — thank you for not letting me settle. The book is better because you wouldn't let me be lazy, and I am better because you wouldn't let me be precious about the parts that needed to go.

To my early readers, who gave me their time and their honesty and occasionally their all-caps text messages at midnight — you know who you are, you know which scenes made you yell at me, and you should know that I changed the thing you hated in Chapter 14 and kept the thing you hated in Chapter 22 because one of you was right and one of you was wrong and I will never tell you which.

To the friends who answered strange questions at strange hours — about Cartagena, about boats, about how long a person can realistically drive through a colonial city at speed without hitting something — your expertise made this book possible and your willingness to not ask follow-up questions made our friendships survivable.

To the online communities of readers, reviewers, and bookstagrammers who take chances on debut authors — you are the reason independent publishing works. You are the reason a book like this finds its people. I owe you more than a mention on this page, but it's what I've got, so: thank you.

To my family, who tolerated the vacant stares at dinner, the "just one more paragraph" that was never one more paragraph, and the emotional whiplash of living with someone who spends half her day in Colombia with fictional people and the other half forgetting to buy milk — I love you, I'm sorry, and no, I cannot explain why I was crying at my laptop. It's a writing thing. You wouldn't understand. (You understand perfectly. That's worse.)

To the city of Cartagena, which I have taken enormous liberties with and which deserves better than being the backdrop for my characters' terrible decisions. Go there. It's more beautiful than I made it sound, and nobody will chase you through the old city in a black SUV. Probably.

And to you, for reading this far — past the last chapter, past the epilogue, all the way to the part where the author gets sentimental and pretends she's not. Thank you. The next one's already started. Cat Sloane has more to fix, more to break, and more questionable romantic decisions to make, and I hope you'll be there for all of it.

— K.L.

ABOUT THE AUTHOR

Kira Lennox spent a decade in international policy and crisis management before discovering that fiction lets you solve crises without the jet lag. She has lived in four countries, has a weakness for complicated men and hotel bars with bad lighting, and writes about women who are the smartest person in every room and the loneliest person in every bed.

The Cartagena Affair is the first book in the Cat Sloane Thrillers. Kira lives on the East Coast and is currently working on the next installment while drinking an inadvisable amount of coffee.

www.ingramcontent.com/pod-product-compliance
Lightning Source LLC
LaVergne TN
LVHW091115080826
845145LV00008B/1923
* 9 7 8 1 9 6 4 9 8 1 1 3 0 *